Never Fear the Dark!

# THE
# LONESOME
# DARK

LISA MICHELLE

For Trent,
I love you always.


"If you meet a loner, no matter what they tell you, it's not because they enjoy solitude. It's because they have tried to blend into the world before, and people continue to disappoint them." —Jodi Picoult

# WIDOW WHITE

# ONE

The pinewood staircase to my attic bedroom is steep, and it whines with each step as I attempt to summit in the dark without killing myself. My costume, a black vintage wedding gown, is heavy and too long for climbing stairs. I stumble. Fall forward and shed the damn thing right then and there, along with the vintage ankle boots.

Rain pelts the octagon window at the top of the stairs like fistfuls of gravel. I reach up, find the chain to the bare bulb, and pull. Nothing. I jerk twice more and still no light. "Shit." Power's out again—not surprising in this storm. I feel for the narrow door to my bedroom and twist the cold antique knob. The rebellious attic seldom lets me in without a fight, especially when it's raining. I slam my shoulder into the door until it gives up. Oddly, from inside, it shuts with no problem. But a few seconds later, it creaks open. I laugh. "You don't scare me anymore."

Blinded by darkness, I crouch and feel along the floor for my night-gown, eventually finding it tangled in the sheet hanging off the bed. In a haze of intoxication, I wrestle into the flannel nightie and fall into bed adrift in a void. It's the dark mixed with sangria that stirs a yearning, allowing the crushing weight of loneliness to suffocate me.

Taking a breath, I close my eyes. The bed spins, lifting me from this world like a ride at the county fair. I'm soaring when something like the sound of footsteps creeping up the stairs intrudes on my crossover into that lovely abyss that only drunken slumber can bring.

The creaking is just the tormented ghost that walks these floors . . . and I'm sick of him. It takes too much effort to open my eyes, so

I listen instead. Waiting for a well-defined noise to confirm my need to worry, or investigate further. Wind and rain threaten the attic roof above my bed. This old Victorian constantly moans and complains about something, especially when its arthritic timbers ache in the cold.

The spookiness of Halloween, like the sangria, is getting the better of me. But just in case, I reach across the bed to the nightstand, slide open the drawer, and finger the revolver hidden under the Bible. I leave the drawer open and the gun accessible.

Sleep comes, and with it another nightmare. In it, something sinister chases me. I can't see the monster, but I know him. Know he wants me dead. I can't escape. Running as fast as I can I'm getting nowhere. He screeches my name—"Pearl! Pearl White!"

I can't breathe.

Fear wakes me. I suck in a breath. It's only a dream, but vivid and violent enough to make me wonder if I've been asleep for minutes or hours. Moonlight illuminates the room a gritty blue as I sit up, situate my pillow. The black and white sugar skull painted on my face smears the white pillowcase like a Rorschach test pattern. My mind is restless, still fogged with booze.

He's dead. "You're dead!" I remind him. "Focus." Don't believe everything you think, my therapist, Maureen Yamaguchi insists. When you feel threatened by darkness, shove it out and shut the door. Envision yourself locking the door. Feel the deadbolt slide into place. Only good thoughts are left in your house.

"Good thoughts." I lie back, close my eyes, and force myself back to tonight's Halloween party.

It was an over-the-top fundraiser that I threw for the county women's shelter. And why not? For the first time in my life, I had the money—and no man to forbid me from doing whatever the hell I wanted. It was liberating. Tucker's probably rolling over in his grave. His money going to abused women is the perfect postmortem retribution.

The wine cellar is an old cave on the northeast corner of the vineyard about a half mile from the house. The previous owners converted it to a massive wine cellar. Decorating it with all kinds of creepy was a blast. There were four life-size wooden coffins that cost a small fortune, but looked amazing. Cobweb-covered mirrors, and two skull bowls filled with blood-red sangria that gurgled with dry ice worked perfectly. Ghosts appeared then disappeared against ancient limestone and timbered walls thanks to a mini-projector hidden in a wine barrel.

I'd even gone so far as to hire the Sheebie Jeebies, an all-girl zombie band.

Outside the cellar, the storm slammed a massive willow back and forth, tangling long, weeping boughs. The trunk went hollow years ago, yet the thing refuses to die, and who am I to put it down? Dead leaves wet with rain scattered like confetti.

In the cave, guests danced and partied in their superb costumes. At midnight, the band departed, but most everyone stayed. My booming Bluetooth speakers, connected to my phone, kept us drinking and dancing through the night. After Michael Jackson's "Thriller," I pulled the plug on the music. Mark Twain passed out cigars to the remaining guests, and soon the cellar was fogged with sweet tobacco.

Through a cloud of smoke, I stepped up onto the stage made of old oak wine barrels and plywood. Everyone cheered as I stood there, trying to think of something intelligent to say.

"Thank you all for coming out in this storm and making my Halloween fundraiser a great success." I lifted my red plastic cup. "And cheers to life insurance." It was funny until I said it. The lighthearted laughter I'd expected never materialized. Someone coughed.

"I'm kidding. Sorry." I hid my face in my drink, and guzzled, wishing I'd simply donated money to the women's shelter rather than forced myself to be sociable. These folks were respectable. The cream of the county. Educated. I, unfortunately, come from a long line of white trash. Life, like Mama, never failed to put me back in my place the moment I tried to step up.

My cheeks were on fire under the skull makeup. "Hope you guys had fun. Drive safe," I said, and scurried over to the punch bowl.

Binging on sangria hadn't drowned my insecurities nor the twang of regret. Neither had fucking J.D. in the coffin. It was a huge mistake, I know. It's what I do best.

J.D. was a long-haired vision of hope with a righteous swagger reserved for cowboys in Western movies. When I laid eyes on him politely holding open the post office door for me, my heart actually pitter-pattered. That was a first. If I were a cartoon character animated red hearts would have sprung from my chest and eyes. He was everything I imagined when reading a steamy romance, but better. He was real. And here in rural Murphys.

At the party, J.D. came as a vampire. Not the goofy black cape and fake-fanged Dracula, but the sexy Victorian, *Interview with the Vampire* kind.

Filled with sangria and need, as soon as the guests were gone, we went at each other like savages in heat. There was something inexplicably hot about a vampire kissing my neck. Sucking. His heavy breath in my ear.

A dark urge to let him devour me consumed my will to behave like the proper lady I so badly wanted to be. He moved behind me, cupped my padded bra, and thrust his tongue in my ear. I leaned back, pushed against him. Felt he was as ready as I was.

When he opened the lid on the coffin, I stepped back and reconsidered. Our Halloween tryst was going a step too far. A serape blanket lined the coffin. Had J.D. planned this? Before I knew it, he'd stripped off his boots and pants and stepped inside the coffin.

"We can't both fit in there." I said.

"We can try." On his back, J.D. opened up his cape, bared his naked flesh as if baring his soul. It was up to me. I shouldn't, but being with a hot guy like him made me feel special. Like I wasn't worthless trash. Feeling loved even if only for a little while was better than nothing at all.

It was wrong on so many levels, but instead of walking away, I lifted my skirt and joined him. For a moment, he was still as he studied me. Then, like a hungry animal, he licked his lips. With deliberate force, he gripped my hips and brought me down. We fit together perfectly in the coffin as if it were custom made just for us.

He touched a void deep inside as intense passion overwhelmed me and fed a hunger. If I didn't slow down, this was going to over in a matter of seconds. On the verge of orgasm, I resisted and threw my head back, took a deep breath, trying like hell to focus on anything other than how incredible he felt inside me.

I watched fake ghosts float by overhead. Thought about my first kiss. It was with my cousin, and when Mama caught us, I got the beating of a lifetime. Visions of being lashed across my bare butt with a cypress switch wouldn't dull the sensuous itch J.D. was scratching.

It had been too long since I'd been with a man, and there was something sinful about doing it in a coffin on Halloween with a vampire. The skulls. Thunder banging in the outside world. Inside, everything seductive and surreal. Worst of all, I liked it.

To be honest, I loved it. Especially when I caught a glimpse of myself in the mirror. The black roses buried in my coiffed auburn hair. The big toothy smile of the skull painted across my face, which expressed my mood perfectly. An enraptured Catrina doll.

I'd likely burn in hell, and I couldn't have cared less.

The coffin groaned as J.D. moved faster and faster. We shook with jagged kisses, our tangled tongues, and oh my god, I couldn't abstain another second. A warmth blossomed in the pit of my stomach, and I gave in. Surrendered all. Let the power of my pent-up sexuality rage and turn me inside out.

We grunted and groaned like wounded animals. The side of the flimsy coffin broke off, and as we laughed, I saw it. From the corner of my eye, a shadow in the mirror. Someone was behind me. My head spun sideways.

Nothing. No one. Could it have been a reflection from the opposite mirror, or was I just being paranoid? Either way, I couldn't shake the overwhelming feeling that someone had been watching us.

J.D. wasn't the least bit concerned when I told him what I thought I'd seen. He said I was too pie-eyed to see straight and drove me across the vineyard, down to the house. We kissed goodbye. How I wanted to invite him in and spend the night wrapped in his arms.

But he's long gone now. And something's wrong. Something bad—I can feel it. My instinct for danger, familiar as standing on the edge of a cliff.

In bed, my eyes shoot open. Terror explodes along with my pulse. I'm *not* dreaming. I'm wide awake and consumed with fear, drowning in my own bed. Weight sinks me deeper and deeper. Something's on me, something heavy straddling my stomach. I can't get a breath. Just one little life-saving breath is all I want. That and my gun.

His face hovers above mine. He's horrid. Deformed. *Get the gun,* I think, and reach toward the nightstand.

Big, jagged stitches zig-zag his forehead, cheek, and chin. His skin is grotesque. Animalistic. Then I realize it's a mask of some sort. Ragged pieces pulled together with gaudy stitches by an amateur. Leather. That cheap, fake leather—pleather.

Oh my God!

My attempts to roll away are futile. He's strong. The grip he has on my neck is like a vise, tightening as I desperately reach for the gun. My fingertips brush the open drawer. I stretch, but the gun inside might as well be miles away. He squeezes harder. Bones crack somewhere deep in my neck.

I fight. My fists connect with his head, his chest—and the one that connects with his throat seems to matter. He coughs. One hand slips from around my neck. I try, but I can't catch a breath. Growls emerge from behind his mask, and both hands are back.

Time slows. Is this how life moves before you die? The final moments linger?

I kick and thrash with every last bit of strength. Why didn't I set the gun within reach? None of it matters now. It's over. I look into his eyes as he strangles the life out of me.

A tear falls from his dark, almond-shaped eye. Holy shit, I thought I'd killed him. Should have known if he wasn't dead, he'd come for me tonight. The one-year anniversary.

He was there—in the cellar, watching me and J.D. If only I'd kept the gun close enough, he'd be dead this time instead of me. I am an idiot. The girl in the horror movie who hears something in the basement and is like, *Let me go down there in my underwear in the dark and investigate*. By the time I realize I should have called the police, or grabbed my gun, it's too late, because I'm getting murdered. And I know I deserve it.

In that final moment, I quit fighting and accept my fate, until I hear—

"Mommy?"

# TWO

Oh dear God, I beg, please don't let my son see me die.

Bodie's at the door with his thumb in his mouth, clutching George, his sock monkey, against his chest. I have to tell him to run if it's the last thing I do.

My hand waves him away, and I pray he understands. Go away. Run *now*! The lack of oxygen to my brain slams shut my peripheral vision. It's as if I'm looking through a dark tunnel. I don't have a clue if Bodie ran, or if he's standing there watching his mama die—doomed to be forever traumatized and sentenced to a life of misery.

The buzzing in my head coagulates into a heavy pressure, echoing like seashells pressed against my ears.

The icy hands are no longer squeezing my neck. He's gone, I think. I hope and pray.

Or is it me? Am I dead?

---

Comprehending time or place is impossible and only adds to the confusion as my heavy eyelids slowly lift, allowing a dreary dawn and reality to pollute me.

My throat is on fire. It hurts to swallow, and my head pounds a familiar hangover beat. Then, a deep, dark fear, like a boulder crashing into my chest.

"Bodie!" I try to scream, but my raspy voice sounds as if I'm still being strangled. I fight the blooming nausea as my bare feet hit the floor.

Standing is a chore. The room tilts and spills sideways as I glimpse what looks like a dead woman. A ghost in a white flannel nightgown. I gasp. My hands come up in surrender, and the woman in the long mirror mimics me. Her long red hair and the grinning skull painted on her face are mine.

Lightheaded and unsteady, I go for the closed bedroom door. The knob seems rusted in place. It's impossible to open because I'm going to be sick. I bend, brace my palms against my knees, and purge last night's sins with a vengeance.

Blood-red sangria splashes the dark wood floor and makes a run for the threshold. I knew I'd be ill when I accepted the third cup of wine from the seductive vampire. Now, remnants are back like regret to haunt me. I wipe my mouth with my sleeve. I'll never drink again, never, I swear. After a few deep breaths, I grab the doorknob with both hands and twist and yank as hard as I can. The old door bleats like a sacrificial lamb before opening.

"Bodie!" My howl is pathetic. My grip on the banister is as weak as my knees, and I stumble but make it down the staircase to the second floor without falling.

Please God, let him be in his bed sleeping with his sock monkey. Dread fills the pit of my stomach like a clot of bile, then metastasizes in my gullet.

My heart races along with thoughts of finding my child dead. It's more than I can take. I won't survive another death. Another murder.

In the hallway, I trip over a toy truck and go down hard. My knee and elbow slap the floor, and I yelp. But adrenaline masks the pain and moves me forward. On all fours, I crawl to his bedroom door. Trembling, I reach up and twist the knob. The door opens, and I pull myself up.

"Bodie?" I whimper. "Sweetheart?"

The blankets on his bed are all balled up—it's possible a five-year-old is under there. Slowly, I reach out. My throat slams, and it's impossible to swallow as panic suffocates me from all sides. I rip back the blankets like a Band-Aid.

George, the sock monkey, smiles up at me. "No!" A mix of relief and terror stomp on me. He's gone. My only child is gone. I jam my hands under my armpits and refuse to accept the possibility I may never see my beautiful boy again. My head shakes from side to side. "No," I whisper as my chin trembles and my teeth chatter. I'm so cold.

"No, no, no." I'm trying convince myself he's here. Somewhere. Hiding or hurt. If I can find him, I can save him.

First the closet, then under the bed. Next, I check the bathroom, even behind the shower curtain. Downstairs, in the kitchen, I inspect every nook and cranny that could fit a little boy. The living room, behind the couch, the curtains, all the closets, every place I can think of. Then it comes to me—the wine cellar.

Barefoot, I rush outside. Rain drills down as I run through the mud. My feet slap the stone steps down to the cellar. The lights are on, but I know I turned them off last night.

"Bodie." My hoarse voice sounds like I just smoked an entire pack of Camels. I clap my hands for no real reason other than that I'm beyond freaking out.

"Bodie!"

The cellar is thrashed from last night's party. My heart lurches when I notice that the coffin J.D. and I fooled around in is now in pieces. Not just broken—demolished, as if someone has gone out of their way to destroy it. The same someone who watched me and J.D., then stole my son.

Three closed coffins remained. The thought of Bodie's little body inside one brings tears to my eyes. I can't take much more of this nightmare. Tearing open each coffin, I find two of them empty. Inside the last is a piece of paper held down by a shiny black stone. I pick them up, taking a closer look.

The paper is a page torn from a book, thin and covered with text. A big red circle draws my attention to a specific passage: *Eye for eye, tooth for tooth, hand for hand, foot for foot.*

I whimper like a child as I climb out of the cellar, crumpling the page pulled from Exodus into a tight ball.

Outside, I run to the narrow creek that cuts through the back of the property and throw the black stone. I throw the note as well and watch it sail downstream. My son is gone. I fall to my knees in the mud—I don't know if he's dead or alive. Soaked to the bone, I scream, then pull myself together and return to the house.

The message light on the phone base tells me the power's back on, but the handheld isn't there. I want to curl up in a corner and sleep until this nightmare and hangover have passed.

Upstairs, I search for my cell. It isn't on the nightstand where I left it. Maybe it was knocked onto the floor during my attempted murder.

On hands and knees, I look behind the nightstand, under the bed, on the dresser for the third time. The wicked bastard took the phones to buy himself more time. That's what I would do. Calling 911 from here isn't an option. I'm wasting time. I slip my frozen feet into a pair of rubber boots and grab a coat.

The key to my Subaru is still in the ignition, and for a moment, I'm grateful that he didn't take it. It's only a quarter of a mile to the neighbors. The car fishtails as I speed out the gate and onto the road.

Outside a newly built A-frame, I lay on the horn until it dawns on me that I have no concept of time. I check the car clock—9:27 in the morning.

I honk again and get out, wishing I'd taken the time to meet my new neighbors.

Banging on their door, I realize they probably have jobs. Halloween fell on a Tuesday, and today is Wednesday—a workday for most. I bang harder and try the knob. Locked. Could this nightmare get any worse?

Dogs bark from somewhere behind the house, and by the sound of it, they're pissed and coming my way.

The hounds of hell appear, and I consider making a run for the car. One looks like an enormous rottweiler, and the other is a brindle boxer. I'm going to be mauled and mutilated any second. The owners will arrive home at some point to find my carcass on their doorstep. I hope it's quick.

"Hey buddy," I say in a raspy yet lofty tone. "It's okay. It's okay." It's so not okay, and I raise my hands in surrender. "Easy . . ."

The boxer attacks, jumps on me and licks my chin while the rottweiler holds back and growls.

"Hello?" A portly man in insulated gray coveralls and a greasy ball cap approaches. "Mike! Get down!" he yells. "Go on. Get!"

Mike the boxer cowers off the porch as the man takes a look at me. I can tell by his expression and raised brow that my appearance is concerning.

The skull paint smeared across my face was creepy last night, but add the white nightgown, my chaotic red hair, and the fact that I'm covered in mud from the waist down, and I'm horrifying.

"I need help. Please. I live next door." I take a raspy breath. "The old Black Springs Winery. And my son—" I sound like I've recently risen from the dead. My throat is so dry, I can't get the words out.

"Call—the police." I clasp my hands and beg.

# THREE

They say if a missing child isn't found within forty-eight hours of their disappearance, odds are they never will be. I have no idea what time that monster stole my child, but it's almost noon, and I feel the clock ticking down with every beat of my heart. The possibility it's already too late gnaws at me.

There must have been at least eight or ten cops in and out of here the last few hours. I refused to be examined by a doctor, even when they insisted. I know my rights. I don't need a doctor—I need the sheriff's department to save my son. Feeling this helpless is like being back with Mama.

They took photos of my neck, and now they're scouring the house, inside and out.

Deputy Martinez, who looks like she belongs on the cover of a romance novel, being ravished by a shirtless brute, comes into the dining room. She places a cup of coffee on the table in front of me. Her long hair, braided to the side, is the blue-black of raven feathers. Wish I had hair like that instead of this out-of-control, curly red mop.

"Thank you." I cradle the cup in my cold hands and wonder where she found a clean mug. Did she wash it or grab a dirty one from the pile in the sink? My kitchen is a disaster. My entire house is a disaster. Keeping a clean home has never been a priority, and now it's likely adding to the deputy's low opinion of me as a mother.

Deputy Clark writes on his yellow legal pad. We've been over the entire episode three times. They want to see if my story changes. I watch *Forensic Files* and *Dateline* religiously. I know they're just doing their job, and I'll repeat the "night in question" a hundred times if it will help bring Bodie back to me.

I'd even tell them about me and J.D. if I thought for a second it mattered, but they already think I'm a terrible person for leaving my son alone in the house while we partied in the wine cellar. No need to confirm it.

Bodie was fine, sound asleep every time I checked on him last night. And I checked on him at least four times. That's what I told Deputy Clark, but the truth is I only checked him once. It has nothing to do with Bodie being taken, yet it adds to the guilt eating me from the inside out.

Another reason I don't mention my relation to J.D. and the fun we had in the cellar is because he has a criminal record. He'll become a suspect, and they'll waste precious time that could be spent looking for the man who actually has my son. If only I'd let J.D. spend the night, none of this would have happened. Not with a guy like that around to protect us.

If only I hadn't gone to bed drunk, I would have heard the sick bastard coming—or at least been smart enough to keep my gun closer. I would *not* have hesitated. I'd have killed him this time. Fired over and over until the gun was empty.

"It's the same guy, the same mask," I say, and I've said it ten times. They're not listening. They'd rather find a way to make me their number one suspect. I'm easier to locate.

Clark asked me to calm down three times. Once when I *was* calm and simply trying to explain that he shouldn't discredit the value of a person's gut instinct and the fact that he wore the same mask as the man who murdered my husband last year. Yes, I'm irritated. Who wouldn't be? It's much easier to classify me as a hysterical woman than a reliable witness.

The deputy stops writing and looks up at me. "I've noted that, ma'am. I agree, it's unlikely this was random. A year to the day of Mr. White's murder is too precise to be coincidental. If it is the same guy, why do you think he came back?"

"Maybe because I shot him. Maybe because I can identify him. Maybe because he's a psychopathic serial killer who murders whoever the hell the little voice in his head tells him to."

I take a breath and start to cry again. I really, really don't want to cry, but there's no stopping it. The aching helplessness has its way with me.

"Do you own a gun?" Clark asks.

"Yes. You guys kept the last one as evidence and never returned it."

"It's my understanding that you did not see the intruder's face. Correct?"

I wipe my nose on my sleeve. "Yes, but . . . I . . ." I can't explain how I know it's the same man who murdered my husband, but I know it just as sure as I know my son is missing. "It's him. I swear to God. You have to find him! Please."

"We will." Deputy Martinez rubs my shoulder from behind, then hands me several paper towels as she takes a seat next to me. She watches me swipe tears from my face—there's something familiar about her.

"Do you think you would know if some of Bodie's clothes were missing?" she asks.

I shake my head. "I don't know." I shrug. "Maybe."

"Would you mind taking a look? See if anything seems out of order." She says this with the kind and caring nature of a therapist. I know I know her, but I can't place how.

"Sure." I stand. I like her. She smells like expensive Chardonnay—and that's when I remember her. She was there the night my husband was murdered. Her hair was different, heavily streaked with blond.

The back door opens, and a man pokes his hooded head inside. Water runs off his long black raincoat.

"Anything?" Clark asks.

"Rain's washed away any chance of tire or foot tracks. Found this, though." He dangles a white plastic bag with a red stripe running across the top. "EVIDENCE" is the only word on it I can make out. "It's a page out of the bible or something. Wanna take a look? It's wet, but lab might be able to pull prints." He sounds hopeful, but the only prints they'll find on the balled-up paper are mine. That rotten bastard is way too clever to leave fingerprints.

"Flag it and tag it."

"Already did, sir. Ground crew's still looking around, and Search and Rescue is en route."

"Good," Clark says, reaching across the table for his recorder.

"KCRA News is here. They'd like a statement."

The deputy doesn't answer, just shakes his head. The soaked man backs out the door and pulls it shut behind him as Clark turns off his phone recorder.

"Thank you, Ms. White. That's all for now. Deputy Martinez has been in contact with the FBI and has put out a bolo."

"What's a bolo?" I ask.

Martinez's voice is soft and deep, like that of a blues singer, attracting attention without demanding it. "It means our entire department, as well as Amador and Tuolumne counties have been notified to be on the lookout for Bodie. They have his photo. An Amber Alert is also underway. I swear to you, we are doing everything we possibly can." She smiles as if it helps.

"You wanna see his room *again?*" I ask.

"Yes. Thank you." Martinez stands.

"Thank you, Ms. White. A detective will be in touch." Clark says. A nod is all I can manage. He shakes my hand and leaves out the front door.

As Martinez follows me upstairs to Bodie's room, our footsteps pressure the old wood staircase to groan in our wake, and I wonder if the intruder's steps were this obvious last night. Would I feel this awful if it weren't my fault?

I flip on the light in Bodie's room. The silence is unnerving and feels claustrophobic. My boy should be stomping around, wanting lunch and his juice box. The scent of Vick's VapoRub lingers from the humidifier that quit working a while back.

"Was Bodie sick?" Martinez is perceptive, and I'm glad.

"He was getting over a cold." I shiver and cross my arms for warmth. "He's gonna get pneumonia out in this weather." In the middle of the room, I look up and down, slowly searching for something to jump out at me, as if a clue is in plain sight and I just can't see it. I sigh.

"Take your time," Martinez says. "Let me know if anything strikes you as odd. Even if you think it's unimportant. Talk it out."

I chew my thumbnail. This feels utterly pointless, like a huge waste of precious time. Maybe I should be out there, trying to track him down myself. Maybe I should pray? Go to church and get down on my hands and knees? I'm going to Google what to do when your child is abducted to be sure I don't overlook the obvious.

I'm so cold, and I can't stop shivering.

"Here." Martinez reaches a fuzzy blue blanket off the bed and wraps it around my shoulders. It smells like my little boy. Like cheese and corn chips.

Tears run down my cheeks before I even know I'm crying. "Thank you."

The thought of never seeing Bodie again is apocalyptic. Guilt and exhaustion crush down on me. Controlling my emotions is impossible. For the first time in my life, I don't care what anyone thinks of me, and I let go. Totally break down, sobbing with each breath.

Bent, on the verge of collapse, Martinez cradles me over to Bodie's bed. She sits down next to me and keeps her arm around my shoulder. It's comforting for sure, and I'm grateful. This is what it's like to have support, and I think maybe, for the first time in my life, I regret being such a suspicious, unsociable loner. Deleting my Facebook and Instagram accounts a few years back cut off the last few "friends" and distant relatives.

Rocking slowly back and forth like a wrecking ball, I hate who I've become.

"I'm sorry," I sob. Strings of saliva hang from my mouth like threads of a web. "So, so sorry."

# FOUR

Slowly, my sobs subside. Maggie Martinez returns to the bedroom with a dampened hand towel from the bathroom and offers it.

"Thank you." My swollen eyes burn as I press the cool, damp towel to my face. I have to get it together and look for his missing clothes. That's what Maggie wants me to do. That's why she's been waiting patiently all this time, never once interrupting my breakdown.

I sigh as I lower the towel, now blackened with last night's skull makeup. I haven't even washed my face. I must look like something from *Night of the Living Dead*. I definitely feel like it. "I'm sorry."

"Don't be sorry. Please. You have every right. No need to apologize."

"Okay." I feel tears welling up again and swallow them down. Taking a long deep breath, I pull myself together enough to study Bodie's room. His closet door is open, and I walk over to it. Nothing looks off. I shake my head and look at his army men and tiny clothes scattered across the floor, under the bed. "I don't know. I'm just not sure if—" I sit back down on the bed next to Maggie.

"That's okay. If you notice anything missing, let me know. I'll give you my cell number. I want you to call me for any reason. Anything at all. Day or night. Okay?"

I nod and close my eyes. "Thanks."

Maggie walks to the door. "Is there anyone I can call for you? A relative? Friend? Neighbor?"

"No." There's no one. I'd love to explain how the second I like someone, or God forbid trust them, they never fail to let me down. Friends and family are less likely to disappoint if held at a distance. J.D. comes to mind. For him, I'd risk heartbreak. What I'd give to crawl into his arms right now. I hide my face in the hand towel.

"I'm here—anytime. I mean it. Okay?" Her kindness is killing me. I don't deserve it, and all I can do is nod.

When I finally lower the towel from my face, Maggie is still there, leaning against the doorjamb. Staring at me, unblinking. Why didn't she leave? What is she waiting for?

I look at her, but she's just staring down at her black work boots. Then, for no good reason other than that I've cracked, I blurt, "My dad died in Hurricane Katrina."

She looks over at me, her back still pressed against the doorjamb, her feet stretched out in front of her.

"He and his Cajun houseboat meth lab floated down the Pearl River." I grin because I've lost it for sure and don't really care.

"How old were you?" she asks. She cares.

"Ten. That's when my mom and me left Louisiana."

Maggie chews her cheek, like she's considering her words carefully. "How'd you end up in friggin' Murphys?" She furrows her brow like she really wants to know.

"Long story," I say.

"Yeah. Seems like everyone here just kind of ends up here. Including me."

"How's that?"

"Long story best told at a later date over an alcoholic beverage."

I snort a laugh and immediately want to punch myself in the face for laughing while my son is missing. "I *could* use a drink." I say, before remembering that it's the middle of the day.

"There's no law against it. Just don't drive." Maggie smiles, then heads out the door and down the hall.

I stand. I will have a drink. If there's ever a good time for a drink, it's now. It'll calm my nerves. I also need to get out of my nightgown and take a shower. I clap twice, and the lamp goes off. Darkness provokes a sick feeling. My hands can't clap fast enough to make the lamp illuminate the room again.

When I pull the disobedient shade, it refuses to retract. Bodie begged for blinds more than a few times. He hated this stained yellow thing that never worked right. He will get his new blinds no matter what.

In one quick swipe, I rip the shade from the window. Then I take another glance around the room. There is something missing. There has to be. I can feel it but can't—then it hits me. Bodie's shoes. "His boots." His little cowboy boots are always at the foot of his bed, and now they're not. I look under the bed. In the closet. All around.

"Miss Martinez. Maggie!" I rush out the door, and she meets me in the hall.

"What is it?"

"Bodie's boots are gone. They were in his room. *Always* next to his bed." I'm out of breath, panting hard for no real reason.

"Okay. Let's look around and make sure."

"That's good, right? Right?" Even I can hear the desperation in my voice.

"We can't jump to conclusions, but if his boots are gone, it's possible the abductor isn't planning— Let's search the house for his boots."

Maggie calls in Deputy Andrews to assist us.

We search the house from top to bottom.

After an hour, like Bodie, the boots are officially missing.

# FIVE

At 3 a.m. it's official. My sweet little angel has been missing for twenty-four hours. I haven't slept or eaten, only smoked and drank. Spilling red wine down my hoodie sends me over the edge, and I hurl the empty bottle against the fireplace. Staying positive isn't happening. It's impossible. Improbable. Even though I keep telling myself that a killer wouldn't go to the trouble of grabbing a kid's footwear if their plan was to murder them all along.

Waiting around is like a time bomb nailed to my heart. Each *tick* hammers the nail deeper. I'm coming undone, and any minute now, I'm going to explode.

It's good the predator stole my phones, because otherwise I would call J.D. Let his soothing voice comfort and talk me down. But that would be a huge mistake.

I step over broken glass on the stone hearth and warm myself next to the fire. Flames claw at me like judgmental talons. I fight the urge to feel guilty and stare back—untangle my thoughts and rein them toward a positive future.

When Bodie gets back, I'm selling this house and leaving Murphys for good. People will understand—there's too much trauma here to stay. I would have left after my husband's murder, but most everyone was so kind, so supportive. And it would have looked bad if I just up and left. Like I was running. Only guilty people run.

Maybe we'll move to Mexico. Maybe Canada—it's safer there. Bodie will love having a family and being with J.D. Then I recall Canada doesn't allow people with a criminal record to enter their country.

We could go back to Louisiana. For what this place is worth, I could live like a queen in Saint Tammany Parish. I wonder if my meemaw Irene is still there. Still alive and able to interpret visions?

Skimming the internet for local updates, I learn law enforcement has already gone door to door for miles, asking if anyone witnessed anything. Everyone's talking about it.

At sunrise, a murky gray dawn casts little light in the house despite the many windows. The perimeter of my home and property line are fenced with yellow crime scene tape. It's like I'm starring in my own episode of *Dateline*, and all I want to do is change the channel.

Soon, volunteers will arrive to once again comb the property, hunt under the house, and search the woods out back. Divers are being brought in from somewhere to cover the pond and New Melones, the same reservoir the Russian mafia used a few years ago. The desolate two-lane bridge is perfect for disposing of a corpse in the middle of the night. The thought of Bodie being dumped off the bridge makes me dizzy. I'm trembling, and when I clasp my hands together, I realize they're ice cold.

I'm not going to just sit around and wait much longer. I can't. I have to do something, even if it's wrong. I pour myself a second cup of coffee and try to force down a bite of peanut butter toast. It's like swallowing a rock.

The house phone rings, but since I don't have the handheld to answer, the machine picks up. "Hello Ms. White, it's Detective Rocha," the man begins. "We'd like you to come in this afternoon. Just a few follow-up questions. You have my number." He hangs up without saying goodbye. I hate when people do that. It's rude.

Last night, Detective Rocha came to the house to have what he called "a look around," and asked if I minded giving *him* my state-ment—"just to be *perfectly* clear."

I didn't mention that I'd already given my statement several times to Deputy Clark. He knew that. He was trying to see if my story changes. If even one little detail was off, he'd run with it.

I invited him in. The hound dog sag to his face had worsened since last year. After making coffee, I relived the nightmare play-by-play, minus J.D. again, and signed my statement. I noticed that the official time of the abduction was between 2:30 and 3:00 a.m.

Before he left, Rocha commented that he loved how I'd remodeled the first floor and all the new modern rustic furniture. "Must have cost a fortune," he said with a wry grin. I knew it was meant to agitate and lure me in. But I refused the bait. He'd been the lead detective on my husband's murder last year, and made it perfectly clear he believed I was somehow involved and would eventually prove it.

"Any plans for your *second story?*" He crossed his arms, widened his legs. A grin grew as if he were particularly proud of the brilliant sarcasm dripping from his forked tongue.

I lowered my head. "No."

As soon as I opened the front door, he left without a goodbye.

I'd leave right now. Go this instant if I had any inclination of where the bastard who has my son might be. My head hasn't stopped throbbing from worry and wine. With lukewarm coffee, I down three Advil, then take a closer look at the bottle.

"Oh no. No, no." Written in blue letters is *PM*. I'd set the bottle on the counter last night, but then decided against taking them in case they found Bodie. I needed to stay alert.

Worrying about what kind of "follow-up" questions Rocha has for me, and how I'll answer if I'm drowsy, scares me. With two Advil PMs in me, I could sleep through a hurricane. I took three. Forcing myself to throw up is the only option.

In the downstairs bathroom, I flip on the light and glimpse someone running away from the window above the bath. For a split second, I think it could be a volunteer, but the way this guy bolted feels wrong. My gut tells me not to let him get away. My gun is in my sweatshirt. I pull it and run out the back door.

It hasn't stopped raining for two days, and before I can get around the backside of the house, my Uggs are soaked. I don't see any signs of search volunteers. I hold the gun out like I've seen in movies. With two hands. Arms straight and serious as I come around the back of the house to the bathroom window. There's no one there.

Big footprints in the mud prove that someone *was* recently there, though. The prints are fresh with deep treads, like those of some sort of work or hiking boot. They lead every which way, so there's no telling the direction the person came or went.

I scan the yard through the blurring rain and see the backside of a hooded figure in a camo-colored coat disappearing into the forest above the cellar. It's him.

"Hey!" I charge.

Calling the police would be the smart thing to do, but that's not possible without a phone. And it's up to me to fight for my son.

Rainwater has formed a plethora of rushing streams crisscrossing the lowest section of woods. I attempt to jump the narrow water, but quickly give up and splash straight ahead. Catching him could mean life or death for Bodie. Life or death for me.

I scramble and see movement ahead. "Stop!"

Blue jeans and the camo coat, no farther than fifty yards.

"I'll shoot!" I can catch him if I don't weaken, but I'm running out of steam. Instead of gaining on the bastard, I'm losing ground. I stop. Raise my gun.

"Stop or I'll shoot!"

It works. He stops, and I rush toward him.

"Don't you move, you son-of-a-bitch!" my raspy voice yells. "I'll blow your head off."

He raises his hands as I step closer. The guy's tall. Much taller and thinner than the monster who has my son.

"Turn around!"

He does.

"Pearl! What the fuck?" His hands drop. Then he clutches his chest, like he's having a heart attack. "Thought you were a goddamn cop. Didn't sound like you. Jesus, what's with your voice?"

"J.D." My knees go weak. I bend over to catch my breath, and the wet gun slips from my grasp as fast as Bodie did. J.D. reaches down and digs it out of the mud.

"What the hell are you doing here?" I gasp and cough.

"Checkin' on *you*. I heard what happened. Jesus, I just— I called about a hundred times—goes straight to voicemail." He shakes water off the muddy gun. "Sorry to scare you, but I was worried sick." He reaches under his jacket, untucks his shirt tail, and wipes the gun. "How come you don't answer your damn phone?"

His hood slips back, revealing wet bangs that stick to his forehead. giving him an innocent, boyish appearance. He tilts his head and pouts just like Bodie, and before I can stop myself, I rush him. My arms wrap tight around his middle as if he can save me.

When he holds me back, I melt. "What do we do next?"

"Find that little bastard that killed Tuck. That's who took Bod."

"Know where he is?"

"Not a clue." Hopelessness blends tears with rain.

"It'll be all right, Pearl girl. I promise." He keeps me upright, and for a moment I believe him. He's the only person, besides Bodie, who doesn't think I'm trash—which makes me think I might not be as worthless as I feel.

"They'll find him."

"What if they don't? What if I never see my son again?" I fully expect some sort of reasonable answer, as if there is one to give.

"What about a ransom? Like does the dude want money?"

"I don't know. He hasn't asked. I'd pay it. Whatever he wants, my house, every single cent. I'd give it all to have Bodie back."

"I know. I know you would." He presses my head against his chest with his big hand. "They got anything? Any leads?"

"They don't tell me nothin'." I shake my head and close my eyes, and we suffer in silence for a minute. What I wouldn't give to start over with J.D. and my son. "Why'd you run?" I ask.

"I knew comin' here was stupid, but I couldn't stop myself. Then, when I got to your house, saw all the crime scene tape and whatnot, I realized they could be watching the house. If they caught me sneakin' about, I'd be history."

"You think they're watching me?" I pull away.

"Depends if they have the manpower. Calaveras Sheriff's is small and limited. I don't know. This gun's fucked. Let me take it home and clean it right." He tucks it inside his jacket.

The thought of being watched hadn't crossed my mind. "Makes sense, though. Think they suspect *me*?" I ask, but I already know the answer.

"'Course they do. They play the odds, hon. Five hundred parents kill one of their own every goddamn year."

"Holy shit." My jaw drops. I can't even fact check him, because the FBI will search my searches. Every single thing I've ever Googled or done or said will be scrutinized and used against me. At least I have fat finger bruises around my neck to prove I didn't fabricate the entire story just to cover my tracks. "If the police get hung up on me, they'll quit looking."

Hot tears warm my icy cheeks as J.D. lifts my chin, his eyes like hands on me. With his big, rough thumbs, he wipes my face, then kisses me. Gently, at first. His lips are warm and full and soft, and they taste like freedom. A way to escape hell.

When he presses harder and pulls me into him, that twinge of desire swirls inside me. What is it about this guy? Am I so starved for affection that the moment someone touches me, my body reacts involuntarily?

His tongue finds mine and stirs the devil in me. For a moment, I want him more than my next breath, right here in the rain, with my son missing.

"No way." I shake my head. "I can't." My conscience whispers, *But why? Who says momentary bliss is wrong? Would a man be considered a terrible father for using sex as a way to lighten the pain?*

His lips work my neck, and his hair smells clean, like baby shampoo. He grinds against me.

"Stop it." I jerk away. "Bodie is missing." Saying it out loud makes it all too real, and I want to take the words back, as if that will somehow obliterate the ugly truth. I cover my mouth with both hands, my sanity hanging by a thread. I let out a sob.

"Hey." J.D. shakes my shoulders. "Come on now. You got to be tough. Now's not the time to fall apart."

"If only I hadn't thrown that stupid party," I blubber. "Why didn't I make it a family thing? Invite kids. Bodie would have loved it. But no, I had to go and act like hot shit!" Snot and drool roll off my lips. "What an idiot!"

"You're not an idiot. You had the chance to do something fun for everyone. You couldn't have known." He cradles my face. "It's not your fault a fucktard tried to kill you and stole Bodie. Blaming yourself is total bullshit. We both know you're extremely kind and have a good heart. That women's shelter wouldn't exist without you. Look at all the money you raised for FFA? And the afterschool program, for Christ's sake."

I burrow into him, my sobs drowning out the silence.

"My truck's parked over yonder in the woods. Let me warm you up? Make you feel good."

I kiss him goodbye like I love him. "Best thing you can do is stay far, far away from me."

# SIX

By the time I get home, the effects of the Advil PMs weigh me down. I'm woozy, and my eyes and legs are heavy as I climb the steps to the attic. All I want is sleep.

Passing Bodie's room reminds me that I may never get the chance to watch him sleep again or see him grow up. Why is it crappy moms can't see they're crappy until it's too late? I'm too tired to cry, but not too tired to let whispers of a maniac taunt me. *"Eye for eye. Tooth for tooth. Hand for hand. Foot for foot."*

In my room, I change out of my wet clothes and into dry sweats and a fleece hoodie. Bed is a welcome relief, and sleep comes as easy as giving up.

Something wakes me. My heart is racing—I'm breathless and I don't know why.

"Pearl White? Hello? Are you up there?" It's a woman.

I sit up, not knowing where I am or who's calling my name.

"Ms. White?"

Shit, I need my gun. Climbing out of bed, I reach into the nightstand, then remember J.D. has it. I tiptoe to the door.

"Hello?" the woman calls. It sounds like she's coming up the steps. "Ms. White? I'm Agent McNulty with the FBI."

"Yes. Coming."

I step into the hallway and look down. It's Kathy Bates with shotput shoulders and the worst helmet haircut I've ever seen atop a navy-blue pantsuit.

"Yes?" I say sheepishly.

She holds out her badge. "Special Agent Sally McNulty—FBI. Given the situation, we were concerned when we couldn't reach you."

The nightmare, the FBI, my missing boy—it all hits like the back of a shovel to the face. I squeeze my temples. "Sorry. I had a headache and took Advil. They were the PMs, and it knocked me out. I'm glad you're here."

"Yes, well. I'm glad *you're* here. Safe. And unharmed." She sounds more irked than relieved I'm alive. "I'm here to find your son. My role is to take an initial report, assess the situation, and report back, before bringing in a task force."

"We can talk downstairs. Let me grab some shoes." I rush back into my room. My Uggs are soaked and muddy, so I dig through the closet for my fuzzy pink slippers with no luck. Under the bed, I locate one. In the corner, under a pile of dirty clothes, I find a thick pair of socks and pull them on and hurry downstairs.

In the living room, the agent makes herself at home, pushing aside a blanket and some of Bodie's toys, and sits on my couch with a briefcase in her lap.

I smile. "Would you like some coffee, or tea, or something?"

"No, thank you." Sally McNulty unbuttons her jacket, freeing ample rolls of belly fat. Then she makes space on my coffee table by gathering Bodie's coloring books into a neat stack. She takes her time boxing up his crayons as I gather a half-eaten bowl of old Fruit Loops and three juice pouches.

My ears heat up. My lack of composure is uncomfortable and likely obvious. "Sorry the house is such a mess." Old milk spills from the bowl and splashes on the floor as I rush to the kitchen. "My cleaning lady quit." I toss everything including the bowl into the trash can before hurrying back to the FBI agent sitting on my couch.

"Haven't felt much like cleaning," I add, even though it won't take a special agent to know this mess has been here longer than a day. She ignores my ridiculous excuse for being a slob and sets her case on the table. It clicks open like the safety on a gun. From inside, she brings out several file folders, the familiar ugly yellow legal pad, and a small digital recorder.

"So, am I being questioned again?" I ask. "I've already given my statement three times."

"The Bureau doesn't like to rely on outside agencies. Including local Sheriff's Departments. When we take over an investigation, we start from the beginning—actually, before the beginning." She clicks her pen and writes my name, as well as the date, time, and place.

"I have to meet Detective Rocha soon. He has follow-up questions for me."

"Not necessary. I'll take care of it. Now, before we begin, would you like some water or something? You seem anxious."

"Anxious? The only thing I'm anxious about is getting Bodie back." I get up, go to the kitchen, guzzle a glass of water, and notice that my throat is on fire. I'm talking too much.

I refill the glass with water from the tap. "Would you like some water, ma'am?" My Southern upbringing sneaks up on me when I'm anxious. Next, I'll be craving crawfish.

"Where are you from, Ms. White? Originally."

"Pearl River, Louisiana," I say as I walk back into the living room. "My daddy named me after the river." I sit on the chair across from the couch while she nods and writes. The timer on the recorder is moving. McNulty notices me eyeing it.

"Do I have your consent to record our conversation?" she asks.

"Sure. I don't mind." I have nothing to hide. "Where are you from, Miss McNulty?" My attempt at making this more of a conversation than an interrogation.

"You can call me Sally." She doesn't answer my question. "When did you leave Pearl River?"

"When I was ten. After Hurricane Katrina."

"Why?"

I take a deep breath and wonder where to begin. "After the hurricane, there wasn't nothin' left of my daddy or his meth-making Cajun cabin."

She moves the yellow notepad to her lap—never stops writing, never looks up. "What's a Cajun cabin?"

"It's a homemade shack built on top of a pontoon boat that lives on the water. He 'bout burnt it down twice."

"Who did you leave with?"

"Mama."

"No brothers or sisters?"

"Nope."

"Where did you go when you left?"

"Reno, first. That's where Mama met . . . someone."

"Please be specific. What exactly do you mean by someone?"

"Her boyfriend."

"What was his name?"

I chew my bottom lip, wishing I could press pause and leave. She stops writing and eyes me with that *don't make me ask again* look.

"Tucker White."

She's writing his name down when it hits her. I can almost see the light bulb illuminate over her head. "Tucker White? As in your deceased husband? That Tucker White?"

I nod and let out a breath. "Yes, ma'am."

Only her eyes move upward, locking on me like it's an *aha* moment. Like suddenly she knows me, knows who I am. This is why I don't like people. They make assumptions based off of an action. I wish she'd just come out and say it, ask directly.

She does. "Tucker White was involved with your mother?"

"Yes, that's right." I try not to sound ashamed as I pinch my ear-lobe—a habit I inherited from Mama.

"At what age did your involvement with the deceased begin? And I think you know what I mean by involvement."

"Yes. I do." My heart is suddenly pounding, and my armpits itch. I'm sweating. "Tuck was a lot younger than Mama. But she lied to him about her age. We were broke and desperate when we got off the Amtrack in Reno. That's where we met Tuck."

I cross my legs and lean back in the chair before continuing. "It was Hot August Nights, and his motorcycle had broken down or something in the train station parking lot. Mama strutted over in her short shorts and high heels with a suitcase in one hand and me in the other. She asked if he knew where we could get a cheap room. Next thing I know, we're staying in a suite at Harrah's Casino and eating at a restaurant. I'd never eaten at restaurant before then."

Sally has gone back to taking notes. "And how old are you at the time?

"Ten." The house phone rings. "Excuse me." I step out into the hallway and then remember I don't have the handset. The answering machine picks up.

"Detective Rocha here—*again*. Why aren't you sitting in my office answering questions? Do I need to send an officer to pick you up? You have one hour." He hangs up without saying goodbye.

I return to the living room and Agent McNulty.

"You won't need to speak to Detective Rocha. I'll take care of it." She taps her pen to her pad. "How long were you in Reno?"

"About six months, maybe. I'm not sure."

"Where did you go when you left Reno?"

"Here—Murphys."

"With whom?"

"My mother and Tucker."

"To this vineyard?"

"Yes."

"Why?"

"I don't know." I shrug. "She and Tucker wanted to." Tucker was connected and had inside information. He knew Calaveras County was going to legalize marijuana cultivation and bought the vineyard to turn it into a grow operation. He eventually replaced forty acres of grapes with weed plants. Locals didn't like us to begin with, but after he destroyed the historic vineyard, they despised us. Another reason I don't have any friends.

"You own the entire vineyard free and clear at present. Correct?"

"Yes." Tucker made a fortune the first two years, until the county repealed their cannabis cultivation laws.

"You inherited it."

"Yes."

"Who paid for it?"

"I'm not sure." That's a lie, but one worth telling. Mama got over a hundred thousand dollars from a life insurance policy she'd taken out on Daddy. Sally might be able to dig that fact up, but I'm not handing it over. I know she'll think the apple doesn't fall far.

"Mama believed the house was haunted," I blurt, because being quiet feels awkward and apparently impossible. "That's why she left."

"She left you?"

"Uh-huh." I nod like we're just two girlfriends hanging out, chit-chatting about our unfortunate past.

"How old were you?"

"Mmm . . . around fifteen." I say, but it sounds like a question.

"And Mr. White?"

"He stayed. Took care of me. Guess that's why I eventually married him." Telling a wise woman that Tucker White said I should marry him because I would become Pearl White and that Pearl White was a totally kickass name will do me no good. Truth be told, we got married in Reno because Tuck was still in love Mama and I was the next best thing. I was also pregnant, but had a miscarriage. Mama swore I'd have a child before turning fifteen. Said the poorer and less educated a woman is, the more children she has. As if it were a way to bring meaning to an otherwise pointless existence. I certainly proved her wrong. At least the part about not having a child by fifteen—or more than one.

"Too bad I can't charge him with statutory rape." She scratches inside her ear with her pen. "I have him listed as the father of the missing child. Is that correct?"

"Correct."

"Are you seeing anyone now?"

"No." My stomach growls so loud, Sally hears it.

"Let's take a break, shall we? Have a bite to eat."

"Okay. I can make you a sandwich," I offer.

"I have lunch in my car."

Sally gets up and goes outside to her black Tahoe, and I go to the bathroom, where I run hot water and wash my face. In the mirror, I hardly recognize myself. My twisted bun sits lopsided on my head. My bloodshot eyes are swollen and tired. I need a smoke before I blow it.

# SEVEN

Daddy always kept his carton of Camels in the freezer. Guess that's why I do the same. Except I like menthols.

Inside the freezer, I dig a pack of Salems out of the carton. The cold air crawls up my arm; I shiver and slam the door. Then, like a dope-sick addict, I tear open the pack and tap out a cigarette, light it off the stove, and suck smoke deep into my lungs. The nicotine rushes to my head but doesn't provide much comfort, as I start to wonder what Bodie's doing right now.

Why can't anyone find this guy? They've had a year since he murdered Tucker. I shot him and assumed he was dead. Now I know why they never found his bones. My mind races, and thoughts spin out of control, bouncing off the inside of my head. That ugly mask with those almond eyes. His pudgy fingers around my neck, squeezing the life out of me. My fingers find my neck, and I rub the swelling. Bodie—poor baby. The scary monster I told him didn't exist does.

I take another drag and look out the window. Sally's in her Tahoe, talking on her cell. If only I knew what she was saying, what's really happening in the investigation. I drop the cigarette in the sink. It hisses under the pile of dirty dishes, and I hurry upstairs.

In my attic bedroom, I grab my laptop off the bookshelf. It takes a moment for the wi-fi to kick in, and I choose the Incognito Search option. My searches can probably be traced, but it's worth a try. I type in *The Pinetree*, our local news site, to see if they know something I don't.

"CHILD ABDUCTED FROM MURPHYS" reads the headline. Before I can stop myself, I click. A picture of Bodie pops up. It's from last summer, when he got lice and I shaved his head. It looks nothing like my adorable, irresistible, innocent child. I scroll down past the photo.

The first paragraph offers little more than to label me Widow White, which sounds oddly creepy for some reason. The next paragraph re-gurgitates the police report and the description I gave of the intruder, including his bogus leather mask.

Then. like an idiot, I willingly venture down the rabbit hole. Can't stop myself from skimming the comments below the article.

Snoopy411: *sounds like Leatherface from texas chainsaw massacre is back. Pleatherface LOL!!!*

Jbflyer007: *Widow White Trash murdered her husband!! Everyone knows it, including the police. They just can't prove it.*

Lilgangstagirl: *OMG! LMAO! PLEATHERFACE SHOULD HAVE BUTCHERED WIDOW WHITE TRASH!!!!*

The comments go on and on. They're calling me "Widow White Trash" and him Pleatherface. People suck, plain and simple. How can they be so cruel? Like this is some sort of joke. A man was murdered and a little boy stolen, and it's funny?

I slam my laptop shut. Grab the pillow from behind me and beat the hell out of the bed with it. Then I smash my face deep into the pillow and scream at the top of my lungs. The minute I'm quiet, I hear her.

"Ms. White?" Sally calls from downstairs. Was she calling while I was screaming? Did she hear me? Does she know I'm teetering on the precipice of sanity?

"Be right there!"

---

Sally spits random questions at me like I'm on a quiz show and the clock is ticking down.

"Do you use drugs?"

"No."

"Alcohol?"

"Sometimes."

"Were you drinking the night your son was abducted?"

This one trips me up, and I seriously consider lying. "I had a few drinks at the party, but I wasn't drunk. Everyone was drinking. It *was* a party, after all."

"How many drinks did you consume that night?"

I don't tell her I started drinking that afternoon while decorating the cellar. "Two at most." I have no idea how much alcohol I consumed. Definitely over the legal driving limit.

"Have you ever been charged with DUI?"

She's baiting me. She knows I have. "Yes."

"More than once?"

"Yes." I take a deep breath. If her goal was to make me feel worse about myself, she has succeeded. "The DUIs were a long time ago. Before I even turned eighteen. I was young and dumb."

"I hope you don't mind, but I took a look around. It's my job. I noticed you don't have much food in your refrigerator or your cupboards. The food you do have is what would be considered junk food. What do you feed your son?"

"Wow." This one knocks me for a loop. I never thought for a moment that what I feed my son would come into question. They're digging for anything that makes me look bad. "I was planning on going to the store. Also, we eat out a lot. I'm a terrible cook, and Bodie loves Rob's place and the Asian Café. Whenever I cook, he won't eat anyway, so what's the point?"

"Are you seeing anyone, Ms. White?"

"No." I'm fairly sure she already asked me that earlier.

"No one before or after your husband's death?"

"No." I say firmly. J.D. doesn't deserve to pay the price for any of this.

"What about life insurance?"

"I have life insurance. In case something happens to me. It goes into a trust for Bodie."

"What about Bodie? Is there a policy on his life?"

"No." I swallow hard. She's jabbing at my soft spots.

"That's all for now. I'll let you know if I need anything else. Thank you for taking the time. I understand how difficult this is." She gathers her things and stands.

"Do you have children?" I don't mean to sound snarky, but I do and stand.

"No," she answers proudly, and I follow her to the door. "Also, it wouldn't hurt to talk to the press. The more eyes and ears on this, the better. And get a cell phone and some security cameras." She opens the door.

"Sally, I answered all your questions honestly. Can you please answer one for me?" I look her in the eye.

"I'll certainly try." Her brow and double chin up.

"Am I a suspect? Do you really think I did this?"

Sally presses her lips inward and lowers her shoulders. "Ms. White," she says sweetly, and I think she's going to reassure me, "everyone's a suspect. Especially someone with means" —she raises her index finger—"opportunity"—she raises a second finger—"and three, motive. M.O.M. A mom."

She walks out and limps down the steps, like her left leg doesn't bend very well. How is she still an agent? The FBI website states agents are required to retire at 57. She's got to be banging on that door.

"Am I being watched?" I yell after her.

"That's two questions," she says without turning around—and there are half a dozen news cameras across the road pointed at me.

Of course I'm being watched.

# EIGHT

Talk to the press, Sally said. The thought terrifies me. People hate me—they won't sympathize with the heartbroken woman whose child has been taken. No matter what I say or do, they'll blame me.

After a shower, I dress in clean jeans and a white sweater. Then I roll my damp hair into a bun, apply a little makeup to hide the dark circles under my eyes, and still look like twenty miles of rough road.

I don't own an umbrella, so I wait until it stops raining. A glass of red wine helps calm my nerves while I tape my son's drawings to the refrigerator. Later, I pull a dusty photo of Bodie presenting a handful of dandelions off the wall. His sweet smile and those big brown eyes are like a warm hug around my heart. I blow away some of the dust and kiss him.

There's a break in the weather, and jagged shards of sunlight sneak out. News vans, cars, SUVs, people—so many I can't count. All waiting behind my gate and the yellow crime scene tape. I take a deep breath and prepare to be crucified.

I'm not even halfway across the yard before they're firing questions at me. I ignore them and open the gate, duck under the yellow tape and out into the road.

A bright light on a camera kicks on, and they swarm like hungry hogs.

"Ms. White, do you know where your son is?"

"No," I say.

A blonde reporter shoves a microphone in my face. "Is it true you were at a party when your son was taken?"

"That's not what happened."

In an instant, a million cell phones are hovering around my head. I wipe Bodie's photo with my sleeve. "My son, Bodie White, was stolen from my home at around 3 a.m. on November 1. If anyone saw anything, please contact the Calaveras County Sheriff's Department immediately. Anything at all—even if you think it doesn't matter, it could be important. Bodie is only five years old." I hold his photo up. "I'm begging anyone who has information to please come forward."

"What would you say to the person who has Bodie?"

"Give him back." Tears sting my eyes. "He's an innocent little boy and doesn't deserve any of this. Please . . . just drop him off somewhere safe. He needs to come home. He needs his mama. And his mama needs him." I can't take it another second—I start crying.

"Are you going to the candlelight vigil tonight?"

"I—I don't know anything about it." I turn and walk away.

"Did you have anything to do with the disappearance of your son?"

I duck under the crime scene tape, through the gate, and press the button. Slowly, the gate swings shut.

"Isn't it strange your son is abducted exactly one year after your husband was murdered?"

I run across the yard.

"Any idea who Pleatherface is?"

I reach the porch steps.

"Come back, Widow White Trash!"

I slam the door, feeling hollow inside. Toss the eight-by-ten of Bodie onto the armchair. With my back against the wall, I slide down until I'm sitting on the floor, staring past my skinny, outstretched legs, taking in the mud on my white Converse.

After hours of tossing and turning and crying, I give up. My attempt to get any rest is futile.

I just about jump out of my skin when the doorbell rings. The police are the only ones with the access code to the front gate. They must have news.

Running downstairs, I peek out the window. A woman dressed in jeans and a black leather jacket is at my front door, holding two pizza boxes and grocery bags.

She sees me in the window and says, "Hey! It's just me, Pearl."

I recognize the sultry voice. It's Maggie, but she's not in uniform. I open the door.

"Hope I'm not being pushy—but it was two-for-one at Pizza Barn, and I didn't really feel like dining alone. Thought *maybe* you didn't either."

"I haven't really been dining at all."

The pizza smells good. Delicious, actually. I can't be rude, and it's the first time I feel like eating. "Come in."

---

Maggie brought me a new cell phone, a cordless house phone, and she says she'll accompany me to the candlelight vigil if I'm up for it. I appreciate all the trouble she's gone to, but I still ask if it would be awful if I didn't attend. She assures me that not attending the vigil would be the wise choice—she doesn't want to go either.

We're at the kitchen counter, halfway through an all-meat thick crust and our godawful back stories, when Maggie guzzles the last of her beer like an expert. She releases an unrestrained burp worthy of poetry. "Nice," I say admiringly. There's something about her. She seems authentic. Protective, like she'd have your back in a bar fight. For the first time in years, I catch myself liking someone and wanting her to like me back. Like I'm back in junior high and giddy with the thought of making friends. She burps again, only longer and louder this time.

"God, if I burped like that, it'd just be gross. You do it and it's freaking cute. You're gorgeous, and smart. Independent. You make me sick." I grin.

She laughs and spills as she refills my wine glass. "Wish my ex thought of me that way. He just thinks I'm a . . . 'cunt' was the word."

"Whoa." I wait. She's not only spilling wine, she's spilling her guts like my new BFF. "He said that?" I cover my mouth.

"Yeah. It got ugly real fast after that, and he left. I don't know—maybe it's for the best. But nights are tough. Being alone in the dark when it's so fucking quiet and that voice in your head won't shut up. That's the absolute worst."

"Tell me about it. After Tuck was killed, I traded a horse for a travel trailer. Bodie and I went to Big Trees and slept in that thing for two weeks. When we came home, he was so scared, I had to sleep with him and his sock monkey."

She nods sympathetically, and I don't want to lie to her. "That's a lie." I sit up straight and confess. "I slept in my four-year-old's room because *I* was scared. He had to comfort me."

"I don't know what I'd do," Maggie says. "There's no right or wrong way to act when something like that happens. And people are so quick to judge."

"Having the kitchen completely remodeled helped. It's where he was killed."

"I know. I was here that night. He was my first homicide."

"I didn't know that."

"Why didn't you move? Get the hell out of here."

"Lots of reasons." I swig some of my wine.

"You were afraid it would make you look bad. Only the guilty run. You started going to church to beg for forgiveness. I worked the case—heard *all* the rumors."

"I had nowhere to go. I would've had to sell the vineyard for next to nothing because no one wants to live in a murder house."

"Ever get spooked?"

"All the time. Mama swore this place was haunted. That's why she left."

"Really?"

"No. She smoked meth. The only ghosts haunting her were the shadow people—they chased her away. All the way off the Golden Gate Bridge."

"Oh. Shit." Maggie pops another beer, and we let the silence linger while we eat. It's nice.

Finally, I say, "Did you see they're calling him Pleatherface because he's imitating Leather Face? You know, with the mask and all."

"The dude from Texas Chainsaw Massacre?" She sounds surprised.

I nod. "And they're calling me Widow White Trash."

"Oh shit. Worst thing you can do right now is get lost in distractions. This is a marathon—not a sprint. Nothing happens fast."

"Why not?"

"Because we have rules—procedures to follow. Even if I thought Bodie was in the house next door, I can't just bust in and take a look. I have to go through the proper channels, get a warrant. Sometimes that can be done in a few hours; sometimes it can't be done at all, if the judge feels there isn't enough evidence."

"Doesn't that make you nuts?"

"Sometimes. But it can save our ass too. People screw up. And if we screw up and get it wrong, it's not as simple as saying sorry."

My cheeks are hot—the wine has gone to my head.

Maggie empties the bottle of red into my glass. I've consumed an entire bottle by myself and have lost all give-a-shit.

"What if Rocha didn't have to follow procedure? He'd already have your ass locked up. After a year, a case is considered cold, and your husband's murder is about to be retired. Rocha's panicking." She raises her brow and tilts her head as she grabs another slice. "He's become obsessed."

"With me?"

"Yep." Her cheeks are filled to capacity as she nods and chews.

"Why? I didn't do anything. Why is he wasting time on me?"

She swallows. "I actually asked him that. He said—Occam's razor."

"What the hell's that supposed to mean?"

"The simplest answer is usually correct."

"How am I the simple answer?" I sip and swirl the wine in my glass.

"In my limited experience, there are no simple answers, ever," she says around another mouthful. "I revisited your husband's file and—" Maggie shakes her head. "Sorry. This is the last thing you need. I came here to make you feel a little less shitty. I'm sorry." She pushes her beer away, signaling that she's done drinking.

"Oh my gosh. Don't be sorry." I set my glass down, slide off my stool, and hug her. "I can't tell you how nice it is to have someone to talk to who isn't scrutinizing everything I say."

"Let's keep it between us, okay? Rocha would hit the roof if he knew I was here hanging out with you, and I'd be in deep shit."

She wants to be my friend as much as I want her to be. But then it hits me—she must know the house isn't being watched, or she wouldn't be here. I can't help but smile and immediately put my hand over my mouth, trying to look concerned.

"The minute Rocha has probable cause—man, look out," Maggie warns me.

"I know parents are always suspect, and since Bodie doesn't have a daddy anymore, of course they're going to look at me. But I swear to you, Maggie, I had nothing to do with this."

"I believe you, but I'd still find a lawyer. Being prepared is never a bad thing. Pretty sure they're gonna ask for a poly when you see Rocha tomorrow."

"A poly?"

"Polygraph—lie detector test."

I rub the back of my neck way too hard. The pain from being strangled is still there, but I squeeze harder. "They really think I'd hurt Bodie?" Tears fill my eyes. The pain of being accused of harming your own child is so much worse than the pain in my neck.

"They don't know, Pearl. Think of it as a way they can exclude you. But I'd still have a lawyer handy. I've seen these things go sideways."

"Everyone already thinks I'm somehow involved. Getting a lawyer just makes me look guilty." I lower my head, and here come the damn tears again. Maggie reaches over and rubs my back. It does nothing to console me. I need to stop, get myself under control. She stands and wraps her arms around me like a true friend until I settle down.

"I'm sorry," I say, wiping my snotty face with a Pizza Barn napkin.

"Your kid is missing. You don't have to apologize. God. Why do women always feel the need to apologize? For everything. Let's both stop it right now. No more 'I'm sorrys' from either of us. Okay?"

I nod. She's right. "Do you believe in a woman's intuition?"

"Oh, hell yes, absolutely, one hundred percent. It's how I knew my ex was seeing someone. I can't explain it. I had zero proof, and believe me, I know where to look, but I damn sure felt it."

"Right?" I blow my stuffy nose. "It's the same with this guy. I know he killed Tucker and has my son." I combined the leftover pizza into one box.

"Unless it's a copycat. But you said his eyes were different. Like almond shaped, right? Do you mean like Asian?"

"A little. The outside corners of his eyes point upward."

The surprise on Maggie's face is on the verge of shocked. "Did you report this? I don't remember seeing this in any statements. All I remember is you saying his eyes were brown."

"I told Rocha numerous times. And the sketch artist." I feel like I have to defend myself.

Maggie shakes her head. "I'm going to request another sketch. You cool with that?"

"Sure. Anything." I shove the empty pizza box down into the overflowing trash can. The silence becomes awkward, and I wonder what she's thinking. "Maggie, I've racked my brain for over a year, tried an online hypnotist, self-hypnosis, anything and everything. I finally called my meemaw Irene. She's my daddy's mama." I clear my throat, and it still burns a little. "Meemaw is very religious, okay? Very, very, religious."

"Nothing wrong with that." Maggie sounds like she's trying to reassure me, and I'm dreading what I'm about to say. I'm going to lose her the moment I utter the word.

"Voodoo." I try not to cringe as I let it soak in for a second. "Yep. Meemaw is actually a manbo—some people say mambo."

"Okay, I don't know what that is."

"Her clients call her a mother of magic. Anyway, whether or not you buy into any of it, and I sure don't, but she said she would do some kind of ritual. I figured what the hell, can't hurt, right?"

Maggie shrugs, looking like she'd be relieved if I laughed and said I was just kidding. "But today, out of the blue, something *really* weird happened."

"Weirder than regular old voodoo shit weird?" Maggie rolls her eyes. "Sorry—*no*, not sorry. Kidding. Alcohol frees the caged asshole in me. Please, continue. I'm dying to see where this is going." She crosses her arms and waits.

"I walked into the bathroom half asleep and grabbed a box of tampons from underneath the sink—and the memory from over a year ago came to me. Just like Meemaw said. She calls them demon visions. While I'm holding this box of tampons, the memory of *him* stocking boxes of tampons at the Murphys Market comes to me clear as day. I remember. He looked at me and turned completely red, like he was embarrassed. I reached in front of him to grab a box off the shelf and saw *those almond eyes*. His eyes."

Maggie doesn't say a word or react. Instead, she stretches across the counter and grabs her beer. After a few long sips, she picks at the label. People who pick are troubled about something. I know because I'm a picker. Mama was too.

Maybe I went too far. She doesn't believe me. I wouldn't if I were in her shoes. Finally, Maggie guzzles her beer and looks at me as if pondering her next words carefully. She sighs and says, "I know a guy who can help."

# NINE

Pleatherface is national news. Bodie White, his mother, and even his dead father are national news. CNN, HLN, MSNBC, FOX—and it's all over the local ten o'clock as well.

"A bizarre twist of events," they call it. "Proof that truth is stranger than fiction."

"A Halloween nightmare straight out of a horror film," Lester Holt begins as I pour another glass of wine that I hope will dull the ache.

It doesn't.

Outside, I light a cigarette. It's raining so hard, the news vans have gone. More likely, they're at the park filming the candlelight vigil. Candlelight vigil in this weather? How's that going to work?

Like Lester Holt said, it's a nightmare straight out of a horror film, only it's come to life and I'm playing the lead. But instead of just sitting around waiting to die, I'm going to fight back. Be brave and meet with Maggie's guy. He's connected and doesn't play by the rules, according to her.

I'm the one who caused this; I should be the one to fix it. I need my gun.

Bonnie and Clyde, two of the friendlier feral cats, are on the front porch, dodging the rain and meowing. Bodie and I found the litter of kittens last year in the haystack after their mama abandoned them. We bottle-fed them and they all survived, then disappeared except for these two. And even they don't like me unless they're hungry.

Their bowl is empty.

I flick my cigarette out into the rain and trot to the garage, grab a ten-pound sack of cat food, and return to set it on the porch. With my pocket knife, I slice open the center of the bag. "Have at it, you two."

In the Subaru a minute later, I start the engine, but I can't see well enough to drive until I stop this pointless crying. It takes a few minutes to get control of myself and pull out. With the headlights off, I drive away slowly through the gate, the crime scene tape, and the steady downpour.

On a muddy back road, the Subaru slips and slides and fishtails uphill. When I finally reach the top and am headed down the other side, I breathe a sigh of relief. It doesn't take long to find a spot to pull off and park without getting stuck.

Rain hammers down, and I cinch my hood over my head. This time, I've prepared by putting on the rainsuit Tucker used to hunt in. The camouflage is perfect on a night like this, because I do not want to be seen.

Ten minutes through the forest along a game trail, I reach the ranch. Another ten minutes across the pasture, and over two fences, I reach the old cabin. It's dark inside, and I stay as quiet as I can, hoping I don't alert the dogs. They're more than likely huddled up somewhere warm and dry.

The backdoor is unlocked, and it squeals upon my intrusion. I step inside and slowly close it behind me. With my back pressed against the door, I wait, listen, and breathe.

A glowing woodstove and a TV are the only light. The eleven o'clock news reporter reminds me of the missing Calaveras County child, in case I forgot. The scene transitions from the news desk to a woman with a microphone catching the wind and rain. The broadcast is from earlier today. That's my house in the background, bordered in yellow crime scene tape.

The remote is on the coffee table. I grab it and press mute. Silence. I breathe. Relax my shoulders. The cabin is a bigger mess than mine and smells like stale smoke and mold. A toilet flushes, and the bathroom door opens.

"Hey." I step across the living room.

J.D. jumps sideways. "Oh, *shit*. Pearl," he says softly. "What the fuck?" His hair rears up in every direction, and I realize he's naked.

"You can't be here," he whispers, grabbing my shoulders and turning me back into the tiny kitchen. "You trying to get me busted?"

"No, of course not. You know I'd never do that."

"Do I?"

His doubt is unexpected, and it stings like a slap. "I thought you'd be happy to see me. No one knows I'm here. I parked far away, in the woo—"

"You best go," he interrupts.

"Okay." Something's wrong. It's like he's irritated or mad at me. Does he think I had something to do with Bodie's abduction?

"I need my gun back," I say, trying not to think about the way his nakedness felt against me. Inside me. He's harder to kick than cigarettes. And just like smoking, I know I shouldn't do it, but the harder I try to force him from my mind, the more I want him, the more I crave him, even just for a few minutes.

"What do you need the gun for?" His eyes are big and bright and beautiful like Bodie's.

"Protection. And—I mostly kind of wanted to see you." Here come the tears. "I don't know what to do." I wrap my arms around his waist and sob. "I wish he would have killed me."

"Don't say that. Come on, they'll find him. You just have to stay strong, 'cause it's gonna get worse 'fore it gets better."

I want to ask how. How can it get worse? But I know. No matter what happens, he's right—from here on out, it is going to get worse. I know it.

Bu right now, at this moment, I don't want to worry about anything that might happen. I don't want to borrow trouble. My fingertips find the soft fuzz that runs from his chest, down his stomach, and between his legs. I force my mouth onto his.

"Stop it." He grabs my wrist, removing my hand from between his legs. "You need to go. Now."

"Why? What the hell's going on?"

J.D. steps back. "I'll get your gun." He leaves me standing with my heart in my hand. I've never felt so utterly rejected. What have I done wrong? In less than a minute, my mind comes up with a dozen scenarios, none of them good. Then, a scenario I hadn't considered speaks.

"What are you doing? Is that a gun?" a woman's groggy voice croaks from the bedroom.

"It's my buddy's. The firing pin was fucked, so I fixed it and now I'm giving it back. Relax."

When he returns, J.D. has a pair of sweatpants and a T-shirt on. He's wiping the gun down with his shirt. Removing his fingerprints, I assume, because he doesn't trust me.

"Sorry." He hands over the gun.

"I thought—" I can't find the strength to finish the sentence. I hate that I've given him the power to hurt me like this.

"Pearl, girl, come on. I was just trying to keep away from you. Now's not a good time for us. You said so yourself. You told me to stay away. I just needed something to take my mind off of you. I swear to God. It's not like—" He stops midsentence.

*She's* standing in the living room. A middle-aged brunette shaped like a frog, wearing nothing but J.D.'s blue plaid coat and a goofy grin. Linda Flowers. Tucker and I met her a few years ago at a Future Farmers of America fundraiser. She owns this ranch along with Mr. Flowers, and is J.D.'s boss.

"Thanks, J.D. Sorry for stopping by so late." I rush out the door, hoping like hell she doesn't know who I am and that J.D. satisfies her well enough that she'll keep her mouth shut and not risk losing her hot young lover. A tiny part of me wants to go back inside and shoot them both, but I'm not that kind of person. I don't have it in me.

I slip the gun into my coat pocket and begin the hike back to the car in the rain. As a girl, I used to love long walks in the rain—no one could see your tears.

You'd think I'd learn. I've *never* known a faithful man. Daddy cheated on Mama every chance he got. My husband preferred prostitutes and was arrested four times for solicitation. I bailed him out. Pathetic, I know.

Why would J.D. be any different? I have no right to feel the sting of a scorn lover. I fell for him way too hard, way too soon, and got *exactly* what I deserve. Still, that doesn't change feeling like I've just lost part of myself.

Daddy was right when he said, "If they'll do it for you, they'll do it to you."

I peel off the plastic rainsuit and toss it into the back of the car.

Inside the Subaru, I blast the heater, wiping at my tears and then the foggy window. It's 11:47. I have ten minutes to get to the cemetery.

I'm late. It's a quarter after midnight when I pull down the narrow side street, heading up to the rusted iron gates of Buena Vista Cemetery. Forged metal in old English-style letters hang overhead, like you'd see in every gothic, black-and-white horror.

I snicker. Buena Vista. The translation of "good view" seems absurd. Good view for whom? The deceased?

Muddy roads and crooked headstones terrace the hillside. I take the driveway to the right; it loops the entire cemetery. Old graves neighbor new ones as I pass plot after plot. Through my wet windshield, a kaleidoscope of shiny beads, like you'd get for lifting your shirt at Mardi Gras, cling to a headstone. I slow.

The bedazzled grave is decorated with a dozen tiny American flags whipping in the wind, pink plastic roses, and a wind chime hanging and banging from an overgrown oak.

I coast to the next plot over and stop on an uphill slope. Branches and a beer can litter the grave. I pull my hood up over my head and rush out.

Working fast, I kick the branches aside and pick up the beer can. It's been a year since Tucker was buried here. I don't want to think of the degree of decomposition, but I can't help myself as I look at his headstone.

*Tucker Benjamin White*
*Beloved husband and father.*

It was *not* my idea to meet here. This is the last place I want to be, but this is where he said to meet him. I get back in the car and drive to an area overlooking the cemetery. The two green picnic tables strike me as odd. Who picnics at a cemetery?

My headlights graze a gray Toyota 4Runner parked along the fence. A man sits behind the wheel. I pull in next to him, and he looks over at me.

I'm glad I have the gun in my coat pocket—this guy looks sketchy as hell when he steps out of his vehicle. He's huge, tall and muscular under a black hoodie and a ball cap. He walks around to my passenger side and opens the door.

"Name?"

"Pearl White."

"Who sent you?"

"Maggie Martinez."

He struggles to fit inside my little car.

Once he's in, he pulls the door closed and reaches his right hand my way. "Woody Harrelson." He takes my hand, and it disappears in his paw as we shake.

I giggle, mostly because I'm nervous as hell. "Woody Harrelson, really?"

His head is an inch from touching the roof as he looks at me. Soon his eyes will glow, he'll turn green, and his muscles will bulge, tearing his clothes—but instead of turning into the Hulk, he smiles. I'm relieved. Surprised at how his smile makes him so much less intimidating. His teeth are perfect and his tone charming.

"It really is my name. Well, Woodrow, but no way anyone's getting away with calling me Woodrow." His breath smells like he just chewed a mint. "Now, why am I in a cemetery on a dark and stormy night?" he asks.

"I wasn't the one who wanted to meet here. Maggie said *you* said I should be here at midnight."

He rubs his face, like maybe he's frustrated with me. Heck, I don't know how these things work.

"What specifically do you want from me, Pearl White?"

"I need you to find a man. Fast. And I don't care what it costs."

"What man?"

"The inbred who stole my son."

"Does the inbred have a name?"

I take a deep breath and lick my lips. This is it. Now or never.

"Kenny Tait."

# TEN

Lightning flashes, so close it illuminates the entire cemetery. A few seconds later, thunder rattles my Subaru. Thunder has frightened me since I was a child.

"That one was loud enough to wake the dead," Woody says, but I don't laugh. It's not funny. I reach into my jacket pocket, pulling out a pack of Salems and a lighter.

Woody reaches into his hoodie pouch and offers me a piece of gum.

"No, thanks," I say, and light up.

He unwraps the foil on a stick of gum and folds it into his mouth. I crack the windows, allowing some of the smoke to escape.

"How do you know this Kenny Tait?" he asks.

"I'd rather not get into that."

"I'd rather not go into a job blind." He gently pinches the cigarette out of my hand, takes a drag, and flicks it out the window. "It's getting late."

"Are you licensed?"

"Depends."

"Do you abide by any sort of confidentiality laws?"

"Of course. I mean, unless—well, it's complicated. Let's just say, if you're a friend of Maggie's, you're a friend of mine. I take care of my friends." He holds up his pinky finger. "I pinky swear." He smiles again, and for some odd reason, it reminds me of J.D.

Hurt rears its ugly head in my heart. Hooking up with this guy would serve J.D. right. I read somewhere that sex is the best way to start the healing process and get over a broken heart. I hook my pinky around his and decide I'm going to have to risk it all if I want Bodie back.

"I met Kenny when he was working at Murphys Market. Me and Bodie were in there all the time shopping, and we'd chit-chat, you know, like you do, and one thing led to another."

"Back the fuck up. Are you saying what I think you're saying?"

"Bodie really liked him. Kenny's kind of a man-child. He was twenty-one, but mentally I'd say he's— I don't know. We were hangin' out all the time, just as friends and—"

"Did you have a sexual relationship with Kenny Tait?" Woody interrupts.

"Eventually. Yes. Once." I reach the pack of cigarettes and pick one out.

"And this is the guy you believed killed your husband?"

I nod.

"Is that a yes?"

"Yes. Yes."

"And then?"

"And then I realized what a nutjob Kenny was. It was just a fling. No big deal. But Kenny became obsessed. Said he wanted to *marry* me. I told him to back off, that I was already married, and a few days later he killed Tucker. Now he has Bodie, end of story." I place the cigarette between my lips and light up.

"I read that you shot the man who killed your husband."

"Obviously, it didn't take." I inhale smoke, hold it until it goes to my head.

"I suggest you go to the police with this information. They have better resources than I do."

I blow it out the window. "I can't! They'll lock me up and throw away the key. Too much time has passed. I should have spoken up sooner. Waiting this long makes me look guilty as hell."

"That it does," Woody agrees, and runs his hand down the lower half of his face. It's quiet except for the wind. "I need a photo of Kenny."

"I don't have any. Just Google his name and add 'missing in Calaveras County.'"

Woody raises one brow at me and pulls an iPhone from the pocket of his hoodie. He doesn't type—probably his fingers are too big. Instead, he holds the phone near his chin and speaks: "Kenny Tait—missing in Calaveras County."

I smoke and hope I didn't just confess to the wrong guy.

Before I finish my cigarette, Woody holds his phone up. "This the guy?"

Kenny Tait's big head and stupid face fill the screen. "Yep. That's him." I take a closer look. "He's a lot younger in that photo, but its him." It looks a lot like a mug shot.

Woody takes a second look, then stares at me in disbelief. "Not to be an asshole, but this dude looks borderline special needs. Like he should be playing banjo barefoot on a porch in the Deep South."

He thinks I'm a horrible, disgusting slut, because I had sex with a homely man. How come guys can have sex with anyone willing, but girls can't? It's such double-standard bullshit. I consider defending my mistake by explaining how Kenny was not only a virgin, he was insecure, and to be honest I felt sorry for him. "I don't care if you think I'm a slut." I flick my cigarette out the window. "A slut is just a woman with the morals of a man."

The rain stops for the moment. It smells clean outside.

"Next question. And think this one over carefully before answering." Woody pauses. "What do you want me to do if I find Kenny Tait?"

"I don't care. Do whatever it takes to get my son back. Torture the son of a bitch, cut off his fingers and toes—just get him to talk. Once you have Bodie—" I hesitate, looking out the window at the clouds floating on a breeze. "I guess . . . maybe you should kill the bastard." I turn to Woody. "Don't you think? So he can't come after us. I don't want to have to look over my shoulder the rest of my life. Or worry that he could take Bodie again."

"I'll need five thousand. Cash. Upfront. Then another five if and when it's done."

"No problem. But how? I have a couple hundred on me, and here." I peel off my wedding ring and hand it to him. "You can have it. It cost twenty-five grand, so it's worth at least ten. And I'll give you more—whatever you want, when it's done."

Woody studies the diamonds and then the band. He tries to shove it onto his pinky, but it stops at his first knuckle. When he looks at me and smiles, I feel a twinge of hope. Wonderful hope.

"Go home and get some rest. I'll be in touch soon."

# ELEVEN

Clips from the candlelight vigil held for Bodie play over and over on all the national news channels. I have to stop torturing myself with rumors and speculations offered by wannabe true-crime reporters.

CNN broadcasts to the world that Ms. White, the missing child's mother, did not attend the vigil and could not be reached for comment. It's almost 3 a.m. Dishes are washed and put away. Floors are swept and mopped. The trash taken outside and counters wiped clean.

I'm out of wine and whiskey, but I found a bottle of Tucker's Ativan. I take two and keep them handy in case I decide to self-medicate myself into a coma. Exhausted, I drag myself to Bodie's room.

George, the sock monkey, smiles at me, and I snatch him up, cradle him next to my face and inhale deeply. He smells like little boy—part dirt, part candy. The two of us crawl into Bodie's bed, and I pull the blankets up around us, then begin my bargain with God.

"I'm so, so sorry. Please, I'm begging you just give me Bodie back. I'll be good for the rest of my life. I've learned my lesson. *Please*, don't let my sins stain his soul." I'm surprised to find that my eyes still produce tears, but the Ativan and sleep dry them.

---

Sunlight fills the room as I wake in Bodie's bed. I actually slept for four hours.

I bring George with me as I walk to the bathroom. The house is freezing, and I wonder if the new heating system has quit. The toilet seat is like a block of ice as I sit.

Pissed that I spent a small fortune on central heating and am now freezing my butt off, I remember needing propane last week. They called to schedule a delivery, and I kept putting them off. Other than the fireplace in the living room, the entire house is heated by propane.

I set George on the hamper and wash my hands in Arctic water because no propane means no hot water. I cup my hands and take a breath before splashing my face.

As I dry, I look in the mirror at my ugly face and want to scratch my eyes out. Instead, I slap myself. Hard. It stings, and my cheek quickly turns pink. I do it again, harder.

"Think, you stupid bitch!" I watch my right cheek redden, and then I step back. That's when I see it—

A way to give them Kenny's name without looking guilty. I open the makeup drawer, find my cranberry Dior lipstick, and remove the lid. Wait. Fingerprints. No, it's fine—why wouldn't my prints be on my lipstick? Maybe I shouldn't, though.

I twist the tube. The lipstick spins up, and I press it to the mirror. It doesn't feel right. But it doesn't feel wrong either. The Ativan, the stress, or simple white trash genetics hinder the odds of becoming a criminal mastermind.

With the dark red lipstick, I write:

Last chanse or Bodie is mine!

Surely, the idiot can't spell correctly.

**U Ken T catch me**

**Pleatherface**

I step back, take a long hard look and change my mind. It's stupid. Too obvious. Nobody would be this dumb, not even Ken T. I use handfuls of toilet paper to rub and wipe away the false evidence.

A funky techno beat buzzes from down the hall. It takes me a few seconds to realize that it's my new phone. The one Maggie gave me. I flush the stained toilet paper, toss the lipstick into the trash, and hurry to Bodie's room, where I left the phone. Maybe it's good news.

It's a text message. No, good news wouldn't come via text message. I open it and read. *At gold country roasters. want something??* The caller ID is M.M. Maggie Martinez must have programmed her number into my contacts.

I text her back: *Yes!! Please!! Lrg chai soy latte T.Y.* I think I love Maggie.

While I wait, I sit on Bodie's bed, wondering if he misses me as much as I miss him. God, why hasn't Woody been in touch? Maybe he's not as reliable as Maggie says. Has she even looked into what I told her about the guy at the market? It's like I need to spell it out for them. But how, without incriminating myself? I scratch my scalp harder and harder, as if I can scratch out the answer.

If anyone can locate Kenny Tait, it's the FBI. I close my eyes and try to think like a criminal. What does he want? Me. He's trying to hurt me by taking Bodie. "Oh my God." I open my eyes. What if he's sorry?

I rush downstairs to the kitchen, grab a black Sharpie from the junk drawer, and hurry to the armchair next to the front door. The eight-by-ten of Bodie is right where I left it after showing it to the press. I pull the lid off the felt pen and use my left hand to write across the glass.

Please FORGIVE me
Ken Tait

In the kitchen, Maggie hands over the most spectacular-smelling chai. She looks in my cupboards and finds a clean plate. The last one. I want to show her the photo on the armchair, but I'm too scared. Fabricating evidence could get me into so much trouble. But if it leads them to Kenny Tait and Bodie, then it's justified. Right?

She sets out warm scones and gingerbread from a white bag. The smell reminds me that there are still a few good things left in this world. I hug her. I can't help myself. She's been so kind. "Thank you," I say, and she waves me off.

"It's nothing. No big deal. I'm on nights now, and sitting around the house alone . . . *not good.*" She rolls her eyes and shakes her head, and I understand exactly what she means. Being around me reminds her that things could be far worse than your boyfriend dumping you.

I sip my latte—possibly the best I've ever had—and pick the corner off a piece of gingerbread. Maggie goes for a scone. "Any new news?" I ask.

Maggie doesn't allow a mouthful to stop her from answering. "They're draggin' your pond today." She swallows. "And probably bringing in cadaver dogs." She takes another bite.

What a huge waste of time and money and manpower, but I don't know what to say other than, "Oh." And sip

"What'd you think of Woody?" she asks.

I shrug. "I don't know. Seems—experienced. Capable."

"He's hot though, right?"

I smile. "I'd officially classify him as a hunk." I pick another piece of the gingerbread and pop it into my mouth. "How do you know him?"

"Better you don't know," Maggie says.

"I wish he'd contact me. I haven't heard a word. Have you?"

"No. No way. I don't want to know anything about whatever you two worked out. That's between you and him." She waves her hands in the air.

I nod. She has to see the photo.

"I just know if it were me, I'd want Woody on my side. He'll do whatever it takes." Maggie smiles. I trust her. She's guided by common sense and a true desire to bring Bodie home. She's not all law and order.

"There's something I need to show you. I was going to wait for Woody. Show it to him and let him handle it. But I trust you."

"What?"

"In here." I lead Maggie to the armchair.

"It's the photo I used when I talked to the press."

Maggie looks down and squints, but doesn't touch anything. "Please forgive me Kenny Tait. Huh." She pulls out her phone. "Have you touched this?"

"Yes. I picked it up earlier to hang it back on the wall. That's when I saw what he wrote. He was here. This Kenny Tait."

Maggie takes several pictures with her phone.

"I should have told you sooner. I'm sorry. I just wasn't sure—"

"Not sure? About what?" She lifts her palms.

"I don't know. I was thinking I should let Woody handle it. You said—" I sound whiny and look down, shaking my head.

Maggie holds her phone in her hand and crosses her arms. "Who's Ken Tait? And why the hell would he leave his name?"

The silence is beyond awkward while I consider what to share and how to share it. "I've been racking my brain. I think it might be the guy I told you about at Murphys Market. Did you check the employee records?"

"Yes." Maggie's face is blank, unblinking. Her fragile nostrils flare. She uncrosses her arms and looks up at the mirror. "I need to report this to Rocha. The entire house should be brushed again for prints. There somewhere you can go?" She sighs.

"There's a travel trailer out back."

"You should stay there for a few days." She seems irritated with me, and I don't blame her one bit. Shaking her head, she looks down at her phone and presses buttons.

When she's done, she looks me in the eye and says, "Mi Wuk people have a saying—every lie is really two lies. The one we tell others, and the one we tell ourself to justify it."

"Maggie, I'm *not* lying, I swear—" I want to work it out, but she walks out the door.

By noon, the house, my entire property, and the surrounding hillsides are swarming with an FBI evidence response team. I peek outside the trailer every now and then. A dozen agents dressed in white hazmat suits search every nook and cranny, including my trash cans. News vans and film crews line the road again.

Divers are gathered at the pond. Mist rises from the surface, the water as smooth and black as obsidian.

It sounds like hound dogs baying somewhere off in the distance. Terrible thoughts float to the top. What if they find him? What if he's dead? Quickly, I drown the idea with a dose of white wine and Ativan.

Detectives have confiscated my laptop, several pairs of shoes, and some of my clothes. At least there's heat in the trailer, and I found a good book. One I forgot I'd bought last year, from Books On Main, and it's been in the trailer ever since.

The first chapter of *Blue Mountain* captivates me. I'm deep into the story when a heavy knock on the metal door rattles the trailer and startles me.

"Come in," I offer from the couch.

The door opens, and Special Agent Sally McNulty leans in without climbing the steps. "Hello, Ms. White. Would you mind coming with me, please?"

# TWELVE

The backseat of Agent McNulty's Tahoe smells like French fries and stale coffee.

"Am I under arrest?" I ask.

"You're being held for questioning." She doesn't take her eyes off the curvy blacktop.

"What's the difference?" I ask, a little too sarcastically.

"There's a big difference. We just want to clarify a few discrepancies."

I'm not handcuffed, so I guess being held for questioning is not as bad as being arrested. So why is my heart hammering, and why are my hands sweating? I pick and chew at the skin around my nails. No one will tell me what's going on. Maybe they found something. Wouldn't they tell me right off if it was Bodie?

"Is this about Bodie? Have you found him?" I ask.

"No," Sally says, and I don't know if I feel better or worse. I should call a lawyer, but that would just make me look like I've done something wrong and need a reason to defend myself. Then again, plenty of innocent people have been jailed for years.

Inside the Calaveras County Sheriff's Office, I'm led through a long corridor to a small room that's as claustrophobic as a cell. Cement walls. Cold metal chairs and matching table. Like an interrogation dinette set. Sally McNulty and Rocha sit on one side, me on the other.

"Do I need a lawyer?" I ask sheepishly.

Rocha's face is peppered with a five-o'clock shadow. He puts his elbows on the table and leans forward. "Have you done something other than lie to us that requires a defense attorney?"

"No," I say, wondering if he can see me trembling.

"You can have a lawyer present if you'd like," Sally says.

"I'm worried you think I had something to do with Bodie's disappearance."

"And your husband's murder," Rocha adds. "Let's not forget that."

"Kenny Tait's who you should be questioning." I look to Sally for support, but she's busy looking down at her phone.

"I'd like to take more photos of the bruising on your neck," Rocha says.

"Okay." I agree. They took photos at the house, before Rocha was assigned.

He gets up, opens the door, and pokes his head out. "Coop. You're up."

A silver-haired deputy who looks to be eighty limps in with a big black camera cradled in one hand.

"Would you mind moving your hair aside?" the photographer asks as he leans into my neck. The smell of Old Spice turns my stomach. Shutter clicks reverberate around the room with each shot, a dozen or more from every possible angle. Rocha stays close. Inspecting. Dissecting every detail. "I'd like you to place your hands around your neck," he asks.

"What?" I say.

"We have to confirm the ligature marks aren't self-induced." Rocha's no-nonsense explanation reveals his desperation to pin this on me.

"You've got to be kidding," I say. "You think I tried to strangle myself? Is that even possible?"

"Please, just place your fingers around your neck, thumbs forward." Rocha waits, crossing his arms. This is nuts. It's one thing to suspect me, but to think I'm capable of self-strangulation is beyond comprehension. It makes no sense, but I do it anyway. The photographer bends down and shoots again from every angle until he's satisfied and straightens up. "That should do it," he chirps.

"Thanks, Coop. Send the file both ways," Rocha orders as the old man exits.

"Thank you for your cooperation," Sally says. "We'd like to rule you out as a suspect. Would you be open to taking a polygraph?"

My heart rate skyrockets, and it might do the same if I'm hooked to a machine that's just waiting for my heart rate to increase and confirm deception.

"We just want to get a read. If you have nothing to hide, we can cross you off the list and move forward. It allows us to focus manpower in the right direction," Sally says with a reassuring grin. "It would be really helpful in Bodie's recovery. We want to bring him home to you."

With the thought of being home with Bodie in my arms, I nod. "Okay. But I need to know, have you found Kenny Tait? Are you even looking for him?"

"We're working on it," Sally answers.

After signing an agreement to voluntarily take the polygraph, I'm moved to another room. The door shuts slowly with an ominous click like the cock of a gun. Another old white guy, FBI deception expert Phil Hansen, introduces himself and fires the deadbolt on the door. "I'm only here to confirm your innocence, not establish guilt. Okay?" His glassy blue eyes under a bushy brow are kind but oddly penetrating at the same time.

"Okay." I nod.

"Let's wire you up." He motions for me to take a seat across the desk in an armchair the size and shape of a padded electric chair.

In no time, Phil straps a band just under my waist and secures it with a Velcro flap. As he wraps a second band above my breasts and tightens it, I notice a camera on a tripod in the far corner of the room.

The straps are cutting me in two, like a tourniquet. I can't breathe. A green light blinks, and I visualize the grainy recordings of the lying murderers I've watched on *Forensic Files*. Phil cuffs my upper arm with a blood pressure monitor. Wires run from a machine to each strap. Florescent lights burn down on me.

It's too hot in here. They're trying to make me sweat. I can't let on that it's working.

Phil seems nice enough, like a grandfather you'd see on a commercial for Consumer Cellular. He smiles and tells me to relax, as if that's actually possible. Who the hell could relax in a situation like this?

Finally, he slips little black finger cuffs on the tips of my index and ring finger as sweat drips from my armpits.

Phil moves to the desk, sits directly in front of his laptop screen, and clicks his mouse. "I'm just going to ask yes-or-no questions. I'll start with simple ones to establish a baseline. Do you understand?"

"Yes," I say, and take a deep breath.

"Is your name Pearl White?"

"Yes."

"Are you an American citizen?"

"Yes."

"Are you sitting down?"

"Yes."

"Are your eyes purple?"

"No." I grin.

"Have you been to the moon?"

"No." I'm sweating like crazy. They probably turn up the heat as a tactic.

"Do you intend to answer each question truthfully?"

"Yes." I count my breaths. Three seconds in and three seconds out.

"Have you ever told a lie?"

"Yes."

"Have you ever used illegal drugs?"

"Yes."

"Have you ever done something you're ashamed of?"

"Yes." I take a breath and focus on my muddy, white tennis shoes.

"Do you know where your son is?"

"No."

"Are the lights on in this room?"

"Yes."

"Have you ever researched how to pass a lie detector test?"

"Yes."

"Do you shower with water?"

"Yes."

"Did you harm your son in any way?"

"No." I fight the urge to let the question upset me.

"Is this 1922?"

"No."

"Do you know where your son is?"

"No." Phil's doing his job, and right now, his job is to confirm my innocence. "I do not," I add matter-of-factly.

"Do you know who has your son?"

"Yes. I believe so."

"Are you in any way involved in your son's abduction?"

"No."

"Did Elvis Presley take your son?"

"No."

"Do you know Kenny Tait?"

"Yes."

"Did you attempt to hire someone to murder Kenny Tait?"

Adrenaline surges. Time slows like the split second you have before being run over by a bus. My heart rate, blood pressure, and anger erupt at the way they set me up. I rip the sensors off my fingers. "We're done, and I want a lawyer. Now, you motherfucking cocksuckers!" I unstrap my chest and throw it aside.

Forgetting about the band strapped around my waist, I jump out of the chair and head for the door. The wires jerk the laptop off the desk and send it crashing to the floor. I fight the Velcro apart and throw the waistband in Phil's direction.

"This is such bullshit!" I open the door and walk out.

As I'm marching toward the exit, Rocha cuts me off in the hallway. I wag my finger in his face. "I'm sick and tired of being accused of hurting my husband and now my son! You either arrest me, or I'm leaving, you fucking asshole!"

Rocha reaches into his back pocket, grabs my wrist, and spins me around.

"You have the right to remain silent. Anything you say can and will be used against you in a court of law."

Cold metal handcuffs bind my wrists.

# THIRTEEN

Spending the night alone in a cold, gray cell offers much too much time to dwell on how repugnant my life's become. What people are saying about Widow White Trash. I try to keep the dark thoughts away and only let the good ones in, like therapist Maureen says. But it's not working. I keep replaying the night Kenny attacked me and stole Bodie. Over and over, reliving every moment again and again as if I can somehow change the outcome.

Not knowing if my son is dead or alive . . .

Living in limbo is breaking me. I imagine Bodie's sweet smile and hold tight to the chance that he *isn't* dead. I'd feel it if he were. Just like I felt it when Mama died. An inexplicable sickening fear that you know you'll never see or speak to the person you love ever again. Looking back, I had the same anxiety when Daddy died. I just didn't know what it was because I didn't find out about his death until weeks later.

Breakfast at the Calaveras County Detention Facility consists of powdered scrambled eggs, an orange, and cold toast slathered with thick, unmelted margarine. I eat a few bites of toast, drink a half cup of cold black coffee, and cry while waiting for my attorney to arrive.

Time crawls back and forth as I lie on a thin mattress atop the lower half of a stainless-steel bunk. My oversized orange jumpsuit smells like puke and piss. Not mine, and I wonder if it's another of Rocha's petty tactics to break me. Either way, I'm cracking.

Hours later, my empty stomach adds to the hollowness inside me, and I occupy my mind by biting my nails to the quick. My pinky bleeds. I wait and watch the blood slowly form a perfect droplet that eventually falls onto my orange pants.

I squeeze, forcing another drop, and wipe it on my shirt—over my heart. Leaving a line. Another drop, another wipe forming a half circle at the top of the line. I spend a long time perfecting the bloody B stain over my heart.

The deadbolt clanks and the door opens. A lanky guard, or deputy, or whatever she is, walks in and hands me a plastic plate with a sandwich and another orange. Then she hands me a bottle of water.

"I can bring you apple juice if you like?" she offers.

"No, thanks." I'm starving, and I bite into the sandwich before she even leaves. White bread, mayonnaise, and a slice of rubbery American cheese. I was raised on fake cheese sandwiches, and I inhale it in a few bites, then wash it all down with the bottled water. The mix weighs heavy and churns in my stomach. It's the first solid thing I've eaten since a piece of pizza days ago.

I'm trying to remember when that was as the door opens. The guard's back. "Your attorney's here. Follow me, please."

I'm led back to the same tiny interview room in handcuffs.

Inside, Ed Manetti, a clean-cut man in his fifties, maybe early sixties, gets out of his chair and removes a tweed blazer like he's ready to get to work. I know Ed—I hired him after Tucker was killed and Rocha began suspecting me.

"Hello, Pearl." He holds out his hand, and I shake it. "Get these cuffs off of her," he instructs the guard, who obeys without a word, then leaves. We sit across from each other. I rub my wrists, even though they don't really hurt. I just don't know what else to do with myself.

"How are you doing, Pearl?"

"Terrible." A lump forms in my throat, but I refuse to cry anymore. I'm so sick of swollen eyes and a stuffy nose. I pinch my arm as hard as I can, until it bites like Mama.

"I can't imagine what you're going through. This is every parent's worst nightmare. All I can say is, I promise I'll do everything I can to help you. Okay?"

"Thank you." I swallow down the tears. Crying is such a weakness. A waste of time and energy better focused elsewhere. "Am I under arrest or just being detained for forty-eight hours?"

"No. You're under arrest. They're pressing charges."

"For what?"

"Solicitation of murder for hire and—"

"Wait—what?" Then, like a slow-motion bullet to the brain, it hits me. "Oh my God." I drop my head in my hands. Why is this happening?

"You met with an agent." He looks at his notes. "Woody Harrelson?"

I look at Ed but don't answer because I'm on the verge of a massive heart attack.

"Unfortunately, Woody happens to be an undercover narcotics agent who was investigating your late husband's involvement with the Hells Angels. And he's also Deputy Maggie Martinez's fiancé. He has your wedding ring as proof of payment and a clean recording of your meeting at the cemetery."

My heart hits the floor, and I want to go with it. I can't breathe. Death would be a welcome relief. "She set me up."

I fall back into my chair and look at the ceiling, but all I can see is how Maggie never liked or cared about me one bit. She was manipulating me the entire time. Lying about her boyfriend dumping her. Lying about being heartbroken. I felt so sorry for her. I truly liked that two-faced bitch—thought she believed I was innocent and wanted to help me. Help Bodie. All she wanted was to bring me down and get a star on her badge.

"Fucking bitch. She *is* a cunt." I mumble under my breath, then doubt that her boyfriend called her that. It was probably just another story. Another lie, to get what they want. I knew better than to trust. "I'm such an idiot."

Ed leans forward his elbows on the table, allowing me a moment for this to soak in. He takes a deep breath and says, "The FBI has you instructing the agent to torture and kill Kenny Tait, then you offered your wedding ring and two hundred dollars cash as payment."

"Wouldn't you want to kill the bastard who took your kid? He may have murdered or abused my son, for Christ's sake!"

Ed nods. "I would, I definitely would. But that's not how the law works. You hired someone to commit murder. Even if the guy deserves it. A jury would likely be sympathetic."

"I'm not getting out, am I?"

"Is there *anything* you can give me? We need to bargain. They suspect you had something to do with Tucker's murder and Bodie's abduction. But they can't prove it. They *can* prove murder for hire. That alone carries a minimum sentence of three years, but up to nine. They have enough to go to trial on that charge alone. But—if you give them something that makes their job easier, they'll likely accept a plea and reduce the charges. Help me help you by being honest."

"Holy shit." I want to crawl into the corner and die. "I swear to God, Ed, I don't know where Bodie is. I know Kenny Tait has him. They have that information. They know what I did and why I didn't share the entire truth. Yes, I want Kenny dead. Who wouldn't? He's the bad guy here. Not me."

Ed sighs, wipes his face with his palm, and clicks his pen over and over again.

My forehead hits the table, and I grab fists full of hair and pull. The pain helps.

"Anything you tell me stays between you and me. Attorney-client privilege. I can't reveal one word of what is said."

"I know all that. You explained it when they thought I killed Tucker," I say without lifting my head.

"Talk to me."

I lift my head and rub my eyes. "I messed up. Screwed Kenny Tait. He murdered Tuck. Why? I don't know." My kinky hair is plastered wildly to my cheek, crawling toward my mouth. "Maybe he thought if my husband was out of the picture, I'd marry him. After I shot him, I think it was clear that wasn't going to happen. Kenny was pissed. He tried to strangle me, couldn't go through with it, and took Bodie."

With both hands, I pull my hair off my face and gather it up behind my head. "They want me to confess, I'll confess. I fucked Kenny Tait! I'm a horrible slut and a shitty mother who doesn't deserve to have a boy as beautiful and sweet as Bodie. He deserves better." I swallow and stare at Ed.

He pinches the bridge of his nose. "Okay. Let's pray they find this Kenny Tait fellow sooner than later. I'm going to put feelers out. Find his mother, father, any relations, friends or foes. The FBI has unlimited resources as well. He can't hide for long."

"He said he lived above the Murphys Market where he worked," I add.

"I'll check it out."

Silence surrounds me like a heavy, choking fog while Ed writes in a large leather notebook.

When his phone chimes, we both jump. He reaches inside the blazer hanging from the back of his chair and brings out his device.

The door buzzes, and Rocha enters. "Come with me, please," he says. If looks could kill, I'd be dead.

"What's going on?" I ask.

"I'm in the middle of a client meeting here. You can't just barge in." Ed stands with his hands on his hips, but Rocha overrules him.

"We found something," he says to the lawyer, then glares at me. "Stand up and turn around."

Ed stiffens. "What *exactly* did you find?"

Rocha pulls out his cuffs. "A body—part."

# FOURTEEN

If I've learned anything from the events of the last few days, it is that I can survive the most heart-wrenching trauma despite my will not to. I don't want to see whatever the hell it is they found. But Ed says at this point, it would be best if I cooperate. "Better to do it now and get it over with. Before it's sent to forensics in Sacramento. Better to know exactly what we're dealing with sooner rather than later."

They'll conduct a DNA analysis, then compare that to Bodie's DNA. It will likely take weeks. I know this because, again, I've watched every season of *Forensic Files*.

"Okay." I agree to look at whatever it is they've discovered.

"I'll meet you there." Ed pats my shoulder and shoves his notebook into his briefcase.

Like a common criminal, my hands are cuffed behind me and I'm placed in the back seat of a green-and-white Sheriff's sedan. A deputy I haven't seen before drives while Rocha rides shotgun.

The drive from the detention facility in San Andreas to the coroner's office in Angels Camp will take around twenty minutes.

Tires hum along the wet, two-lane highway as we ride in silence. The rain intensifies, and the driver kicks the wipers into high gear. The slapping rhythm reminds me of the Eddie Rabbitt song. I can't recall the title, but I know the words. Tucker and Mama sang it over and over while we drove from Reno to Louisiana for Daddy's funeral. I still can't believe she had it in her to bring her new boyfriend to her husband's funeral.

I'd much rather sing than worry about what's coming next. "*Well, the windshield wipers slapping out a tempo, keepin' perfect rhythm with the song on the radio oh. But I got to keep rollin'. . .*"

Then my give-a-shit gives out, "Ooh, I'm drivin' my life away, looking for a better way—for me. Ooh, I'm drivin' my life away, lookin' for a sunny day."

Rocha turns around, looks at me like an obnoxious child, and I stop singing. He raises his brow. He's going to tell me to shut the hell up, and when he does, I'll sing even louder.

"I love that song," he says, then turns forward. Advanced psycho-analysis of criminal behavior 101.

The vehicle slows. The tick-tock of the blinker counts down the remaining seconds. The driver stops and waits for the flow of passing traffic to make a left. Utica Park is on my right. I stare at the empty swings and slides. Bodie's laughter fills my head, visions of the first time he raced for the playground. The car moves forward, then left.

Angels Memorial Chapel looks like one of those cookie-cutter homes from a suburban neighborhood randomly plopped down on the outskirts of Angels Camp—a beautifully preserved gold rush town. Tucker and I used to love visiting historic gold rush-era towns. Ghost towns especially.

When I was seventeen, Tucker took me to Bodie, his favorite ghost town in the Eastern Sierra. It was dark and eerily lonesome as he led me through the back-skirts of town.

"Here. This is it." Tucker took my hand and pulled me up onto a back porch made of old timbers. "This was the whorehouse." He grinned and kicked in the door open with zero regard for breaking and entering. We stepped inside.

The air was stale and lifeless. Dust and cobwebs covered everything, including the antique kitchen table and chairs. A black, potbellied stove sat in the corner. "I don't like how it feels in here," I said.

Tuck turned around, took me in his arms, and kissed me. "Feel better?" He asked.

I didn't want to admit that I did. Most of my life, Tucker was the only one who'd ever made me feel safe. Twice, he stepped in and stopped Mama from punching me and he'd never been cruel or unkind, unlike most everyone else in my life.

"Don't go tellin' your little friends I kissed you neither," he warned with a wagging finger.

"I won't." Why would I? I had no friends. Everyone in school hated me for so many reasons. We ruined the old vineyard and brought a criminal element to town. I was accused of the hit-and-run on an old dog that used to wander the school grounds when I didn't even drive or have a car. Girls called me a ho. Rumors that I'd blown most the seniors weren't true. I'd never sucked or screwed anyone in town.

"You like me kissin' you?" Tucker sounded like a boy.

I shrugged. I knew it was wrong, and disgusting, but truthfully, I did like it. Liked how it made me feel important. Made me feel loved. Plus, it was a huge "fuck you" to Mama. And probably Daddy.

I stood in front of him, looking up, waiting—wanting more. He lifted my chin and kissed me slowly. Soft. His tongue gently parted my lips. I couldn't help but open my mouth and allow him in. Something ached in my stomach.

Tucker stepped back. "You tell me if you want me to do more."

"Lots more," I whispered.

Tucker waited a long moment, contemplating, I supposed, running his hands through his hair. "You're gonna destroy me," he said as he lifted me up and set me on top of the rickety table.

On my back, I imagined starring in my own porn video—*Naughty School Girl*—as he removed my pink terry-cloth shorts and underwear. Then he looked at me a long while, before gripping my ankles and sliding me to the edge of the table. My stringy legs hung like weights, pulling me to hell. He knelt and began by kissing my knees. When he spread my thighs and kissed high inside, I thought I'd burst into flames.

His hot, velvety tongue touched places it shouldn't, and I writhed. He licked and sucked, satisfying a hunger, before finding his way inside me.

I fell back and let pleasure destroy my morals.

---

The Angels Memorial Chapel is quieter now than it was for Tucker's funeral. That day, the parking lot overflowed with bikers, their engines rattling the chapel windows.

Now, it's only us and a white hearse hiding under a canopy like a wolf waiting for passing prey. Rocha opens my door and I step out into a puddle, soaking my white slip-on jail-issued tennis shoes.

We rush through the rain to the front door, where Ed is waiting. A small metal sign under a door bell directs visitors to call a local number for entrance. Rocha presses the bell and waits. He digs out his phone and dials, looking up at the number on the sign. "Craig, we're here. No, the front." He waits. "Open the front door." Rocha hangs up, shoves his phone back inside his jacket, and adjusts his grip on my upper arm.

Eventually a tall, mustached man opens the door. It's him, the same man I spoke to when Tuck died. He's the funeral director and the Calaveras County coroner.

"Hey. Sorry about that. I assumed you'd come through the back." The man, Craig, wears a blue button-down with a paisley tie, as well as khakis. He steps aside and allows us in.

Rocha ignores him and leads me inside like an unwilling puppy, past cornsilk-colored walls. Our steps are stifled above double-padded carpeting.

The empty pews were full for Tuck's service. The chapel was over capacity. Mourners stood outside, on the sidewalk and in the tiny side street. Until recently, it was the hardest day of my life. The closed black coffin with Tuck lying there dead inside. Shot to death. Images of a tiny coffin replace memories of Tuck's. Tears drip, and my lower lip quivers.

Suddenly, a hand touches my shoulder, and I look back. It's Ed. He leans forward and whispers in my ear. "This is all just a tactic. He's trying to break you."

I nod and take a deep breath. "Mission accomplished."

My handcuffs chime, mutilating the coerced tranquility as we march in line down a long narrow hallway to the gallows. Craig unlocks a metal door.

Inside, the concrete flooring echoes our wet, squeaking footsteps. Cold air and the overwhelming scent of citrus air freshener hit me. In less than a second, the stench of feces enters the mix.

"Let me grab that hallux for you," Craig says, then opens a refrigerator door in the wall.

*Oh my God, what's a hallux?* I look at Ed for support.

He watches Craig bring out a clear plastic bag and set it on a stainless-steel exam table. Rocha pulls me closer to the exam table.

I look but have no clue what it is. An acorn, I think at first. A translucent bluish blob inside a plastic bag. Why?

"Digit appears to have been removed postmortem." Craig presses down on the plastic.

Digit. He said digit. "Is that . . . a toe?" I ask. A little big toe. A child's. All the breath leaves my body.

"Is that your boy's toe?" Rocha sounds sympathetic. "Is it, Ms. White?"

Ringing in my ears fills my head like a helium balloon. "I don't know," I say, but I can't hear myself speak.

The toe isn't Bodie's. But how can I be certain? It looks a bit shriveled, like when Bodie's been in the tub for too long. And the color is wrong. A good mama would know for sure. Even a decent mama would recognize her own son's toe.

Then the thought of Kenny actually cutting off the toe . . . post-mortem . . .

"No." I can't hear the word come from my mouth. I try again, but my feet lift off the floor. A lightness comes over me and I rise—then go down fast. Lightning fast, headfirst into a black hole. Deeper and deeper, I venture alone in the dark, where time and worry evaporate.

---

When God decides he isn't done torturing Pearl White, he brings me back. My eyes open and shut a million times, and my head feels like an anvil fell on top of it. I don't know where I am or why I don't know where I am. I cough and try to swallow, but my mouth feels like it's chockful of gauze.

The room is dim, and a heart monitor beeps, reminding me I'm alive. In bed. In a semisitting position. I think I'm in a hospital. There's an IV attached to my left arm. Handcuffs keep my right wrist attached to the bed's side rails.

There's another bed, but it's empty. I have the room to myself. "Heerrooo?" I call out. Pronouncing the word is not possible. My mouth and jaw are throbbing along with my head. I can't feel my tongue. What the hell is happening? I wonder for a split second, then recall the last thing I can.

A child's toe. And I no longer care where I am or why. I close my eyes and think of how good hugging Bodie will be when he returns.

His little arms around my neck. Squeezing. All his toes attached. I'll kiss each and every one of them. Play "this little piggy" as he squeals with laughter.

I don't know whose toe that was, but it wasn't Bodie's. I'm not the sort of mama who can't even recognize her own child's—

"You're awake. Okay. I'll be right back." All I see is the backside of a female nurse in pale blue scrubs and a black French braid walk out the door. It closes slowly behind her.

I'm certain I'm in a hospital room but have no memory of how I got here. Or how long I've been here. There's a window, but the heavy curtain is drawn. No light seeps in. It must be dark out.

The door buzzes, opens, and in walks a bald man. Lanky and leathery.

"Hello, Ms. White. I'm Doctor Navarro. How are you feeling?" he asks, but never looks at me. His eyes are reading through what I assume is my chart.

I don't answer because I can't.

"Oh. Sorry. I see here you suffered a traumatic lingual laceration. Speaking will be very difficult for a while." He finally looks at me, smiling like he has a reason to be happy. Taunting me. He squats onto a rolling stool.

I widen my eyes at him, shake my head, and turn my palms up to gesture that I don't understand.

He looks down at my chart and flips the top two pages over. "Apparently, you suffered syncope—that is, you fainted—fell, and bit your tongue, quite critically. Almost all the way off, actually. Doctor Boggs sutured the laceration."

That's why my mouth feels like it's full of gauze. It is.

"Do you know where you are? You can either nod or shake your head."

I do neither. I look at him and shrug.

"You are at Mark Twain Hospital in San Andreas. An ambulance brought you here after you passed out. Do you recall—the, uh, events of the day?"

I nod.

He runs his closed pen down a page on my chart.

"Because of the fainting, and the procedure, and subsequent pain management, it's standard procedure to run bloodwork. Looks like congratulations are in order."

I look at him. "Hmmm?" I wait for an explanation.

"You are aware of your pregnancy, correct?"

—•—

# FIFTEEN

Since I was a child, men have been infecting me. Like cancer that's reached my marrow, and there's no cure. I'm ruined. I should have been more careful.

When I was a girl and messed up, Daddy would say, "You mess with the bull, you get the horns." Mama used the old cliché, "Play with fire, you get burned," after burning my arm or leg or whatever was within reach with her cigarette.

Sometimes, I think I never had a chance. The instant white trash infiltrates your genes, you're bound for generations of suffering. Maybe Bodie's better off without me. I'd surely infect him and his children.

A woman knocks as she opens my door. She's in an all-too-familiar uniform. Apparently, I have a guard from the Calaveras County Sheriff's Department now.

"Hello?" Ed Manetti walks in and the guard steps out, closing the door behind her. "How you doing?"

I tilt my head and glare at him. Lifting my cuffed wrist, I bang the metal, and use my free hand to point at my swollen face. I feign a smile.

Ed nods. "Sorry. Bad habit, I guess." He sits on the empty bed opposite me and pulls the familiar yellow legal pad from his briefcase. "Since you won't be able to speak for a while, we'll have to communicate the old-fashioned way." He sets the pad on my lap and starts to hand me a pen, then realizes my right hand is cuffed to the bed. "Oh. Let's get that off of you."

He opens the door and instructs the guard to uncuff me. She refuses. "Any change in procedure must be determined by Sergeant Ortiz."

"I need to communicate with my client. She can't speak, and in order to write, her right hand must be free. Cuff her left hand if you must. Where the hell's she going to go, for Christ's sake?"

The guard comes at me in a hurry, like it's a competition and the fastest time wins. She unzips a hidden compartment on the side of her leather belt, pulls out a key, and shoves it into the pawl, freeing my wrist from the cuff. She does the same for the cuff attached to the bedrail.

If I wanted to escape, now would be the time to snatch the gun from her holster. I consider it but decide it's too risky. I don't have the strength or the will. She'd overpower me, shoot, and put me out of my misery.

In less than a minute, my left hand is cuffed to the bed, and it's too late—she's on her way out the door.

"Your arraignment is set for Monday morning." Ed hands me a pen. I take it and roll my wrist in a circle.

"Just write the answers to my questions. Okay?" Ed has his fancy leather-bound notebook open. "Who's the father?"

My eyes open wide, and I throw the pen across the room. I should have taken my chances with the guard. How the hell does he know this already?

"Pearl, cooperate or I can't help you. And you being pregnant, while not exactly copacetic, will add a degree of sympathy to your case." Ed finds the pen and returns it to me. "I'm going to be perfectly frank. If you don't trust me and start being honest, I'm going to withdraw representation. Understood?"

I put the pen to the paper and write *NOT Bodie's toe!* Stabbing the pad with the pen. Ed leans over and reads what I wrote.

"Good. I'll relay that to Rocha. Place your initials next to the statement just to be safe." He taps his index finger on the page. "I have a sneaking suspicion the toe was another one of Rocha's tactics to break you down. The report says it was left in his mailbox. Too convenient—I don't buy it for a second."

Ed scooches back on the bed and wipes the corners of his mouth. He looks excited as he nods. "A week ago, a kid in West Point wandered off and got hit up on Winton Road. Four-year old, Caucasian boy. Hit and run. His body's still at the coroners. Doesn't take a genius to figure it out. Add in the fact that Rocha and Craig are golf buddies."

I initial the page and wonder what I've done to deserve such cruelty from a man who took an oath to uphold the law in an honest and professional way.

"Wouldn't be the first time Rocha played dirty. I'm filing a motion to see if the corpse has both big toes."

Ed's cell rings. He pulls it out of his blazer, looks at it, and silences the ringer.

"Pearl," Ed says, shoving his cell back into his pocket. I look at him. "I'm going to need a name. Or names. No judgement. Just list everyone you've been with in the last three months."

He thinks I'm a trashy whore who likely has a long list of candidates for her baby daddy. He sees me as a guest on Jerry Springer.

I write *J.D. Lewis*, then underline his name twice. That's it. Widow White Trash only has one baby daddy.

J.D.'s going to lose his shit when he finds out I'm pregnant. Guess I can't blame him. Maybe it's a good thing I have a guard outside the door and he can't get to me.

"Okay. Good," Ed says. "Where can I find him?"

I write *Flower Ranch*. I wish I could tell J.D. to run. Disappear before it's too late. This mess is not his fault. He shouldn't have to suffer for my sins, but I don't see any other way out of this. I hope I get the chance to tell him how truly sorry I am and that I love him.

# SIXTEEN

Losing track of time is one thing, but I've lost track of what day it is. In my jail cell, I'm in limbo. Wondering if they're even trying to find Bodie or if they've just decided I'm the one. Widow White Trash killed her husband and her son.

My arraignment was yesterday. Judge denied bail. Ed says it isn't unusual in these types of cases. He filed a bail hearing and thinks the odds are good it won't be denied. It's just the way the system works, he says. Everything takes forever.

Time crawls around backward in here. There isn't a minute that goes by that I don't wonder what Bodie's doing. Where he is, if he's cold, hungry, alive? In spite of my best efforts, I can't determine how long he's been gone. Maybe it's better I don't know.

In the cafeteria, I pick at my powdered eggs. According to the doctor I saw yesterday, or the day before, my tongue is healing nicely. Chewing is still far too painful, though. And there's no chance of serious pain meds in here. I asked, then begged. They offered Tylenol. It doesn't help.

I eat yogurt, bananas, and overcooked vegetables that I smash with a plastic spoon. Last night, the fake mashed potatoes actually tasted good until the salt I added stung my stitches.

My speech is improving, though I've chosen not to talk. The less I say, the more people tend to listen. I sip my imitation orange juice. The acid stabs my wounded tongue. Before I can set the little plastic cup back on the table, my head jerks back.

Juice goes flying. I'm ripped over backward, away from the table, flipped off the bench seat and onto my back. Women are yelling. Whooping and cheering just like they did back in school.

A fist slams across my face. My nose feels like it's spreading across my cheeks. Splattered. A warm wetness runs into my mouth. I recognize the taste of blood. This isn't my first beat-down, far from it. I know the drill and immediately raise my hands.

Punches or maybe kicks connect with my head and face in rapid fire until I take cover behind my arms, my palms gripping the back of my head protectively. My forearms now take the burden of blows.

Someone's pulling my hair, pounding my head up and down and back and forth against the floor. The hammering reverberates in my ears and drowns out the cheers.

Their hatred hurts as much as the kick to my chest. Air leaves my body, but my knees make it up. Balled up tightly in a fetal position is the best I can do. I don't scream, don't fight back, just close my eyes and take it. Fighting back just makes it worse.

"You fucking baby killer!" someone yells.

"Piece-of-shit bitch!" another adds.

Kicks to my ribs refuse air in my lungs. I can't breathe.

"Widow White Trash cunt! How do you like it? Huh, puta?"

It's like being strangled all over. I walk the line between make-it-stop or kill me.

"Beat her ass, Bianca!" By the sound of it, there are more than four. Maybe five or six. I try to open up, uncurl my body, and accept my fate.

"Fuckin' whore!"

Momentarily, I lower my arms.

"What did you do to him?"

But the natural will to survive is spontaneous. I can't force my body to uncurl as blows to my back and arms continue.

"Where's Bodie, bitch?"

A whistle blows, interrupting my punishment but prolonging my pain. I fight to catch a breath as footsteps scurry away like rats.

———

In the Emergency Room at Mark Twain Hospital, I savor the pain, letting it temporarily fill the void my missing child has left.

A full-figured nurse administers something for the pain, a wonderful concoction of I-no-longer-feel-anything injected directly into the vein. The relief is almost instant, and it warms my blood. Scrapes my heart off the floor, and the nightmare no longer matters.

I laugh inside, eavesdropping on the obese guy in the cubicle next to me who choked on a hunk of sushi. He literally inhaled fish into his lung, and now it's become infected. They're referring him to a specialist. I wonder if it's possible he's happy. What's it like to go around not giving a shit about what you look like? Must be liberating. I'm deep in the dilemma when the doctor nods at the deputy sitting outside my cubicle and comes in.

He doesn't bother shoving the X-rays into the lighted frame and sharing my results. Just hands me a plastic clipboard with a pen hanging from a string.

"You have two broken ribs. Nothing detrimental. You'll be fine," he says. "Sign that."

I scribble Widow White Trash along a line at the bottom and hand over the clipboard.

"What day is this?" I ask, just above a whisper.

"Excuse me?" the doctor asks as he scratches the pen against the paperwork.

"The date. What is it?"

"You don't know what day it is?"

I shake my head no.

"Do you know where you are?" he asks. His bushy black brow crinkles a little.

I nod, staring at his big brown eyes behind black-rimmed glasses.

"Tell me where you are."

"Hell," I say and he writes something on a page behind the page I signed, then walks out on me without revealing the date. He doesn't give a shit about me or my well-being. I'm garbage, a prisoner, no longer human.

"Tuesday. November 7," the obese man chimes in from next door. He can't see I'm a criminal. Doesn't know he's responding to the infamous Widow White Trash.

The next morning, I wake on a skinny foam mattress and narrow metal bedframe screwed to the wall. I breathe through my mouth and can't help but cry out. It's as if someone shanked me in the night and the blade is stuck in my rib cage. But that's impossible—I'm in solitary.

My pathetic whimpers go nowhere, absorbed by gray cement walls that lack the typical jail cell etched penis, flowers, names, numbers, and *fuck you*. The cell is the same size as a top-of-the-line, side-by-side refrigerator box. I know because I helped Bodie make a fort out of ours.

A small stainless-steel toilet and sink on one end. A tiny window high on the metal door on the other. Allowing a pregnant woman right back into the general population would be a flagrant liability if I were to be killed. An attorney's dream, really. A pregnant woman beaten to death in jail because no one cared enough to protect her.

Everything hurts when I sit up. My left eye is swollen shut, and I imagine it's blossomed into that lovely shade of plum. I'm a pathetic excuse for a mortal, but I still love and miss my son. It's been a week since his abduction, and there's still no word. I try not to cry because it does no good.

A guard brings breakfast into my cell. Oatmeal, a carton of milk, and a side of Tylenol in a Dixie cup. I down the pills with a swallow of milk. Force a few bites of cold, pasty oatmeal and wonder how long it would take to die if I quit eating. Then I think of the child inside me, who's already survived her first beatdown. A life and a tiny reason to live. No more thoughts of wanting to end things. "No more," I promise myself, Bodie, and my baby.

After lunch, I'm escorted to a large interview room. Ed Manetti's sitting at the table inside. I take the orange plastic chair next to him. What is it with orange in here? The guard reaches down and removes my handcuffs.

"I get bail?" The words sound slow in my head.

Manetti sighs. "Thank you," he says to my escort.

The guard salutes and leaves.

The door clicks shut, and Ed places his palm alongside his leather notebook on the table.

"Am I getting out?" I sound drunk.

Ed looks down at his closed notebook as if contemplating life itself. "Afraid not. There's been several developments. Rocha's on his way to question you."

"Why?"

Ed leans over and points up to the camera. Whispers in my ear, "Friend of mine says they got a guy related to your case."

"Kenny!" I jump out of my chair. "Where's Bodie?" My speech is perfectly clear.

"That hasn't been established."

I sit back down. Hope—like an invigorating injection of vitality that lifts my entire being.

Ed leans in again, whispering. "The guy's being held for questioning. That's all I know."

"But, *who?* Who is it?" I don't whisper. I don't care. This is the way back home. Back to Bodie. Back to the land of the living.

"I told you, I don't know." Ed shrugs and quits whispering. He laces his fingers together behind his head. "We have to wait and see."

It's got to be Kenny Tait. Please God, let it be Kenny Tait.

The door buzzes and opens. In walks Rocha, followed closely by a grinning Maggie Martinez, carrying a box of tissues.

Dread hacks at my flesh like an ax, chopping deep into my bones.

# SEVENTEEN

Maggie and Rocha prepare for battle across from Ed and me. Maggie slides the box of tissue my way, like she expects me to break and is worried about drying my tears. What a load of shit.

I keep my head and eyes down. Stare at my handcuffs to avoid Maggie's evil, backstabbing eyes.

Rocha clears his throat. "Pearl, would you please explain your relationship with Mr. Jackson Davis Lejeune?"

"Excuse me?" I heard him.

In a more vocal, no-nonsense tone, he says, "Explain your relationship with Jackson Davis Lejeune."

My heart plummets. I refuse to answer. Refuse to look up with my one good eye and acknowledge his bullshit accusations—especially after what he did to me with that kid's toe. Fuck him.

"Who's Jackson Lejeune?" Ed asks Rocha.

"Best to hear it from your client," Maggie chimes in. "Don't you think?"

Ed looks over at me, and I whisper in his ear, "Can I take the Fifth?"

"I don't recommend it," Ed says, shifting in his chair.

Rocha's jaw is clenched, his leg bouncing vigorously under the table. "Seems Mr. Jackson Davis Lejeune has been in a relationship with Ms. White for the *past seven years*. A month after he escaped from Angola. During the prison rodeo. Maybe she's forgotten. He uses the alias of J.D. Lewis now. We ran his prints. He has quite the résumé." Rocha sings slowly, emphasizing each charge. "Manslaughter. Armed robbery. Possession of an illegal substance. Oh, and"—he chuckles—"now we can add the crime of incest to both their charges. In California, it carries a sentence of three years."

"Incest? What the hell are you talking about?" Ed won't look at me. He doesn't need to. His bewilderment is tangible as my chest tightens. Heat surges like a jolt of electricity, every nerve firing as I hold my breath.

Ed chews his lower lip, then looks at me. "I need a moment with my client."

Rocha and Maggie leave the room, grinning at each other. The heavy door clicks shut, and I'd bet the farm they high-five each other in the hallway.

Ed drags a chair over to the corner and steps up on it, reaches in behind the camera and unscrews the cable. The blinking red light slowly dies. As soon as Ed steps down off the chair, he kicks it across the room.

I jump but don't look at him. Tears sprout and fall from my closed eyes.

"Okay. You had better come clean, because I'm about two seconds from walking out of here."

I cross my arms on the table and bury my head in them. I don't want to say it out loud, but I do. "I love him. I've always loved him. I can't not love him—I've tried!" My lip and voice quiver the same way they did when I confessed to Mama that I loved Jacks after she caught us kissing in the river. Jacks was thirteen. I was nine.

"What did Rocha mean when he referenced incest charges?"

"Jackson's my cousin. And maybe—*probably* Bodie's real daddy."

"Haaa! The hits just keep coming! Motherfucker!" He slaps his hands on his head.

The room is silent after that. I wonder what Jacks told them. Wonder if he's here, maybe in the next room. When I finally lift my head and open my eyes, Ed is sprawled across the chair, staring at the ceiling. He loosens his tie and looks at me from across the room.

"I'm not evil because I love my cousin. I know how awful this looks, but I swear to God, and I'll burn in hell if I had anything to do with Bodie's disappearance."

"You *do* realize you've lost every ounce of credibility you ever had. And this fellow, your criminal cousin, is going back to prison. Unless he loves you more than freedom, he'll make a deal, trade what information he has on you to reduce his sentence."

Jacks would never do that. We're both in this thing way too deep. And now I'm carrying his child. "Can you talk to him? Tell him I'm pregnant?"

"No." Ed shakes his head.

"Please. Just get a message to him."

The lawyer sighs. "No more favors, Pearl. You've made me look like a complete *fucking idiot*. So—no." He unbuttons his collar. "Never in my entire thirty-year career have I been at such a loss as to what to do next." He rubs his face up and down and up and down. "Guess we call them back in and see just how deep this shit hole goes." Ed walks to the door and knocks.

Within seconds, the door buzzes open. Rocha comes inside without Maggie. He doesn't sit, just hands Ed a file and leans against the wall with his arms crossed.

"That's an updated list of charges. Likely still incomplete at this point. Mr. Lejeune has so much to say, and he's biting every bit of bait we're throwing at him. I highly suggest you do the same."

The door buzzes again, and in walks Maggie. She slides a chair under the camera and climbs up. She reattaches the cable and waits for the blinking red light to confirm it's recording.

"Thanks," Rocha tells her, and takes a seat across from me.

"No worries," she says, sliding the chair next to him out and sitting down.

Ed studies the file Rocha offered and continually scratches his chin.

"Come on, Pearl. Just stop with all the crap lies. Tell us what happened to Bodie, and let's all move forward," Maggie says.

"Fuck you! I'd never hurt him, you phony bitch!" I can't hold back—I stand. Rage turns my hands into fists. All I want is to rip that smirk off her face.

Rocha tilts his head toward the door.

Maggie takes the gesture, gets up, and waits for the door to buzz. When it does, she leaves, but not before looking back at me and grinning. It dawns on me that she purposely wanted to rile me. It's part of their procedure, and I fell for it. I'm beyond pissed.

"We've found Kenneth Tait." Rocha steeples his fingers under his chin.

Hope and vengeance wrestle in my mind. "Where's my son? What did he do with him?" I scream.

"Tell me about your relationship with Mr. Tait." He waits patiently. Stoic.

"I slept with him. Once," I confess. "He said he was a virgin. And I don't know, I guess he fell in love with me. Wanted to get married. He wouldn't leave me alone and finally lost it. Killed Tucker. I shot Kenny, trying to save Tucker, and he went completely nuts. Came back a year later, and tried to kill me, then took Bodie to torture me. Now stop wasting time and find out what the fuck he did with my son!" I slam my hands on the table.

"We will," Rocha says, calm as could be. "Problem is, we can no longer question him."

"What! Why the hell not?" My head is about to explode, along with the rest of me.

"One reason is he's a minor, and legally, minors must have a parent present."

"He's no *fucking* minor. He's twenty-two. We celebrated his twenty-first birthday together last year!"

"According to our records, he turned seventeen on his last birthday, and you're also being charged with statutory rape."

The punch to the gut is as real as when Mama would catch me off guard. I grab my belly with both hands and gasp. "You're lying—just like the toe. This is pure and utter bullshit." I shake my head. "No. There's no way." I'm drowning in a never-ending, raging river of shit, and I fill my lungs with one last breath. "Y'all are lying sons a bitches."

I look to Ed for help, but he's still reading through the charges.

Rocha leans across the table toward me. "Kenny claims *you* set him up."

"Set him up. How? For what?" I ask, and slap my hands on my head. "I can't believe this is happening. He's a lunatic!" My hands flail as I attempt to defend myself. "A lying, mentally ill lunatic! Why, for one second, would you believe him?"

"Motive. Profit. And gain," Rocha says. "The pieces are falling into place, Pearl White. Kenny's story is very compelling. Worthy of an episode of *Forensic Files*, if you ask me."

I fake laugh, but there's nothing funny about him mentioning *Forensic Files*. I drop my chin to my chest and shake my head.

"You watch a lot of true crime, like *Forensic Files*, don't you Pearl?" How does he know this?

"And *Dateline*," I say. "It's how I know most investigators are incompetent. Specially once they've set their sights on a suspect who turns out to be innocent." I wipe my mouth with the back of my hand. A trail of blood streaks my fingers. My stitches are irritated—I'm sick of all the back-and-forth bullshit.

"Did you ever see season eight of *Forensic Files*? Episode 34, about Sharee Miller and how she went about having her husband murdered?" He waits as if I'm actually going to answer him. I swallow down the metallic iron taste of blood as nausea overwhelms me.

"It's called 'Web of Seduction.' Come on, you've seen it, I'm sure. The resemblance the episode has to Kenneth Tait's version of events is incredible."

Blood fills the back of my throat as I take one deep breath after another.

"Watching all those true crime shows should have taught you that no one ever gets away with murder." Rocha nods. "Not even you."

Ed slaps the file closed and tosses it on the table.

"Sharee Miller didn't accept her plea deal, and a jury gave her life in prison," Rocha says. "When she finally confessed, all she got was peace of mind. We can make a deal if you confess right now."

I lower my head between my knees. A pathetic amount of vomit hits the floor as I retch and spit.

Rocha gets up, pulls tissues from the box, and brings them to me.

"I can summarize what Kenneth claims happened." Rocha offers the tissues. Strings of saliva hang from my mouth as I lift my head.

I take the tissues and sit up. Wiping my mouth, I take several deep breaths.

"Let's hear what sort of fucking fiction Pleatherface has been spewing." I spit.

# PLEATHERFACE

— · —

# ONE

**HALLOWEEN 2022**

It's almost midnight, but the numbers on the digital clock are stuck at *11:59* forever. I stare. And stare, waiting for the numbers to change. But they don't, and I wonder if it might never be October 31. The rain pouring down my window makes me have to pee.

When I return from the bathroom, it's 12:03 and officially Halloween, but there's no way I can sleep with only twelve hours left to prepare. My stomach hurts just thinking about it.

To get pumped, I make myself watch *Texas Chainsaw Massacre.* Seeing people get ripped to pieces with a chainsaw makes my arms tingle and my hands go numb. Like nails on a chalkboard, except it's like the chalkboard's inside me. There are ten *Texas Chainsaw Massacre* movies, but I only watch the first two, plus the latest remake. Every time Leatherface starts his saw or the murder music plays, I close my eyes and cover my ears. After the killer cuts a guy's face off and makes a mask out of it, I almost die and press pause.

Leatherface's, mutilated stolen face fills the screen. He glares at me like he can actually freaking see me. I'd never mess with that guy.

That's when I get the idea to make myself a mask.

Tutu has a fake leather pillow in the hall closet. It's pleather. Animal products aren't allowed in Grandma Tutu's home. It's not a dietary thing—she just hates that ranching has destroyed twenty percent of the rainforest. I love meat, just not around her.

It takes a minute, but I find the pillow smooshed under a cardboard box marked *Xmas* and slide it out. It looks exactly like a giant piece of dried-out caramel.

"Pu?" Tutu yells from the kitchen. "Breakfast's almost ready."

"'Kay." I toss the pillow into my room and pull the door shut.

In the kitchen, Tutu's cooking with long, lavender hair. Yesterday, her hair was black.

"Nice hair," I say.

"You like it?" She runs her hand down the length of it. "Serena did it for me."

"Who's Serena?"

"My yoga gal." She flips what look and smell like pumpkin pancakes.

"Your yoga instructor dyed your hair lavender?"

"Yeah. Why? You don't like it?" She sounds hurt because, unlike most, she cares what I think.

The light lavender accentuates her brown face. "I think—yeah. I like it." I step back, examining her, and nod. "Makes you look younger." She actually does look more like a mom than a grandma.

"I am *young*—ish. Fifty-six is *not* old. Anytime you wanna arm wrestle?" She flips the pancakes again.

"No way." Tutu and I arm wrestled all the time when I first moved in, and I swear I think she let me win. She'd always let me struggle and sweat before suddenly tiring out.

I reach to pull down a plate from the cupboard. "You're the hippest hippie I know." I hold out my plate.

"Fo sho, homie." She plops four pumpkin pancakes onto my plate. "Happy Halloween, Pu." Tutu's smile is so big and white, it makes me feel good inside. I kiss the deep dimple in her cheek.

"Happy Halloween." We don't have a jack-o-lantern or one spooky decoration. It's fine. I'm too old for that stuff anyhow. But I love Halloween. It's always been my favorite. There's just something about this time of year. Dressing up and becoming someone else, *Hocus Pocus*, and free candy.

I sit down at the table, and Tutu sits across from me. "You're not eating?" I ask.

"I'm cutting out gluten. See if it helps my digestion." She watches me eat. I don't get it, but it seems to make her happy. Tutu makes a big deal out of a lot of little things.

"How are they?" She sips her mug of tea.

"Good," I say through a mouthful. "No. Superb." Pancakes aren't my favorite, and food was the last thing on my mind until I smelled warm maple syrup and nutmeg.

"Rent's due today."

"'Kay." I reach into my back pocket, pull my wallet, and peel the Velcro apart. Handing Tutu three hundred bucks makes me smile inside and out. Finally, I have a decent job at the market and can contribute. Sponging off Tutu the last few years was not cool.

"Thanks, hon." She doesn't want to take my money, but she doesn't have much of a choice, and neither do I.

We live at the Murphys Diggings Mobile Home Park in what we call the wobbly box, since the entire double-wide wobbles when you sit on the toilet or do jumping jacks. I'm not supposed to be living here. The place is only for old people—fifty-five and over—but Tutu needs me here, and I don't have options. I come and go on the down low so hopefully no one reports me. I'm pretty sure the neighbors know what's going on, but everyone likes Tutu and keep quiet.

Once me and Pearl move in together, Tutu will live with us. Help babysit and stuff. Pearl said it'll be perfect, and it will.

"You go for Halloween?" Tutu asks with remnants of her mother's Hawaiian pidgin. It sneaks in every once in a while, especially when she's worried or upset. I'd say probably when she's mad too, but I don't remember ever seeing Tutu mad. My heart sputters a little as I wonder what's brought her pidgin up. But there's no way she has a clue of what I'm up to tonight. I hope.

"You should go." She's rearranging the money I gave her so all the Ben Franklins are facing the same direction. "Get out and have some fun."

Oh, I will, I think. Killing Tucker White will be a blast. "Nah. Supposed to rain. Probably watch scary movies all night." Lying to her makes me shaky inside.

"Ahh! I hate them movies. Come to bingo with me." She looks hopeful as she waves the cash. "My treat."

"Maybe," I say, because it makes her happy for a minute, even though there's no way I'm going to bingo. I have more important things to do.

I open the junk drawer. "Bingo." I find the scissors and hold them up. "Thanks for breakfast."

"You welcome."

In my room, I press play and listen to Leatherface commit gruesome murders as I cut the pleather pillow into four jagged pieces. I flop two pieces over my eyes and mark holes by scratching the material with my nail. Then, I do the same for my nostrils and mouth.

I poke tiny holes every so often and work leather shoelaces in and out to stitch the mask back together. It actually looks pretty badass.

As I stitch, I think of Pearl. The smell of her soft red hair. Like ice cream, something about her hair soothes me. It always has, from the first time I met her at the market.

I was stocking boxes of feminine product when she smiled and said hello. Normally, people like her don't waste their precious time talking to guys like me. Most people don't notice me at all, and if they do, they're not nice. But Pearl was different. Not just nice—hot. Like, ridiculously hot and nice. I'd never met anyone like her.

It gets dark early now, and I like the way my mask looks in the mirror. It covers my entire head. No way anyone will ever recognize me, but it's kind of hard to breathe.

"Arrivederci," Tutu says from outside my bedroom door.

I pull off my mask. "Good luck. Have fun."

"Sure you don't wanna come?"

"I'm sure."

"Love you."

"Love you too," I say.

"Lock the door behind me, Pu." The front door squeaks open.

"Okay. Bye!" I shout.

The door rattles the double-wide when Tutu slams it, because if you don't slam it, it doesn't shut. I pull my pleather mask back on and look in the closet mirror. The mouth hole sits crooked, which makes me look even creepier.

On my bed, I lie back, pull the mask off, and go through the entire plan from start to finish, over and over in my mind. I cannot screw this up. Our entire lives depend on it.

I must have dozed off, wiped from not sleeping last night, because the next thing I know, Tutu's back, opening my door.

"Goodnight," she whispers sweetly.

"Night."

I lie around watching *Stranger Things*, checking the clock every few minutes until eleven. Then, slowly, I open my bedroom door, tip-toe into the kitchen, and lift Tutu's keys off the key rack.

Without a sound, I go back into my room, grab my pleather mask, and climb out my bedroom window. With the key in the ignition, I release the emergency brake, stomp the clutch, and push the gearshift into neutral. The Astro Van inches forward on the gravel, sounding ridiculously loud. Tutu sleeps with the TV on, and I'm pretty sure she'd never hear her van start, but I'm playing it safe. When the van refuses to roll any farther, I start the engine and take the back way to Black Spring Road—these days, there are too many cameras watching every move you make. Rain swells my anxiety. Always has, ever since the night they took me away from my mom. Saying I hate rain is a massive understatement.

I turn up Black Springs Road and follow the curves uphill until the pavement ends. After parking behind a massive stack of logs left over from last summer's logging, I kill the engine. My hands shake so bad, it's like they're vibrating as I work on a pair of leather gloves. I stuff the van keys into my pants pocket, then check that my mask is tucked securely inside my jacket.

Cold wind bites at my cheeks as I slide out of the van. I zip my jacket up as far as it will go, then pull a black plastic poncho on over everything. The hood flops off. I tug it back on and begin my hike to Black Springs Vineyard.

Last week, I practiced the half-mile hike along the creek bed. Staying just inside the water prevented tracks and only took about fifteen minutes, but tonight, with all the extra adrenaline rushing through me, it only takes twelve.

The gun is right outside the cellar, under the fake rock, like Pearl said it'd be. It's heavier than the one we practiced with. The first thing I do is check the safety, because I don't want to forget and fire with it on. It's off, and I leave it that way, being extra careful as I near the house.

The front porch light is off. Pearl has flipped the breaker, cutting off the power as soon as Tucker fell asleep. Just like we planned. A fat-faced pumpkin flickers inside the narrow window next to the door. Smiling, watching as I set the gun down, remove the poncho, ball it up, and stuff it inside my coat.

The oval rainbow rock Bodie painted is exactly where Pearl said it would be. I lift the rock and chuck it as hard as I can. The window shatters, but the pumpkin is unharmed.

I have less than a minute to get inside before Tucker comes downstairs to investigate. Carefully, I reach my gloved hand through the busted-out window and unlock the front door. My heart is thumping so hard, I can't hardly think straight.

As soon as I open the door, I jack the gun from my jacket. I cock the hammer with both hands and keep the thing front and center as I step inside.

Even in the dark, the living room is super nice. Big. With black leather furniture that matches. A million times better than the wobbly box. I take a step forward, broken glass crunching under my feet, and get a whiff of pumpkin pie. Pearl doesn't cook. Must be a scented candle inside the pumpkin. It momentarily improves my mood.

There's a staircase off to the left, and I think I hear footsteps coming, but maybe it's my own heart banging in my ears. I run fast to the kitchen and duck behind the counter, willing my ears to work. I take a deep breath.

Maybe Tucker won't come downstairs. Maybe he's too high. Pearl says he wakes and bakes before getting out of bed in the morning, if you consider ten or eleven still morning. Plus, it's Halloween—another good excuse to get wasted.

I wait. Rub at my forehead, and realize I don't have my mask on. Holy crap!

I set the gun down, rip the mask from inside my jacket as fast as I can, and jerk the pleather down over my head. Situate the eye holes so I can see.

God, that was close. Too close. I should go. Run, now. Forget this whole damn thing. The mask amplifies my heavy breaths. I should have cut ear holes—it's hard to hear anything other than my own heartbeat. I'm out of here.

With the gun in my hand, I start to crawl away, then freeze. Light slices back and forth through the dark, blinding me.

# TWO

Time slows as I get to my knees. It takes forever for my eyes to adjust. Squinting, I hold the gun up and shade the beam stinging my eyes, trying hard to see who's there, who's coming at me in the dark, before I shoot. The shadow behind the light is tall. Taller than Pearl, I think.

All at once, a man yells, "Motherfucker!" and the clink of an aluminum bat hitting a home run travels faster than the pain that shoots up my right forearm. I go down screaming, but I keep the gun.

The flashlight hits the floor and rolls away a split second before a whack to my back knocks my rib cage sideways.

"Stop!" I beg. "Tucker! It's me!" He doesn't know me, but he thinks he might, and hesitates.

"Who?"

Instantly, I raise my head and gun—and fire. The boom is deafening. My ears ring. Spent gunpowder smokes and snakes its way through my mask.

Tucker stumbles back and drops the bat, but I can't hear it hit the floor.

On my knees, I aim the gun at him with both hands. I have to make sure he's dead, or Pearl will have to stay with the man who will kill her. Adrenaline surges, and I scramble to my feet like a guy who just got the shit beat out of him.

Tucker's lying on the floor. Screaming. I can't see any blood, but he's holding his stomach with both hands and squirming like crazy.

Definitely not dead. I have to do it. Have to finish what I've started.

I bend over, press the gun against his forehead, right between his open eyes, then turn my head away. My finger on the trigger. His screams turn to cries.

"Please. Oh God. Please," he begs, and I don't know if he's talking to me or God or maybe Pearl. He should beg for forgiveness.

I'm ready, but unwilling. I hesitate. Can't resist the urge to look at him. Something's off.

His dark eyes meet mine. "Please don't! Please!"

I can't do it. The blast is crazy loud. My right shoulder is slammed backward. It's on fire, and I drop the gun. It's like someone is shoving a claw hammer through my shoulder. I wince and howl while the claw twists its way out. Panic interferes with reason.

That's when I see her. Standing there. It doesn't make sense. She has a gun, and it's aimed at me.

"Pearl?" She doesn't answer, just fires again. Instinctively, I dive behind the counter like it's home base. Did Pearl, *my Pearl*, just try to kill me?

"Come here, Kenny," she says. "Come on, it's okay. You have to get out of here, now. I have to call the police."

"You shot me!"

"I had to. Now come on. Don't be a pussy and screw this up."

I don't know what to do. I don't have a gun. It's somewhere on the kitchen floor, and Tucker won't stop screaming and moaning. The pressure in my shoulder is ballooning, about to explode. I can't think—I pull the mask off my head.

"If I wanted to kill you, I'd walk over there and kill you. Don't be an idiot. Take the money and go!" Pearl says.

The money. Shit. I'd forgotten all about the money. This was supposed to look like a robbery. Tucker has tons of cash from selling weed under the table. I get to my feet, holding my shoulder.

"I love you, Pearl." I say it like it's a question and I'm waiting for her answer. To make this right.

She lowers the gun and holds out a plastic grocery bag double-knotted at the top. The money. "Love you too. Now get the hell out of here."

I tuck the mask deep into my back pocket and cautiously start toward her. Slowly, doubt crawls up the back of my skull. I just broke into a house and shot a man. It won't take long—I'll be arrested and put in prison for murder. Pearl will be a rich widow. My entire body trembles. Fear rushes me and it's far worse than the pain in my shoulder.

She dangles the bag, and just as I reach for it, her gun comes up. Time slows. The bag falls. I'm about to die. She's going to kill me.

Without hesitation, I rush her. Snatch her wrist. Force the gun and her arms above her head. As we struggle, the gun goes off. Pieces of the ceiling rain down, and we both scream.

She's taller than me, but I'm stronger, and I'm fighting for my life. I bend Pearl's wrist along with the gun, straight back, and Pearl cries out. "Stop! Kenny!"

But I don't stop. I won't stop until I break her damn wrist. She wants me dead. She wants to be sure her self-defense shooting is clearly justified. Shooting me while I cowered behind the counter would have thrown reasonable doubt into her story.

Pearl stops fighting. I'm grateful and release my grip on her. Now, I have the gun, and she's running away. Up the stairs.

Tucker howls like he wants to die. His eyes are wide open. Maybe he'll live. If he lives, I'm not a murderer.

I've got to go, but I'm trying to digest what the hell just happened in less than a minute. All I know for sure is that I'm completely fucked. No matter the reasons why, I just shot a man in cold blood.

The pain in my shoulder is worse than anything I've ever felt in my entire life. I press my fingers at the wound, but it doesn't help.

I don't know if I should take the cash or leave it, and I don't have time to calculate the consequences of either. Surely Pearl is calling the police by now.

The front door is open. I reach down and swoop up the money bag as I hurry for the exit. On the threshold of escape, a blast from behind obliterates the once-happy pumpkin.

I run. And keep running. Back through the property, down the way I came, along the creek bed.

My shoulder is wet, and I'm unbelievably weak. I shove Pearl's gun in my jacket pocket. Doubt I'll make it back to the van before collapsing. Can't go to the hospital. Odds are good I won't make it through the night. If only I could start this day over with Tutu's pumpkin pancakes. Funny the things you think of when you're dying.

I can't run any farther. Walking is a chore, and breathing hurts too. My entire right side is asleep, tingly pins and needles. Probably nerve damage, but I make it up the last hill, one slow step at a time.

The van comes into view. It won't surprise me one bit if the police are there, waiting to arrest me. I won't resist. I'll go willingly. And I'll tell them the entire story. They'll never believe me—I wouldn't believe me either.

If I were a good guy, I would never have slept with a married woman, and I'd never have tried to kill someone. That fact will tell them all they need to know.

Before crossing the small clearing where the van's parked, I wait, watching from behind an oak, wondering if the cops are there just waiting for me to step out. I don't think I've ever seen a night this dark.

My heavy breaths cloud my face, and silence buzzes in my ears the harder I try to listen. Sweat drips into my eyes. After a minute, there's no sign of the police, so I go for it, half expecting them to rush me any second.

I get the van door open and toss the money onto the dash. Climb into the driver's seat like a hundred-year-old man. My hand shakes uncontrollably as I slip the key into the ignition and start the engine.

This was not the plan. Not even close. What do I do now? Where do I even go? Fucking Pearl!

"Fuck!" I shift into drive, pulling around the log stack and onto Black Springs Road. It's very likely I'll pass the cops on their way to the scene, and Pearl would have described the van. They'll spin around and take me away. End of story.

At Highway 4, I stop. Look both ways at the empty options and just sit there. Still no sirens speeding toward me. Maybe Pearl didn't call the cops. No, she had to, or it would look like she was in on it. The coroner will know exactly what time Tucker was shot, so she can't wait too long.

None of it makes sense. All this bleeding has probably resulted in a lack of blood to my brain, but I do know I shouldn't sit at this intersection any longer. There are only two choices. Left or right? I could turn left, head east into the mountains. Hide out deep in a cave, or cavern, or old mineshaft—and bleed out.

Maybe I should just turn myself in. Save the police the headache and cost of finding me. But the thought of spending my life in jail quickly takes that option off the table. I've spent time in juvenile hall, and this time they'll try me as an adult. I'm *not* going back—not ever. Death is a much better option.

I turn right, downhill, and drive home. The least I can do is give Tutu this money before I disappear or die. She deserves it more than Pearl or me.

Lightning flashes as I head for home. More fucking rain.

Nearing the driveway, I turn off the engine, coast quietly to a stop, and park. Pearl's gun is in my coat, along with the mask in my back pocket. It takes forever to pull them out and shove them way back under the front seat.

I grab the money and make it to the side of the wobbly box, soaked to the bone with bloody rain. Climbing back through my window is way harder now than it was only an hour ago. It's mind-boggling how fast I ruined my life. And Tutu's.

Inside, I toss the cash onto my bed and shut the window, then peel off my wet bloody jacket with that small hole in the shoulder. The balled-up poncho falls. I shake it out and fold the jacket up inside, then shove the entire mess, including the cash, between my mattress and box spring.

Slowly, I open my bedroom door and tippy-toe the few steps to the bathroom. In the mirror, blood stains the right side of my favorite long-sleeved camo jersey. I try to pull it off using only my left hand because my right arm is useless. It's not working. Screw it, my shirt is trash anyway, so with my left hand, I dig into my right front pocket and pull out my knife. I jack the blade and slice the shirt in half from the neck down.

It falls to the floor. I glance down at the inside of my shirt. Blood, lots and lots of blood, along with little white chips. I reach down and lift one of the fragments, squeeze it between my thumb and index finger. Holy shit, it's rock hard.

Bone. The bullet splintered bone on its way out.

I avoid the mirror. I know it's going to be bad. Worse than *Texas Chainsaw Massacre*, and I can't take it because this is real. This is me. And it hurts worse than a bad *mother*.

I turn on the hot water and wait, then wait some more. It takes forever for the water to get warm. It never gets hot. I'll clean myself up, leave Tutu most of the money, and get the hell out of here. I soak the hand towel under the faucet and try to squeeze out some of the water. I don't have the strength.

Gently, I wipe my stomach and notice that the blood has run past my waist. Even my jeans are wet. I'm Pretty sure I'm bleeding out. I think of Tucker, holding his guts, bleeding, and wonder if he's dead or alive. Or if it matters at this point.

If Tucker didn't die, I'm not a murderer. But I'll still go to jail for attempted murder. My body feels heavy, water logged, like a blood-soaked rag. After a few deep breaths, I work up the courage to look in the mirror. It's gross, but not as bad as I'd imagined.

With this amount of pain, I assumed she'd blown my entire shoulder off. Instead, there's only a tiny hole I could plug with my finger, between my shoulder and armpit. Blue bruising discolors my super-white skin. Blood oozes from the hole.

I lean over the sink. Little red bullets firing, splattering faster and faster. Sweat trickles down my temples. I hold my breath, turn around, and check the reflection of the exit wound.

"Ughhh!"

It's a million times worse than the front. I'm gonna barf—if I don't pass out first. My backside is painted red. Bits of bone stick to the meat, and stringy white sinew hangs like a shredded tongue. A hole the size and shape of a screaming mouth—Tucker's screaming mouth.

My head spins. I turn away and splash water on my face. Breathing hard and fast, I hurl into the sink.

The retching is loud enough to wake the dead, and I realize I'd better keep it down. I bury my head in the sink and puke again, and then the bathroom door opens.

—·—

# THREE

"Oh, sorry." Tutu takes a step back as I raise my head out of the sink. Our eyes meet, and I watch terror take over her smiling face.

"Ahhh!" Her mouth drops and her hands hit her chest. "Pu! Oh God!"

For a split second, we freeze, taking each other and the situation in.

"What happen? I'm call ambulance." Tutu turns and goes.

"No! Tutu, wait!" I go after her. "It's—it's not real."

She stops in the living room. "What?"

"It's fake! Fake blood. For Halloween." I say it like it's true. It sucks that I'm getting so good at lying.

"Naw. You're so pale." She spins me around and inspects the hole in my back.

"I been drinking," I say.

"Pu, for God's sake, you gimme heart attack." She shoves me by my shoulder, and I can't help but scream. "What!" Tutu screams, and I bite my lower lip, holding my shoulder.

"Just kidding," I manage.

Her eyes narrow in on me, and doubt forces her hand to the glasses on her head. She slides them down onto her face and lifts her chin as she inspects the wound closer.

I force a sorry laugh. "I swear. It's just makeup and—" Tutu pokes a finger in the hole in my back. Pain slices through every nerve and I drop to my knees, yelping like an injured puppy.

"You bleeding—blood! God!" Tutu's eyebrows rise. "What happen?"

I can't answer or breathe. The hurt makes me dizzy.

"Pu, you tell me now. What happen?" She puts a hand on my good shoulder.

"I fell . . . in love." That's all that matters.

Tutu helps me to my feet and sets me on the couch. She tightens her bulky robe as she runs to the kitchen and grabs a clean dish towel from the drawer.

Next, she opens the freezer and brings out a bag of peas. As she hurries back, she folds the bag of peas in the towel and gently places it over my wound.

"We're going hospital. Right now. Get in the car"

"No! I can't!" I start to shake. "I did something terrible. If you take me to the hospital, I'm going to jail forever. You'll never see me again."

There's a long silence. Maybe for the first time in like, ever, Tutu doesn't know what to do. There's a pitiful, all-too-familiar sadness taking over her eyes, and I want to cry. I dread telling her what I've done. Maybe she's better off not knowing.

I'm suddenly freezing and shivering, though I'm sure the house is warm enough. My teeth chatter.

"Tutu. I love you—but it's better you don't know anything. When the police come, you won't have to lie. You won't get in trouble. I'm sorry, I screwed up again." Hot tears warm my face.

"I think you should tell me."

"I had to save her," I say as my ears ring. "He was gonna kill her. I saw the bruises on her belly after . . ."

\*\*\*

Next thing I know, there's light. Maybe this is the way to heaven. No. That can't be right. I can't go to heaven after what I did. The darkness comes again. Like waves. In and out.

I'm face down and too heavy to move a muscle. On Tutu's musty brown carpet, I'm staring at the black tourmaline stone she keeps next to the door because she believes it keeps negative energy from getting in. I never noticed how intensely dark that rock is. How much it looks like a bundle of long black needles.

*Get up*, I think. But I can't. Why can't I move? I can't feel my arms or my lips, come to think of it. Fear of the unknown jacks my heart and my breath. Why am I on the floor?

"Kenny, I'm going to need you to be still, okay?" It's a woman's voice, one I don't recognize. "Lula, he's waking up," she says, excitement bleeding through her voice.

Lula—that's Tutu's real name. Talula.

Who is this woman giving orders? I try with all my might to roll over. To lift my head.

Blurred movement interrupts. Someone presses down on my back and left shoulder.

"Be still." Tutu's voice comes toward me. "This is my friend, Teresa—she was ER nurse and gonna fix you up."

"Well, I'm going to try," the Teresa lady says. "These aren't optimal conditions, and his shoulder blade might need reconstruction or it's never going to work properly."

There's a tug, then a drastic pull, on the shoulder that isn't resting on the floor. I want to ask what she's doing. I find pieces of the words, but they're garbled when they leave my mouth. "Whaa do nnn?"

The sound of scissors cutting and clipping.

"Think I got most the bone frags. I put the big piece in a Ziplock, in case you want it. Some people like to keep that stuff. Not sure why, but hey, whatever," Teresa says, and there's more pulling.

My shoulder. I'm injured. I injured my shoulder? My head, then the rest of me, spins. What happened? I want to ask, but I can't bring the words to my mouth.

"I administered some Midazolam. Be grateful, it's good stuff."

"We're more than grateful—I owe you," Tutu says. "Can't believe I shot him. Gonna get rid of that damn gun for sure."

Tutu shot me? Why? What did I do? Tutu doesn't have a gun. This isn't right. None of this makes sense.

"Happens more than you'd think. People hear someone in their house, they get spooked, and shoot their husband or wife. There's usually drugs or alcohol involved, in my experience."

"No drugs here. Maybe too much *Dexter* at bedtime."

"I *love* that show. Wish there really was someone who would kill bad guys," Teresa says.

I killed a bad guy. The memory hits like a tsunami, sucking me down under. I want to tell Tutu. I really do.

Wait—Tutu watches *Dexter?* She hates horror—books or TV.

A tear rolls sideways across the bridge of my nose. Pearl. My Pearl shot me. I was better off when my mind was trashed.

"You're a lifesaver, Teresa. For real," Tutu says. "If we'd gone to the hospital, they'd call the police. Too much investigation. I can't afford a lawyer and I'd probably lose my housekeeping bond."

Tutu cleans vacation homes for a living. Says she loves it, but I don't believe her. It's a coping mechanism, because saying you hate your job just makes every day worse. Tutu's great at always finding the good in the bad.

"A while back," says Teresa, "a guy shot his girlfriend's kid when he showed up from college without calling. It was the middle of the night, and he thought the guy was an intruder, same as you. It was an accident, but the shooter had a hell of a time. Lost his business because of it. Court of public opinion isn't always fair. Your secret's safe with me."

"I almost killed my Pu." Tutu's lie sounds believable.

"Glad your aim isn't very good."

"Ha! Yeah. Me too!" Tutu laughs and I think maybe everything will be okay.

Rubber crinkles and snaps as Teresa pulls off her blue disposable gloves. Tutu bends down and looks at me. It feels like I'm drooling, but I can't help myself or do anything about it but slurp.

"You're gonna be okay, Pu." Tutu smiles, then winks at me. "You came in wearing that spooky Halloween mask. Scare me to death and almost get killed."

I love Tutu so much. Once again, she saved my ass. The first time, I gave her my word. Promised with one hand over my heart and one on the Bible that I'd never let her down. Guess that's shot to hell. Literally.

"You take it easy, Kenny. And Lula, if you can find a way, I'd get him to a specialist."

"Yeah, yeah," Tutu says.

Teresa rolls up a towel with bloody gauze, scissors, a syringe, and all kinds of junk on it. "Left some antibiotics on the counter. One pill three times a day." She gets up.

"I'll throw it away." Tutu takes the rolled towel from Teresa.

"Keep that shoulder elevated and iced. Let's move him into the recliner."

"Yup," Tutu says.

"Kenny? We're going to get you up." Teresa starts rolling me onto my left side. I try to help her, but it's too late—I'm already on my side. Next, she slides my right knee toward my stomach, then pushes me upward using my left shoulder. "I'm going to put you on all fours—okay, Kenny?" Teresa's voice trails off.

Before I can answer, Tutu lifts me from the back of my belt. It amazes me how strong and agile she is for an old lady. I'm on my hands and knees, feeling no pain.

"Call me Pu," I say, but don't know why. Tutu nicknamed me Pu when I was a kid. It stands for Pu'uwai. Hawaiian for "heart." Tutu says I'm her heart because she couldn't live without me. "Pu."

Teresa slides the coffee table close to my head. "Okay, Kenny, can you put your left hand on the table?"

I do. And now I'm on my knees. The recliner is out of place, right behind me.

"Walk your knees toward the table, Kenny."

I do as instructed, but it's an incredible effort.

"Stay there a sec. Let me get this sling on you." Teresa places a sling over my right shoulder, then gently folds my arm and works the Velcro straps until they're just right. Her glasses are thick, making her eyes huge under her long gray curls.

"Are you dizzy?" Teresa is suddenly holding my left arm. My right arm rests comfortably in the sling. I didn't see her move. She's smiling at me, looking like she's waiting for something. What? What's she waiting for? She looks like a nice lady, and I smile back at her.

"Do you feel dizzy?" She asks.

I nod, but I don't really feel anything at all.

"Let's just stay here a second."

I need Pearl. "To love."

Teresa laughs. "Let me know when you feel like you can stand up, okay?"

With my hand on the table, Tutu behind me pulling my belt, and Teresa lifting my left side, I try. It's awkward, but I'm up.

"Just sit back," Teresa says. "Sit back."

All I have to do is sit back in the recliner, but I can't do it.

Tutu raises her voice. "Got you, Pu. Sit down."

I want to say that I can't. I try to lower my butt, then plop down hard.

"Good job!" Teresa claps.

"Oh—kay! Yeah," Tutu gasps, out of breath.

I close my eyes and suddenly remember to breathe. Oxygen feels great each time it fills my heavy lungs.

"You still have the Norco I gave you?"

"Yup."

"Good. They're addictive, so only as needed. Ice is best. Ice his shoulder front and back, every hour for twenty minutes," Teresa says.

"Ice, ice, baby." The ridiculous words fall out of my mouth before I can stop them. A creepy laugh winds up, and suddenly I'm sobbing.

--·--

# FOUR

Pearl takes off her top. She isn't wearing a bra, and her nipples are hard. She's the most beautiful thing I've ever seen. I love the feel of her long hair on my chest—soft as a warm sunrise, filling me with hope. We kiss. Her petite hand finds my dick. Gripping my hardness.

"I love you, Pearl." Her hot tongue slithers in my ear. I'm about to come as she slams the gun into my chest and pulls the trigger. My heart shatters like glass, into a million little pieces. I gasp for air and take in my surroundings.

Panic has me practically hyperventilating as gray light fills the living room, a heavy comforter over me—I silently thank God it was only a dream.

A deep ache throbs in my groin and shoulder. My throat is dry, and I have a major boner. A drink of water would be nice, but I also have to pee. A dull sensation stimulates my brain, and the nightmare of what I've done returns.

"You're awake," Tutu says, sitting up on the sofa, still in her robe. Her lavender hair is a mess. I'm grateful for the comforter over my lap.

"How you feeling?" She struggles off the sofa.

"Fine," I lie as she puts her hand on my forehead.

"I'll get your pills." She heads for the kitchen. "Maybe some toast?"

"Naw." The thought of food turns my stomach upside down. "Who was that lady? Last night."

"That's Teresa." She turns on the kitchen light. "Friend of mine—from bingo. Good to have friends."

Everyone loves Tutu. There's just something special, something likeable about her that I failed to inherit. She opens a pill bottle and shakes one out. Then a second pill from another bottle. "Teresa knows how it is," she says while filling a glass of water from the tap. "She's good people."

Tutu drops two pills in my palm, and I pop them in my mouth. Then she hands me the glass, and I guzzle every last drop of water.

"Why?" I ask.

"Why what?"

"Why'd you call her and not an ambulance?"

Tutu's face drops. "You know why." She gives me a moment.

I nod.

"What you said, about going to prison if I take you to the hospital."

"I did?"

"Yup, you did. And I'm not losing you again." Her eyes brighten. "I know Teresa a long time. I helped her get sober. I feel bad for lying to her. Saying I shot you on accident when you came sneaking in last night. She doesn't know you're living here. And I—"

"So you just called her and she came. No questions asked?"

Tutu looks out the window and cocks her head. I know this look. She's contemplating. She does it a lot; it kind of drives me nuts. "Come on," I say, "why would she do that?"

She shrugs like she has no idea. "I gave her some money."

"How much?"

"Twelve hundred bucks, you want more water?" She's trying to gloss over the payment.

"Where'd you get twelve hundred dollars?" I know Tutu lives paycheck to paycheck.

"Oh." She pauses. Surprise on her face. "Let me get you more water." She takes the few steps required to reach the sink.

"Tutu. I don't want water. Where'd the money come from?"

She hovers over the sink. "Okay. Geez. You."

"Me?"

"Yeah. You." She fills the glass with water anyhow. "The three hundred per month you've been paying. I saved most of it. In case, you know, down the road later, you wanted to take classes. Go to college." She says it like it's no big deal.

To me, it's way more than a big deal. She works her ass off most every day cleaning up other people's shit. And now, she has to clean up mine.

She hands me the glass of water, and I set it down alongside the chair, Looking at her sweet face that wants nothing more out of life than to love her grandson. Me.

I hold out my one good arm, and she bends down. I hug her and cry—I can't help it. Her dedication to me is overwhelming. She will never not love me. *This* is true love.

"I love you, Pu."

"I love you." I'm crying so hard, I can barely get the words out. "Love you *so* much. I'm sorry, you don't deserve this."

"It'll be okay. We're tough, we can handle anything you and me. We always do." Tutu stands, smiling. "Now, what happened?"

"That's a really long story, Tutu. I can explain everything and I want to, I do, but it's better you don't know."

"I think it's better I *do* know."

We stare at each other, neither of us blinking. I have two choices here. Lie, or trust Tutu with the truth. I look away first. Scratch away a speck of dried blood from the back of my hand. "Someone wants me dead." It's not a lie, just not the whole truth.

"Who?"

"A girl I was dating."

"Why?" Her voice rises in pitch and volume. "You do something bad to her?"

"No. She tried to kill me so no one will know she set me up."

"Set you up? How?"

"Tutu, not now. Please. I can't. I have to pee. Can you just trust me? Please?"

Tutu crosses her arms and closes her eyes, deep in breath and thought. Here we go again. I wait because I know better. This is her way of letting the universe supply the answer. She stays perfectly still, breathing loud in rhythm with her lulling head. Palms upward.

I'm going to piss myself if this goes on much longer.

Her eyes open wide, looking hard at me. "This girl know where you stay?"

"No." I shake my head. I never told Pearl I live with my grandmother. "She thinks I live alone, above the market."

Tutu nods then shakes her head. "This is bad. Real bad."

"I know."

"Let me think." Tutu taps her heart. "Okay, I trust you."

"Good. Now, I got to get outta here, before I'm arrested." With my past, they'll lock me away for the rest of my life. I'll never see Tutu again. "I need a place to hide. Where no one will find me." I lean forward. "And I gotta pee, like now."

Tutu pulls the handle on the side of the recliner, and my feet hit the floor. "I'll help you. Pee and hide." She moves to my left side. I move the comforter, my boner at bay, and wrap my good arm over her shoulder. She lifts as I stand. That wasn't as hard as I thought it would be. She helps me to the bathroom and leaves.

After the longest piss in the history of the world, I look in the mirror. My wound is completely bandaged, front and back. It doesn't look bad, but I hate how pudgy I am. I won't stand a chance in prison. They'll crucify me like before, but worse. Way worse. The thought of being someone's bitch and taking it up the ass twists my stomach into knots.

I'd rather die, but I don't have the nerve—plus, I couldn't do that to Tutu. She'd be heartbroken for the rest of her life. So that leaves only one option. Run.

In my room, I reach behind the door, pull my black Pearl Jam zip-up sweatshirt off the hook. Pearl gave it to me for my birthday. It still smells like her. I hold it over my face and inhale. A lump swells in my throat, and my eyes burn. I don't want to cry anymore.

"I got it!" Tutu yells, rushing from her room, shaking the wobbly box as she runs across the house. Then she's at my door, dressed in jeans and a green wool sweater. "Pack plenty warm clothes. And hurry."

# FIVE

The five o'clock news begins with a breaking story. "A shooting in Calaveras County." The dark-haired woman with too much makeup sounds shocked. My heart stops. This is it. Please God, let Tucker be alive. Please.

Tutu quits loading canned goods into a cardboard box and moves from the kitchen to the living room. She folds her arms as we watch, shooting me a knowing look.

"Calaveras County Sheriff's Department investigators report that units responded to a 911 call on Black Springs Road in Murphys at approximately 12:40 a.m., where they discovered a man had been shot. KCRA's own Brandy Hall spoke with the Sheriff's Department. Brandy"

The reporter stands outside Pearl's gate on Black Springs Road, yellow crime scene tape strung out behind her. "The early report is that this appears to have been a robbery gone wrong. The victim, forty-one-year-old Tucker White of Murphys, did not survive. Investigators are asking for your help. Anyone who may have noticed something or someone in the vicinity of Black Springs Road last night or early this morning should contact the Calaveras County Sheriff's Department."

All hope vanishes. I am officially a murderer. Without a word, Tutu slaps the television off and goes back to the kitchen. Starts packing boxes of quinoa from the cupboard into the cardboard box. She knows it was me, she just doesn't understand why.

I'm going to hide out—Tutu calls it "healing up"—in one of the cabins she cleans on Mosquito Lake. The place is inaccessible in the winter when the road closes and the lake freezes. There's no way in or out, other than snowmobile or cross-country skis, and the owners are on a European cruise for six months.

Tutu has to close the Mosquito Lake cabin up for the season—drain the pipes, board the windows, close the damper in the fireplace—but she's not doing any of it. Instead, I'll be "vacationing" there a while.

We decide to wait until cover of darkness to deliver me to the cabin, in case someone happens to be hiking, or fishing, or kayaking. It's late in the season and very unlikely someone would be out there, but you never know.

Tutu warms up vegetable lasagna for dinner and insists I explain what happened last night. Neither of us feels like eating, but Tutu insists we try. Between forced bites, I explain the gory detail. From watching *Texas Chainsaw Massacre* and making my pleather mask, to running for my life after Pearl shot me.

Now she wants to know. "How'd you meet this girl?"

"I was stocking shelves at the market. She came in and we just started talking. She was really friendly and nice." I can't tell her I was filling the top shelf with boxes of tampons when Pearl reached in front of me and her boob touched my arm. I liked how soft it was—before I jerked away like I'd been burned.

Pearl smiled. Said, "Hi, I'm Pearl White," and held out her dainty hand with little pink nails. Heat radiated through me like a furnace. My face on fire. I looked down as we shook hands. I'm such a pussy—I couldn't think straight, let alone react like a normal adult. "I see you here all the time. What's your name?" Her voice felt like when you lie down at the end of a hard day.

"Kenny." I force myself to look at her, and oh my God, her eyes are unreal. Big and green and hypnotic. Like a painting I want to stare at forever without blinking.

"Nice to officially meet you, Kenny," she sings.

"Yeah" is all I can manage. She's the most beautiful thing I've ever seen, including the fake girls on TV.

Tutu gets up from the table and brings me back to reality. She reaches down her abalone shell off the top of the fridge.

"Oh God," I say because I know what's coming. Bundled sage and a lighter are inside. She lights the sage and blows it out. Smoke rises and circles. She waves the smudge stick in my face like a magic wand and looks away as she asks, "Eh, you make love to her?"

"Tutu!" I can't do this. Smoke burns my eyes and I cough. Tingly heat prickles my cheeks, and I'm sure they're cherry red. The thought of telling Tutu about me and Pearl and what we did is worse than confessing to murder. No way. Not happening. "I—I don't want to talk about it." My eyes water.

"You're no killer." She relights the sage. "How'd this happen?"

I rub my eyes. "I told you. I fell in love."

I get up from the table and hurry to my room, then shut the door and lie on my bed. This isn't anything like how I imagined things turning out. Pearl and me are supposed to be together. "Forever," she said. That familiar sting in the back of my nose means tears are on the way. I close my eyes, and Pearl's face fills the dark space in my head.

I have to find a way to hate her. *The bitch shot you,* I remind myself. You'd think that'd be enough to convince a guy she's not the person she pretended to be. And she definitely does not love me.

A soft knock on my door gets me off the bed. I wipe my eyes and open the door.

"Here." Tutu hands me a thick leather journal. "I was saving for you till Christmas. Take it with you. If you can't tell me how this thing happened, you write it. You'll have time at the cabin and it'll be good for you. Writing is the absolute best way to purge demons. Trust me, I know."

"Okay." I swallow. "Thanks."

"Good thing you're left-handed. See, the universe wants you to write. To tell the truth." Tutu turns and walks away. "Truth is important."

"Wait. I have something for you." I go to my bed and dig out the money bag from under the mattress. Tutu comes in.

"What's that?"

I hand it to her. "Karma."

She takes it, unties the handles, and looks inside. Then she looks at me.

"I didn't steal it. I swear. Pearl, she gave it to me."

"Why?" She reties the bag.

"To make it look like a robbery gone wrong, instead of a setup."

"You can show this to the police. Maybe they'll believe you and . . ." She trails off, knowing how ridiculous it sounds. We both know my past and the evidence is stacked against me. I don't stand a chance in hell.

"I'll hide it in the dryer."

---

We drive northeast, up the mountain for an hour. By seven, Tutu pulls the van off the highway and onto a muddy side road that follows the lakeshore. After only ten minutes, she parks and turns off the headlights. It's dark. I can't see two feet in front of me.

"Got your headlamp?" Tutu asks.

"Yep." I pull it out of my coat pocket and wiggle it on over my beanie.

"Let's load the canoe." She clicks on her headlamp and jumps out of the van like a kid.

I power on my headlamp, wondering if we're doing the right thing. The side-door slides open, and she grabs my duffel bag of warm winter clothing, holding it up as I shove my left arm and shoulder under the strap.

She totes the two bags, and I follow her down a narrow trail to the shore. A rim of ice around the edges. Wind whips the trees lining the shore as Tutu sets her bags down and unties an aluminum canoe from a sturdy pine.

I drop my duffle and help her drag the canoe to the water as best I can with one arm. Waves rush in and out, and Tutu and I do the same until the canoe is loaded with gear.

The narrow vessel rocks from side to side as Tutu climbs in.

"Think this is safe?" I ask.

"Safer than breaking into someone's house in the middle of the night and shooting them," she says, and I don't know whether to laugh or cry. She's always been outspoken. If you don't want to know what she really thinks, you don't ask. I learned that years ago when I asked her if she thought I was chubby. "Let's go."

I climb in and sway side to side. Tutu grabs my elbows and helps me find the seat. "Turn off your light," she says, and paddles us away from the shore.

"Shouldn't we have life vests or something?" I yell over the wind and waves.

"Yup." Tutu doesn't look back, just paddles for the far side of the lake.

Mosquito Lake isn't very big, but with the wind working against us, and Tutu doing all the paddling, I feel worthless. Maybe we'll sink and I'll drown. I kind of sort of hope so. Sure would be a cold way to die. I hate being cold almost as much as I hate being locked up.

Tutu turns her head and yells. "Doesn't make sense. Pearl knows you shot her husband. If she's told investigators, they'd have come for you already."

"I told you, she doesn't know a thing about you, or where I live. She thinks I have a room above the market," I yell back.

"But still. They can track you down if they want to. I think she doesn't want the police to find you."

"I wouldn't know what the fuck she wants," I say, hopeful Tutu doesn't hear me curse over the wind and waves banging the boat. Clouds scurry across the sky and the moon appears. Bold and bright. For a moment, I take it in, appreciate the beauty.

"I think she's not going to tell them who you are." Tutu's paddle whacks the side of the canoe. "Because if they find you, you 're going to tell on her. And she can't have that. They hear your story—they'll doubt hers. Bitch can't spend her husband's insurance money from prison."

I've never heard Tutu say a bad word. Not ever.

"She might try to find me herself—finish what she started. Obviously, she wants me dead." It dawns on me that I left the gun in the van. Under the front seat. Shit.

Tutu stops paddling. "Dead men tell no tales." The canoe rocks hard, side to side, and I grip the rail.

# SIX

The little green and white cabin is perched on a triangle slab of granite that slopes gently into the water. Lake in front, mountain out back. A cool place to hang if it were summer and not a sufferfest situation.

Tutu unloads my duffle and hangs it over my good shoulder, then passes me two canvas bags. She takes the box and another heavy bag all the way to the cabin. I barely keep up. By the time I reach the porch, Tutu's stuff is on the steps and she's unlocking the door.

The cabin is half the size of the wobbly box, with two rectangular windows next to the door and one above the sink. Plain and simple, with wood-paneled walls that were probably an update about a hundred years ago. A log bed and fireplace on one side, kitchen table and what looks like a wood-burning stove on the other. I'm guessing, because there are no knobs and bits of wood poking out of a hole where a burner should be.

The kitchenette looks unfinished. "No microwave, no coffeemaker, no phone?"

"No police." Tutu makes a pitiful face and tilts her head. "No Pearl trying to kill you. Oh, and no power." She wipes her nose with the back of her sleeve. "Also, don't use the generator. Someone might hear it." She steps out onto the porch and brings the box of canned goods in. "Better get this place warmed up. Start a fire," she says. "Matches and kindling are right here."

She reaches inside a metal box next to the rock fireplace and tosses me a box of wooden matches. Then she balls up a section of newspaper and tosses it in. I follow her lead and do the same until Tutu says we have enough. Next, she uses the kindling wood to make a tee-pee around the paper. "Light her up." She stands and looks at me.

I strike the match and hold it to the bottom of the newspaper. It ignites, and the flames go from small to supersized in a few seconds.

"Soon as the kindling gets going, add bigger pieces." I watch the fire as Tutu brings the bags in off the porch. She closes the door. "No fires during the day until they close the highway. Someone sees the smoke and . . . you just never know. Better safe than sorry."

I add two small logs to the fire while Tutu stacks cans of who knows what into the cabinet.

"I'll do all that," I say. "It'll give me a reason to live."

"Okay." She doesn't stop putting stuff away. Better to let her do her thing while I explore my new vacation home. Looking for the bathroom, I open a skinny door. It's a closet full of crap jackets, hiking boots, snowshoes, blankets, and towels. "Where's the bathroom?" I ask.

"Around back."

"What do you mean? Like outside?" Panic squeezes down on my chest.

"Yup. Only a few steps," she says, likes it's seriously no big deal. "And you got to board the windows first thing."

"With one hand?" My tone gains a few octaves.

"It's easy. They're already attached. Up top. You just unlatch and pull 'em down. Geez, Pu—it's no big deal."

I shake my head. I can't do this. There's no way in hell. I've never even been camping. The only thing I could list on my outdoor skills resume is watching two seasons of *Naked and Afraid.*

"And, don't forget, keep the water trickling, or the pipes will burst when it freezes. Okay?"

At least there's one thing I can do.

"You're gonna need firewood. There's an ax on the porch. Get that soon, but don't be out during daylight until they close the highway. Stay invisible. Just in case."

"Okay." I can't believe she's going to just leave me injured, out in the woods—all alone.

"Tutu, I really, really, really don't think I can do this."

"I think you can, because unless you have a better idea, you have to. It'll be all right. I promise you'll be stronger in the end. I know you will."

"How do you know?"

"Because"—she shrugs—"I did."

"You did?"

"Yup. Now, close your eyes."

I do, but I want to know what Tutu survived. What exactly made her stronger? My father's death? How could that have made her stronger?

She taps two fingers between my eyes while patting my heart. Drumming my chakras. The tapping goes on and on. Way too long. "Okay. That's enough." I open my eyes and step back.

Tutu tilts her head as if trying to decide what to do with me. Then she goes toward the door and pulls down a fishing rod from the wall. "What doesn't kill us makes us stronger. In my experience, it's true." She gives me that goofy grin of hers. "And, who knows, maybe someday we can trade journals."

She hands me the rod. "You can fish when it freezes, make a hole in the ice with the ax. I used to love fried fish and potatoes for breakfast."

"You ate fish? When?"

"Long time ago."

Since when did Tutu fish? I never thought about it. She was raised by the ocean—of course she fished. There's so much I don't know about my own grandmother. Every time she'd start telling stories from her past—"talk story," she called it—I'd find something better to do. I wasn't interested one bit, and it must have hurt her. I'm such an awful shit.

"What kind of fish?" I don't want her to go.

"All kinds."

I want to go home and let her talk story forever. "Can you stay for a day or two?"

"No. I need to be home if anyone comes looking for you. Life as usual, you know. And it's time you get along without me." Tutu walks to the door and pulls something from her coat pocket. She sets it against the wall next to the door. Black tourmaline the size and shape of a candy bar, to keep bad energy from getting in.

God, I wish she didn't have to go. And I wish I didn't kill Tucker White. Mostly, I wish I'd never met Pearl. This sucks more than anything has ever sucked before.

"I'll check on you if I can. But you'll be okay." She winks at me. "Just use your head. And stay busy, write, that'll keep the cabin fever away." Tutu pulls a necklace off and drapes it over my head. The thing falls and dangles below my chest. I lift and look at it.

"This obsidian?" I ask.

"Yes, and clear quartz. Pairing the two has a powerful effect. Obsidian draws out the negative, and quartz replaces it with light and positivity."

I force a smile. "Thank you." I don't believe in the healing power of crystals or sage, or most things Tutu does, but it makes her happy, so I go along with it like always, and it can't hurt.

Tutu hugs me. "I love you so much, Pu."

"Love you too."

"Don't forget take your medicine."

"Okay."

She looks at me and pats her palm over her heart. The urge to cry sneaks up on me, so I fake cough. Anything not to cry like a little bitch.

I follow her down to the canoe, watch her climb inside and get situated. "I put the money in your bag. Under your clothes. In case you need to get away," she yells.

"What? No." I wanted Tutu to have that money. That's so her. I wave goodbye.

The wind is quiet as she disappears across the glassy lake. My lower lip quivers and I wonder if I'll ever see her again. Alone, I cry all the way back to the cabin.

---

Coals glow in the fireplace. I survived my first night alone, cold and haunted by guilt. Last night, I shoved the double-sized bed closer to the fireplace to catch some heat, but I woke up every few hours, shivering. My shoulder ached all night, and now the pain is eating through the bone, sucking at the marrow.

My pain pills are on the stone counter, and I pop one in my mouth. Water trickles from the faucet, and I turn it up, cup icy water in my left hand and wash down the pill.

Outside, rays of sunlight split the sky into shards. Mother Nature rocks as I pee off the porch, steam rising as my piss rolls down the cold granite. The scent of wet pine is so strong it's jarring, but it brings an unexpected sense of hope. The ax leaning under the window reminds me I need wood. I can do this. Tutu's wise—she thinks I can handle it. I should believe in myself as much as Tutu does.

I have no idea what time it is, none whatsoever, and it gives me a weird feeling of déjà vu. Like I've been here before—in these woods, on this lake, pissing off this porch. It's unsettling, and I don't know what to make of it.

Coffee. I decide I need coffee, whether it's nine or noon.

Someone has left newspaper and kindling in the stove. After wasting a half box of matches trying to get the damn thing going, I give up. Instead, I cuss and pace. Simple things are ridiculously hard. I can barely wipe my own ass. Little things take forever when there's no electricity and my shoulder is wrecked.

But I need coffee, so I decide to try again and again. When the flames reach from the burner hole, I cheer. "Finally." This is going to be a long day, even if it's already half gone.

I fill the coffeepot with water and dump some Folgers in. Push the iron griddle back over the flames and set the pot to boil. All this just for a crappy cup of coffee.

By the time I have the groceries somewhat organized and put away, the coffee is boiling over and hissing on the stove. I find a towel and move the pot to the sink. Adding cold water is supposed to help settle the grounds, so I add a splash and pour a cup. It actually smells amazing, and it tastes pretty damn good.

Thunder booms overhead, and I jump, knocking my coffee over and down my front. "Shit." But who cares if my pants and coat are stained? Who cares if I smell bad because I haven't showered? Or brushed my teeth? Or shaved? No one—that's who.

I stand by the stove to dry myself and open up the griddle hole. Flames and smoke strike like snakes trying to escape. Smoke. Suddenly, I remember—I'm not supposed to have a fire during the day until they close the road. "Shit." It's the pills. They're making me super sleepy and goofy. I stare at the fire. It's impossible to see how I'm going to get away with what I've done. Honestly, I don't deserve to. I'm going to get caught, and go to jail where I belong.

But I'm taking Pearl White with me.

# SEVEN

Wind and rain rattle the antique windows as I sit at the kitchen table, eating lukewarm ravioli from a can. Staring at the old floor, I wonder if any other criminals used this place as a hideout. My mind jumps to the owners of this place cruising somewhere in the world. I wish I was on a ship cruising somewhere. Anywhere.

The leather-bound journal is spread open in front of me, waiting for the truth. There's nothing else to do, so I pick up the pen. It's like a weight in my hand as it hovers above the thick, handmade pages. Why is it so hard to begin? Where to begin? I close my eyes and think of the first time I ever saw her face. When I open my eyes, the words and the truth spill from the pen to the page.

The day after Pearl's boob touched my arm, I saw her at the Fourth of July parade. She seemed happy to see me, like she knew me, and asked if I'd like to watch the fireworks with her and her son.

"Sure." I shrugged, wondering why someone like that would want to hang out with me. I'm not cool. Not good looking or rich. The only good thing about me is that I'm nice. At least, I think I am. I try to be. Maybe being nice matters to Pearl.

That night, we drank Red Bull and vodka that Pearl had premixed in a big thermos. She asked if I was twenty-one and I said "almost." Told her my birthday was next week, July 13. That was the truth, my birthday is July 13th.

The sky exploded with vibrant bursts of light, but it was nothing compared to being close to Pearl. I couldn't take my eyes off her. When she smiled and clapped her hands, I felt it in my heart. The fireworks ended, but we chilled on the blanket. While Bodie slept, we drank and talked.

"Twenty-first birthday pretty soon. Gosh, you're still a child," Pearl said.

"No, I'm not." I sounded exactly like a child.

"No, I'm not." She mimicked me. "You're definitely too young for me." She leaned back on her elbows, and her nipples poked through her yellow T-shirt. I tried hard not to notice, but that was like trying not to notice fireworks exploding in your face.

My heart revved. It could have been the Red Bull, but I doubted it. "How old are you?" I asked.

"Old enough to know better than to fool around with a player like you." Her smile stretched across her face. The pinkest, plumpest lips I'd ever seen parted just enough to see her teeth. So straight and white. Not too big like mine, and not too small like some people's. She was flawless—absolute perfection. But the best part about her was it seemed like maybe she was into me.

"I'm no player," I confessed, because that was the truth.

Pearl sat up. "You're married, aren't you?" Her shoulders and face sagged like she was disappointed.

"Not yet," I laughed, and almost told her I'd never even had a real girlfriend, but quickly decided the less I said, the less chance I'd screw this up.

"Good." She cocked her head. "In a relationship?"

I shook my head.

"I don't know if I believe you. Guys lie."

"Not me."

Bodie woke up and crawled into Pearl's lap. "I'd better get this kiddo home. Call me. Let's hang out."

"Yeah. When?" I nodded. She wanted to hang out with me. She liked me. I played it cool, stoked beyond words.

"Want my digits?" she asked.

"Yeah. But I don't have my phone." I didn't have it, because I didn't own a phone. I didn't really need one.

"I bring Bodie to the park on Sundays. From noon to like, whenever. Come by."

"Yeah, okay, maybe." I watched her walk away, waiting, hoping like hell she'd turn around and look back at me. Waiting and watching, fingers crossed, I held my breath. And then it happened. She turned around and waved. Holy shit!

Sunday seemed like it would never arrive. Five agonizing days I waited to see Pearl again. Visions of her kept me up every night. Just the thought of her sparkly lips and her braless boobs gave me a massive boner. She'd keep me up all night if I didn't relieve myself.

When Sunday finally arrived, I woke up at five, and couldn't go back to sleep. It was like time crawled backward as I waited for noon.

At the park, Pearl pushed Bodie on the kid swing. I stood back and watched. As soon as she saw me, she waved and ran over. She was hotter than Pamela Anderson in a red bathing suit running on the beach in slow motion.

"Hi!" She hugged me, and I hugged her back. Felt those perfect tits against my chest. She could turn me on as easy as flipping a switch. I knew I'd better cool it.

"Hi yourself," I said. Lame.

She smelled like coconut suntan lotion. All smooth, tan legs in shorts and flip-flops as she ran back to Bodie and helped him off the swing. "Want a sandwich?" she asked me.

"Okay." We walked to a picnic table, where Pearl had an ice chest.

"Peanut butter and jelly okay?" She opened the ice chest as Bodie jumped on the table and helped himself. He pulled out a sandwich in a baggie and handed it to me.

"Thanks, Bode dog." I high-fived him.

We sat at the table and ate sandwiches and potato chips. Pearl and I drank beer and talked. She wasn't like most people. I never felt judged, just understood, and shared more about myself with her than I had with anyone else—including Tutu.

Pearl told me about her father cooking meth then drowning during hurricane Katrina, while Bodie pushed his toy tractor in the sand.

"What about your dad? You guys close?" she asked.

"Never knew him."

"How come?" She frowned and pushed her lower lip out, like it made her sad. In spite of not wanting to talk about my father, I did.

"He didn't want me. Tried to make my mom get an abortion. Least that's what she said. Could be bullshit." I swigged my beer, adding to my growing buzz.

Pearl covered her mouth. "Your mom told you that?"

"Yeah. Way before I even knew what the hell an abortion was."

"Ouch." She rubbed my arm. "I think I hate her."

"She shouldn't have had kids," I said

Pearl's eyebrows slammed together. "Well, I'm glad she did!"

"Yeah, guess that's true." I shook my head. If she suspected I was an idiot, I'd just confirmed it. God, what a stupid thing to say. I shrugged like it didn't really matter, then tried to save myself. "I was two when my dad rolled his truck down the Licking Fork."

"Oh, fuck." She slapped her hand over her heart, and it got real quiet while she downed the rest of her beer. Was I trying to impress her with my shitty childhood like some guys might with their money? Fuck. I was trying to get her to feel sorry for me and hadn't even realized it. It was just cool to talk to someone besides Tutu. And the beer. The beer was superb. I had like, four. I'd never drunk that much beer in my life.

"I been through that canyon." She tossed the empty bottle in the recycle can. "The Licking Fork, it's a treacherous son of a bitch."

"Especially when you're driving shit-faced with a kid."

"No! You were not in the truck?"

"I was, but I don't remember any of it."

"Well, that's good." She chewed her thumbnail.

Bodie picked dandelions and loaded them in his dump truck. I wondered what Pearl was thinking and what she'd do if I leaned over and kissed her.

"So, where's your mom?" she asked.

"Good question. I have no idea. She liked partying better than me." I guzzled my beer until it was gone and I felt better. Pearl didn't respond, just opened the ice chest and dug out two more bottles of beer. I wondered what the fuck I was doing here, besides getting wasted.

"Sounds like we had the same mother." She handed me a beer. "Hope we're not related." She laughed and struggled to open her beer, then handed it to me. I popped it with no trouble and handed it back.

"Cheers to surviving!" She held out her bottle and we clinked, then chugged.

Bodie brought her the wilted dandelions. "Thanks, Bode." She kissed the top of his head, then looked over at me. "I think we turned out pretty good, even if we did have shitty parents."

Instead of telling her why I'd spent a good portion of my life in the N. A. Chaderjian Youth Correctional Facility and ruining her opinion of me, I said, "Least we're not in prison. And you're a great mom."

She smiled like she appreciated the compliment. "Thanks, Ken."

I laughed.

"What's so funny?" she asked.

"Nothin'. Just—no one's ever called me Ken. Sounds, I don't know, weird."

"Really? You remind me of the Ken doll I had when I was a kid."

"And you're Barbie." Oh hell no. Did I just say that? I regret the words as soon as they leave my lips. "Sorry."

"You're sweet." Pearl got up and shook her ass all the way to the girl's bathroom.

While I helped Bodie on the monkey bars, Pearl talked on her phone. I wondered who she was talking to for so long, but it was none of my business. After I pushed Bodie on the swing and caught him at the bottom of the slide a million times, Pearl spread a blanket in the shade of a gnarly old oak. We snacked on grapes while Bodie fell asleep.

"Think you could keep an eye on him while I run to the market?" she asked.

"Sure. I don't have to be to work until five."

"Awesome." She stood and tossed a grape at me. "He'll probably just sleep the whole time." Pearl tossed another grape, so I opened my mouth. "I'll be back in an hour." She took aim with another grape and missed. "Shit."

Then, all at once, she knelt, shoved a grape in my mouth, and kissed me. On the lips. I almost choked as the grape slipped down my throat.

"See ya later." She got up and left without giving me a chance to kiss her back. I was dazed, drunk, and confused, coughing and catching my breath. "Holy shit," I whispered, "holy shit."

Bodie slept for over an hour, while I imagined getting another chance to kiss Pearl. Next time, I'd use my tongue. My tongue swept across my lips over and over, trying to taste her. I replayed the moment so many times, I got a semi. I didn't know what was wrong with me lately—breathing seemed to make me horny.

Pearl should have been back. I tried not to worry. Like a child, I joined Bodie on the swing set. He wanted to see who could swing the highest, and I let him win.

We moved on to the slide. I helped him on and off, and he insisted I go down too, so I did. It was fun. I slid a few more times to keep my mind from worrying about Pearl not being back. I had to work in an hour.

Bodie and I split the last peanut-butter-and-jelly sandwich, then played hide-and-seek. He was crouched behind the big oak. I was crawling across the picnic blanket to tag him just as Pearl came up from behind. "Boo!" She squeezed my middle, and I rolled over like a puppy wanting his belly rubbed.

"Mama!" Bodie ran out from behind the tree and hugged her hips.

"I'm so sorry," she said. "The car died. I had to get jumped. You really need a cell." She seemed irritated with me.

"Yeah. I know. Sorry." I said it because she was right.

"Hey, Boogie." She kissed Bodie's head. "You ready to go?"

"No. I wanna stay wiff Kenny." He ran to me and hugged my waist. I lifted him up, and he wrapped his scrawny arms around my neck and squeezed. This was the most awesome little kid I'd ever met.

"Whoa, little dude, you're strong." I acted like he was choking me. Pearl looked at me and smiled that sexy smile, and all I could think about was kissing her again. I put Bodie down.

"You need to go wash your hands and face," Pearl told him.

"Okay." Bodie ran to the bathroom.

"You need to wash too." She licked her thumb. "You've got jelly all over that beefy face of yours." She wiped the corner of my mouth.

I tried to think of something witty to say. "You're a good kisser. I mean—I like how . . ."

She looked at me like, duh, she already knew that. She glanced around the park, and I wondered why. The place was almost empty—except for an old man and his two dogs.

Then she struck like lightning. I closed my eyes and, like a complete dork, didn't open my mouth until she grabbed my chin and forced her tongue against my teeth.

"Open up," Pearl whispered, and pressed her body against mine.

I let my jaw fall, and our lips and mouths and tongues played like new best friends.

"How was that?" She stepped back.

"Yeah." My lips and mouth were wet, but I didn't want to be rude and wipe them.

She raised her eyebrows and looked down at my crotch. I wanted her, and she knew it. My chest got tight, and my stomach hurt. My damn dick had a mind of its own.

"I have to work," I blurted like Rain Man.

"Looks like maybe you should stay." She grinned, and it was like being killed with a feather.

"Yeah. No. Sorry. I got to go." I stepped back and turned away. "Bye." I shoved my hands deep into my pockets and walked fast, hoping to hide the corndog in my pants.

"Ken!" she yelled, and I stopped. For crap's sake, there she was. Standing in front of me. Running her fingers through my belt loops. Tugging at my sides. Pulling me toward her. Teasing me. I couldn't look her in the eye. "What are you doing for your birthday?"

"I don't know." Probably what I did every year. Tutu would cook eggplant parmesan and bake me a carrot cake. We'd pig out, watch a movie, and fall sleep around ten. I couldn't tell Pearl I lived with my grandmother, but I didn't want to lie either. Best I could do was avoid specifics.

"We should party. You get free drinks at the Irish Pub on your twenty-first birthday. Oh! Dude! Guinness and Jameson." Her eyes lit up.

"Okay." I couldn't help but smile, and then I noticed Bodie running back to the ice chest.

"I'll be there at eight." She removed her hold on my belt loops. "Don't be late." Pearl walked away, shaking that ass. Shrinking my nut sack.

"I'll be there." I never thought I'd regret those words.

# EIGHT

The sun melts and smears flames across the frozen little lake. That I even notice the beauty makes me realize Tutu was right. Writing is cathartic. I open and close my left hand to work out the kinks. I've filled pages, and I can't believe how easy the words come. As easy as my love for Pearl. But what good is love if this is where it gets you?

I swallow down my meds and heat up a can of baked beans. Eat them right out of the can so I don't have to bother washing a bowl later. I hate baked beans, but figure I should save the food I do like for later. When I'm snowed in.

After dinner, I toss wood on the fire. It pops then crackles explode. Sparks shoot out and up like fireworks. Like the last Fourth of July. It was hella hot that day. I close my eyes, trying to remember the heat, how it felt to be sweaty. The band played country, mostly Toby Keith songs, but when they played "Independence Day" by Martina McBride, Pearl cried. I wonder now if her tears were real or only for dramatic effect. To win me over.

It's too early to go to bed, but there's nothing else to do. Changing into my long underwear takes forever. Finally, I add sweats and my Pearl Jam sweatshirt. With my headlamp and journal, I crawl under the covers and kick my legs to circulate warmth, letting out a groan.

I open the journal to where the pen holds my place. The fire distracts me with its hypnotic flames. The heat is saving me from a frigid existence, but if I get too close, it burns and scars. Pearl is fire. With the pen against the page, the memories flow faster than the ink.

The Irish Pub was dead on Wednesday, July 13. I'd been waiting on the bench outside the front door for nearly an hour when a bearded black guy in dreads came outside and locked the antique double doors.

"You're closing?" I asked.

"Yeah. We close early on Wednesdays. The hotel is still serving."

"Okay. Thanks." I watched him walk away.

It was almost nine when I heard the click-clack of heels on pavement and looked down the empty street. A dark-haired woman in a short skirt and a long jacket came prancing up the sidewalk. It wasn't Pearl. This chick had short black hair, red lips, and thick-rimmed glasses.

"Ken," the woman said.

I'd have recognized her huge smile anywhere. She waved and trotted over. When she hugged me, I inhaled her sweet vanilla perfume.

"Sorry I'm late. My babysitter didn't show, and I couldn't call you. You need your damn phone, dude."

"I know," I said through a ridiculously big smile. "You look different. Nice, but different—I didn't even recognize you."

"Oh. Ha! Yeah, thanks. I love dressing up for special occasions. I get bored so easily and . . . I don't know—it's your birthday!" She rubbed my arm. "Let's get this party started."

"They're closed," I said.

"Oh. Shit. Right. Forgot they close early on Wednesdays." She grabbed my hand. "Come on. I'm not letting this ruin your twenty-first birthday." She led me up the street and down a dark alley. "I know a much better place to party in private."

I'd have followed her off a cliff, but instead we got into her car. She reached into the back seat and handed me a gift bag with curly rainbow ribbons dangling all over the place.

"What's this?" I asked.

"Open it and find out."

I carefully pulled out the silver tissue paper and reached inside to find a black sweatshirt. I stretched it out in front of me for a closer look. "Pearl Jam!" I loved that it was a zip-up. I always hated the ones that go over your head—takes forever to get them on and off. "I love it. Wow. Thank you."

"Now, whenever you get chilly, you'll think of me and get warm."

"Yeah, I will. I definitely will." I worked the sweatshirt on as Pearl drove out of town. She turned off the two-lane highway, up Black Springs Road. When the pavement ended, Pearl spun the tires through dirt curves.

"Where we going?" I asked.

"It's a surprise." She looked over and winked, and suddenly I didn't care where we were going. She was so sexy in that black wig and those glasses, her lips painted dark red. I felt like I was in a movie. Like this wasn't real. I thought about kissing her, and was just leaning over when she slammed the brakes, skidding. to a stop as I braced my palms against the dash.

"Buckle up, buttercup. It's going to be a bumpy ride." Her voice was weird and low. I slid my seatbelt across my lap and buckled it.

"You don't get it, do you?" she asked, looking at me.

I shrugged and shook my head as Pearl turned left, uphill, past a sign that read:

### PRIVATE ROAD
*Black Springs Winery*
*Deliveries Only.*

She threw her head back dramatically and laughed as she floored the gas pedal. "It's from the noir film *All About Eve*."

"Oh, yeah." I'd heard of noir. Old black-and-white crime films.

"Betty Davis?" she asked, like I should know this woman.

It took a few seconds, then it dawned on me. "She's that old lady from the Golden Girls." I used to watch that program with Tutu every Saturday night at nine o'clock. It was actually pretty funny.

"Nope. That's Betty White."

"Oh. Sorry." She had to know she was dealing with a dumb shit.

"You've lived a sheltered life, haven't you?" She was joking, but it's true.

"You got that right."

Pearl slowed down. We followed the private road to a paved parking area.

"Where are we?"

"Come on." She jumped out, and I followed.

A massive full moon lit the night like an eerie black-and-white film. Almost grainy. Our monstrous shadows crept along behind until Pearl disappeared down a dark stone stairway. Her footsteps echoed, and the musty air cooled as we descended. She shoved open one of two giant wood doors. The iron hinges moaned as we entered.

Pearl hung her jacket on a rack and flipped a switch. Fake torches flickered on.

"This was an old wine cellar."

"Oh. Cool." It was way more than cool. It was a huge, badass underground cavern. The roof and walls were limestone, with giant timbers every so often. Oak wine barrels stood stacked on both sides. I wanted to ask if we were allowed to be in here, but I didn't want to sound like a complete pussy. "Wow."

"I thought you'd like it." Pearl flipped another switch. A row of fake lanterns hung above us, leading deeper into the cave. I followed her down a tunnel into a small chamber.

Inside the door, she turned on a string of overhead bulbs. A pool table sat front and center, and a colorful jukebox in the corner. Against the far wall, the rear section of an old black Cadillac had been made into a red leather couch. "What is this place?"

"Choice man cave. I knew you'd dig it." Pearl opened the refrigerator and brought out a bottle of champagne. "Turn on the jukebox."

I went to the jukebox, but I finally had to ask. "Do you have permission to be here?"

"Better to beg for forgiveness than ask permission. Right?" She popped the cork, and champagne exploded. She shoved her red mouth down over the hole and sucked the foam.

"Damn." That was all I had.

After three games of eight ball and two bottles of champagne, Creedence Clearwater's "Born on the Bayou," came on the jukebox. Pearl went nuts.

"I love this song. Let's dance." She started without me. I'd never danced before, but for her, I would've tried anything. It was a lame attempt—I have zero rhythm—but she didn't mind. She snatched my hand, and we danced until the song ended. The mood changed when we slow danced to an Adele song, "Make You Feel My Love." That was when we kissed with fucking tongues.

Pearl brought my hand to her boob, the same one that had brushed my arm not that long ago. She liked me enough to let me touch her boob. Oh my God. I wondered if she could hear or feel my heart pounding.

We swayed to the music, and all of a sudden, she grabbed my cock. I jumped, but she didn't let go, just started rubbing me over my jeans. Before the song was half over, I was about to burst.

The song ended, and Pearl unbuttoned my Levi's.

"Oh my God." She smiled. "Get naked."

I'd never been naked in front of a girl in my entire life, other than my mom when I was little. Part of me wanted to run, but I kicked him to the curb and undressed. Pearl tossed the pool sticks and cue ball off the table, then slowly shoved me backward.

Naked on green felt, I watched her climb up onto the pool table in her short skirt and high heels. There she stood above me. All legs and ass and tits. An angel looking down without any underwear. *Oh my God.*

Then she got on her knees and straddled me. This was about to happen, and I was going to blow it. "Hurry . . ." I had to get inside her, or it didn't count. I put my hands on her hips to help situate her.

"What's wrong?" she asked.

"Nothing, I just—oh, fuck." I sounded like a wounded animal.

Pearl slapped me. Hard. "Ken! Are you a virgin?"

The urge subsided a little. "No." I couldn't lie to her. "Yes."

"You should have told me," she said sweetly. "I just assumed a dude like you had been around."

"I'm sorry. I thought you'd—you know—a guy my age."

"Kenny, you need to tell me things. Honestly, you can trust me. Okay?"

I nodded.

"Okay. Now lie back. Relax. Breathe."

I trusted her. From that moment on, her wish was my command.

"Close your eyes."

I took a deep breath and did so.

"Happy birthday to you," she sang as she slowly slid down, angling herself perfectly, simple as stepping into a warm bath. I was inside. *Holy shit.* This was it. I was fucking this gorgeous woman. *I'm not a virgin.*

"Happy birthday to you." A hot wetness wrapped around me, sucking and stroking with the beat of my heart.

"Happy Birthday, dear Ken."

*Happy birthday to me. I should move,* I thought. *Make it good for her.* I raised my hips and pushed deeper. She moaned, threw her head back, and that was all it took.

"Oh, oh—uhhh, uhhh, uhhh." I did it.

"Happy birthday to you." Pearl smiled.

It was without a doubt the best sixteenth birthday ever.

# NINE

I jolt upright in bed, my heart racing, and I gasp. The dark night is having its way with me just like Pearl. Hard to believe I thought meeting her and losing my virginity at sixteen was the best thing that could have ever happened to me. Now look at me, freezing my ass off alone in the middle of nowhere, unable to sleep.

Staring at the ancient, water-stained ceiling, I try to calm my nerves with deep breaths. The wind in the trees used to feel good, like music, but now it's just noise, static no matter where I tune my thoughts. I lie back and pull the covers over my head.

As soon as I start to doze off . . .

*"Kenny . . ."* Like being hit by a bolt of lightning, I thrash out of bed. There it is again, *"Keeennny."* It whispers, but it's not her. It's only the wind. I know it is.

I put a log on the fire. The stacked wood is dwindling. Then I open the door and step outside in my socked feet. Icy wind slaps my face, stings my lungs, and I cough.

My shoulder aches as I piss off of the porch. I need another pill.

Inside, I fetch a Norco from the baggie and rush back under the covers. I'm wide awake and in pain. There's no way I'll get any sleep until my shoulder quits stabbing me. I situate the headlamp on my head and flip it on. Find the journal. The thought of someone reading what I wrote, the parts about what Pearl and I did, sparks dread that quickly turns to fear.

I consider tossing the whole thing into the fire—and I will, as soon as I'm done. I can't chance Tutu or anyone else reading the sex stuff. But right now, it feels good to let it out. Purge Pearl from my mind and hopefully my heart.

*"What the fuck?"* The monstrous voice screams in my ear. *"What the fuck?"*

---

"What the fuck?" he yelled, and I jumped up off the pool table, naked and afraid. He came at me through the door, screaming, "What the fuck are you doing?" His arms flew every which way, and just before he reached me, Pearl cut him off.

"Tucker, stop!" She looked tiny, standing in front of him. Her arms braced against his chest as if she could stop him. Fear rushed me, ignited adrenaline and rocketed my heart rate to maximum velocity. I gathered my clothes off of the floor.

"I'm sorry." Who was this guy? "I'm sorry."

"I'm gonna fucking kill you!" He grabbed Pearl's hair, and her black wig came off in his hand. She screamed, and he threw it at her. "You fucking whore!"

"Hey. Stop it." I snagged his arm, and he shoved me aside without much effort. He could definitely have kicked my ass with one arm tied behind his back. Maybe both.

"Get the fuck out of here right now," he growled at me, "or you never will."

"Go!" Pearl cried. "Get outta here." Her red hair twisted in little buns, and her red lips smeared down her chin like she was a sad clown. She looked awful.

With my clothes in my arms, I hurried toward the door, then stopped. "I can't leave you like—"

"Kenny, please!" she screamed, and waved her arms. "You're making it worse!"

The guy stood with his legs spread and his fists ready to beat my ass. "When you fuck my wife, you fuck me. Kenny." He spit as he spoke. His red face seethed. "You don't want to fuck me, Kenny."

"You're *married*?" My voice squeaked and cracked. "Pearl?"

She looked at the dude. "I'm sorry."

"How could you fuck someone named Kenny?" he asked. What a dick.

"I didn't fuck him. We were just fooling around. I swear, Tuck. It's not what you think." She held his face and kissed him. "Calm down."

I ran as fast as I could. Out the door, down the tunnel, through the cave.

Outside, the night was hot and humid as I hid behind Pearl's car, pulling my pants on. Pearl was married. She had a husband. What the actual fuck? It made no sense. All I knew for sure was that I needed to get out of there, like now.

The driver's window was down, and I opened the door. Felt the ignition. "Yes."

The keys were inside, so I stole her car and drove back to Murphys. Left the car at the park. Fuck her. She lied and almost got me killed because of it. She can find her own damn car.

The walk home wasn't long enough. The intense back and forth between the guilt of sleeping with a married woman and being lied to gave me a screaming headache. Or it could have been all the champagne, I guess. All night, I went from being pissed off to worried he'd hurt her. He seemed the type.

She'd knocked my entire world into a deep dark hole. The next day, food lost its taste. After a few days, Tutu asked if I was sick. She even brought me a cheeseburger, French fries, and a chocolate shake. I forced down a few bites and thanked her. Things that used to make me feel good inside, like Tutu's flower garden and the little birds we fed, lost their appeal. I couldn't see beauty no matter where I looked.

Misery lingered, along with the dude's big red face. The way he screamed, his foul whiskey breath—low and guttural, like Satan himself. Why didn't Pearl tell me she was married? I never would have done it. Never.

Maybe she wasn't happy being married to an asshole and was attracted to me because I wasn't an asshole. She liked being with a nice guy for a change.

Even Bodie liked me. And I liked him, a lot. But I loved Pearl, and I couldn't breathe without her. The torment of wanting to kiss and strangle her was taking a toll.

I stop writing. Regurgitating the affair is making me ill. My stomach gurgles. I can see my breath, so I know it's cold in here, but I'm sweating. Maybe it's the flu. Or the beans. Pearl, probably.

Tucker's face the night he found Pearl and me on the pool table takes up all the space in my head. I try not to dwell on it, to think of something else. Anything else. But a sharp pain stabs my side and I grab it, groaning in pain.

The night I shot Tucker in the gut . . . He gripped his stomach the same way I am now. His face twisted in pain like mine.

I saw him. His face. Looked him in the eye for less than a second, but that face is burned into my memory. My jaw drops when I realize.

The face in the cave that night and the face of the man I shot were not the same.

# TEN

The Tucker that wanted to kill me was tall and slender and good looking. The Tucker I killed was short and stocky. Not all that good looking.

Who the fuck did I kill? The question eats at me through the night until I can no longer think straight.

I need sleep, but that's not an option. There's nothing else to do, so I write.

The market closed two hours ago. Usually, it takes me two, sometimes three hours, to stock the shelves, but I was wound up and finished in a little over an hour.

The parking lot was abnormally dark and empty and smelled like wet cement. I've always loved that smell. That night, it made me want to get in the van and just keep driving. I dreaded going home to stare at the ceiling all night.

Out of the corner of my eye, I glimpsed a shadow emerging from behind and rushing toward me. I frigging froze. Too scared to react. Too scared to save myself from Tucker. I was dead.

"Ken," Pearl said.

I whipped around. Chills rushed me as I returned to the land of the living and held my chest. "Shit, Pearl." My heart punched inside my chest like it wanted out.

"I can't take this. Can we please go to your place and talk?" she asked, all nice. She thought I lived above the market. I wasn't going to tell her I lived with my grandmother. Why should I?

"I'm not allowed visitors. Why?" I ask.

"I'd like to explain, if you'll let me." She hung her thumbs through the belt loops of her cutoffs.

"That's okay. I'm good," I lied. And why shouldn't I? She'd lied way more.

Pearl crossed her arms, hiding her tits from me. "I really am sorry. I never meant—" She bit her bottom lip with her top teeth. "I just want to know you're okay?"

I was pretty sure my eyes bulged. "Seriously?" Pearl knew damn well I was not okay. Did I really have to say it out loud? I shook my head. "No. No, I'm not—okay. I'm nowhere near fucking okay!"

"Get in the car. Please. Let me explain about Tucker and me."

I didn't want to know about her husband, so I ignored her and walked to the van. Tutu and I shared it, since she worked days and I worked nights. It was a close call, but I officially had my license.

"Please, Kenny. It won't kill you to just listen."

I opened the door. Pearl stepped in front of me. "Don't be stupid. Being with you is easy. I didn't know it then, but I know it now. That's love, Ken. Love. Something I've never had my entire life. And it's too fucking good to just throw away. I love you."

I looked at her, and I swallowed. Tears filled her big eyes. I wasn't expecting love or tears. Not hers—mine.

We did have something special. She consumed me, made me sick to my stomach and gave me the shits. I couldn't eat or sleep. I just wanted it all to stop, and she had the power to take all the hurt away. It had to be love. I blinked back tears and pressed the unlock button on the door. "Get in."

We got in the van and drove. "Did he hit you?" I strangled the steering wheel.

Pearl looked out the window. "That shit don't bother me anymore. He just slapped me around a little. At least Bodie was asleep this time."

"Why do you put up with him? Leave!"

She glared at me. "I tried. He almost killed me. You don't know what he's capable of. Besides, where would I go? I don't have shit."

"Stay with me and—" I stopped, reconsidering being honest about living with Tutu. She filled the momentary silence.

"Tucker's involved with some very bad people. All he'd have to do is pick up the phone, call in a favor, and they'd never find my body."

Her body. Her beautiful, sexy, perfect body. The thought of her dead and rotting in some backwoods grave made me ill. I rolled my window down, sucked in the crisp air, then crossed the two-lane into Feeney Park.

"Are we in danger?" I asked.

"No. Tuck's in Reno. At a biker thing."

"Think he has someone watching you?"

"No, no, no." She waved me off.

"Does he hit Bodie?"

"No. Never."

It was after midnight, and the park was deserted. Normal people were home, asleep in their beds. Not sitting in a van in the back of a parking lot, next to a shitty skate ramp, watching a cat eat a mouse, listening to an abused married woman cry and beg for forgiveness.

She told me about her mom and the drugs and how Tucker practically raped her when she was underage. We had so much in common. I understood Pearl's loneliness.

Finally, I asked the question I just couldn't make sense of. "Why do you love me? You're gorgeous and smart and could have a million other guys. Rich guys. What do you want me for?"

Pearl swung her legs to where a center console would be if the van had one. She leaned in and kissed me. "That's why." She tasted like Red Hots and made my tongue tingle.

She kissed me again. Her long, silky hair tickled the side of my face and smelled minty. "Tell me you don't feel that. Tell me and I'll leave right now and never bother you again." Her eyes pooled with tears.

"I feel it," I said, and she snatched my hand.

"Show me." She tugged me up and out of my seat. Bent over, I followed her to the bench seat in back. We kissed, and it felt like an anvil had been lifted off my chest. I could breathe again. The world had been put back together. Saved by true love.

I squeezed her tit. Harder than I meant to. "Oops, sorry."

"I like it." She took my hand and forced me to squeeze harder. She bit my ear and snatched my balls.

"This is wrong. You're married." My body didn't give a damn about her marriage, but Tucker scared the shit out of me. He wouldn't put up with a guy screwing his wife more than once. "Pearl, stop."

"Will you just hold me? Please."

I reached over the seat and found the lever. I pulled it, and the top of the bench seat fell back. We stretched out, and she snuggled in.

"Finally, a chance to spoon," she giggled. "You're the big spoon." Her sweet hair in my face. "We fit together so perfectly," she said, wiggling her tight ass against me.

I wrapped my arm over her waist and held her as we breathed in rhythm. She was right. This could be so easy. So perfect. She took my hand and guided it down the front of her shorts, between her legs, all soft and hot and slick.

Together, our hands massaged her. Every time she moaned, my erection grew. "We should stop. Seriously."

"I want you inside me," she whispered, and fucked herself with my fingers. "I love you."

"I love you too." I said it because it was true. Right or wrong, I loved her.

She flipped over and faced me. "You do? Truly?"

"I do." I kissed her.

She unbuttoned my jeans, jerked them down with surprising strength and put her mouth on me. "Oh shit." I never knew anything could feel that good. That night, for the first time, we didn't have sex. We made love.

---

The writing helps with the details, but reliving the nightmare upsets my stomach. I need to get to the outhouse, fast.

By the time I get my boots, jacket, beanie, and headlamp on, I'm close to shitting myself.

I run, but pucker hard, and just about rip the outhouse door off its hinges. The toilet seat shocks me. "Ahhh!" It's like sitting on a block of ice. It's a painful relief. The gurgling gas seems to echo across the lake and reverberate off the granite below. I promise myself to never eat an entire can of baked beans again.

My headlamp searches for toilet paper. The roll sits on a stick poking out of the wood frame. Light spooks a spider, and she disappears inside the cardboard roll. Spiderwebs stick and break as I lift the TP and shake the creature out onto the rotting wood floor. I can't wait to go home and crap in a clean, warm bathroom.

Nightmares consume what little sleep I get, but it's better than being awake, and I'm grateful for the light of day. Still, my shoulder is a bitch in the morning. It burns deep, with an unbearable stabbing pain.

I can't open the sealed baggie, so I rip it apart. Pills scatter across the counter. I snatch up two and double the dose.

Today, at some point, no matter what, I have to get firewood. "Lots," Tutu said, and I hear the way she dragged it out, accentuating the word: "Laaahh-tsss." Her voice rings in my foggy head.

Banana chips and two granola bars help me feel better, but it's the pills that bring a wave of wonderful relief.

I skip coffee and drink hot cocoa instead. It doesn't rattle my nerves.

Next, I realize I need gloves to gather firewood and search the cabin. No gloves, but I do find a half-full bottle of Jim Beam. I take a swig. It burns my throat but warms my insides.

My eyes and nose run the minute I step outside. The cold is extreme, and there's a dusting of snow that sends a feeling of dread through me. Gathering firewood is going to be awful without gloves.

I decide to go back inside and wait until it warms up. Add a little whiskey to my cocoa. It's not bad. With the last of the wood in the fireplace, I sit on the edge of the bed while the gyrating flames seduce me into a trance.

I can't remember what day it is. I try to think backwards, recall what I did yesterday. Everything's whack. Out of place. Like I've been here a week, but I don't think I have. Maybe I can't remember because time doesn't matter anymore; maybe it's better I don't know what day it is or how long I've been here. Maybe it works the same way the brain represses traumatic experiences. Wish I could forget Pearl. And Tucker.

My jaw hurts. I didn't realize I've been clenching my teeth so long. Every muscle in my body is tense as random thoughts bang around inside my head. Here's Johnny! Jack Torrance's crazy face as he busts through the door. Leatherface. Glenda the Good Witch. A tree. A tall tree. A baby stuck up in the tree, wedged between its branches, crying, about to fall.

I'm sweating and notice my stench. Catch myself rocking back and forth, repetitively scratching the back of my neck. I itch all over. There are bugs in the bed. Bed bugs.

I need to get a grip, so I slap myself in the face. Hard. *That's odd,* I think. It doesn't hurt. Why doesn't it hurt?

The firewood's gone—I need more. I walk outside. It's beyond cold and snowing.

I wish I had gloves. An extreme feeling of déjà vu unsettles me, like a premonition of my death. I go back inside and shut the door.

# ELEVEN

Inside the cabin, I flop on the bed to pick up where I left off. I reread the last page I wrote in the journal and try to recall how it all went down. Pearl and I were having an affair. It's a terrible, awful thing to admit, but it's the truth.

We couldn't get enough of each other. Whenever Pearl could get away, she'd show up at the market after hours. One night, we snuck into the stockroom and did it.

A week later, she stuck a note under my windshield wiper asking if I'd like to *play pool? The ogre is gone a while.*

The best was Big Trees. Pearl and I screwed standing up inside a giant sequoia while Bodie napped inside a neighboring tree. Sex in nature is the best.

---

I'd kept track of our lovemaking. By September 13—our two-month anniversary—we'd done it four times. But that night, in the back of the van, at Lake Alpine, we did it twice. Technically, we were on number six when she gave me the news.

"I'm pregnant."

I sat up. "Pregnant?" Shock, then confusion silenced me for a long while. "But, you're on the pill. You said—"

"I was," she interrupted. "Doesn't always work—especially if you miss a day or two."

The back doors of the van were open, and we stared out at the blood moon turning Lake Alpine red. A million thoughts rushed and tackled me. And then the big one—"It's mine, right?" She swore she hadn't slept with Tucker since we'd met.

"How could you even ask that?" She sounded hurt and scrunched up her face like she might cry. "Jesus Christ."

"Oh—no, I'm sorry." I hugged her, kissed the top of her head. "I just— I never expected this."

"Me neither." She squeezed my waist. "You're going to be a daddy."

I'd never been more excited and petrified at the same time. I dreaded to ask the question. "You getting a divorce?"

"I'm gonna try." She took a deep breath and sighed. "Just the thought of asking Tucker for a divorce makes me ill. He's gonna go ballistic."

"Is there someplace you can go? You and Bodie, until we figure things out?"

"I can't think of anywhere."

I wondered if I should tell her about Tutu. Confess that I live with my grandmother in a seniors-only trailer park. No. There was no point. It was hard enough for me to sneak in and out without getting caught. We'd never get away with two of us and a baby. Then Tutu would get kicked out and we'd all be homeless.

"Maybe you can stay with me above the market," I said, hoping like heck she wouldn't go for it.

"We'll figure it out. We've got a few more months." Pearl gathered her hair and pulled it to one side. It lay over her shoulder like a horse's tail. "Don't let tomorrow ruin today. Here, check this out." She got up, reached into the passenger seat, and dug in her purse.

"Look at this." She handed me an undersized black-and-white photo.

"What is it?" A grainy, blurry blob.

"A sonogram. That's your son."

"What? No way!" I turned on the overhead light and took a closer look. "It's a boy?"

"Yep." She knelt next to me and pointed her pinky at the picture. "See? That's his little pee-pee right there."

"Whoa." I squinted and stared at it. "Looks like a nose." I'd never even met this kid, and already I loved him so much it was insane. "This is a miracle."

"It's the universe at work. We're meant to be together."

"I love you, and I love our son," I said.

"I love you too."

"Can I keep this?" I asked, waving the sonogram.

"I'll make you a copy. Oh, and one more thing. I got you something." She took the sonogram out of my hand and went back to her purse, where she exchanged the photo for a Walmart bag. "Happy anniversary, and congratulations on becoming a father." She handed me the bag. "Sorry, I didn't have time to wrap it all nice and stuff."

I opened it up and pulled a box out. "A phone." I laughed. "Thanks."

"It's just a pre-paid Tracphone."

"Like drug dealers use so they can't be traced. Awesome—thank you."

"You're welcome." She helped me get the phone working, then gathered all the trash. I sat in the driver's seat while Pearl went out to use the bushes. Her purse sat open where the console should have been. I looked inside, then dug around to find the sonogram. I couldn't help myself—I tucked it into my back pocket.

Sometimes it's better to beg for forgiveness than ask for permission. That was Pearl's philosophy, and I agreed.

I dropped Pearl off at her car, hidden behind the big log stack, then drove home and fell asleep staring at my son.

\*\*\*

The phone Pearl gave me rings and rings. She's calling. I need to talk to her. It's dark, and I can't remember where I am. My hands and feet are freezing, and my shoulder gnaws on me from the inside out.

I locate my headlamp under the covers and turn it on. I'm at the cabin, and there's no way the phone could have been ringing because I don't have it anymore. It's just a dream. Or Pearl's everlasting, infectious mind-fuck.

Getting warm is all I can think about after taking three pain pills. There are only four or five left. The antibiotics, the fire, and the day are all gone.

I need wood, but it will have to wait until daylight. I'm not gathering firewood in the freezing dark.

Hunger pangs force me out of bed. I look through both cupboards, and there aren't many options left. Two cans of corn, more beans, SpaghettiOs, and lentil or split pea soup. "Yuck." Even though I can't remember the last time I ate, nothing sounds good

There's about six inches of new snow, and I watch a bazillion fat flakes fall in slow motion to earth as I pee off the porch. The county will close the road soon, if they haven't already. Hopefully Tutu gets here before too long.

When I turn to go back inside, I catch a glimpse of myself in the window. The guy looks nothing like me. His chin is covered in whiskers, hair so matted and greasy I can smell it. There's something feral about him.

He scares the living shit out of me when he smiles and waves.

# TWELVE

Inside the tiny closet, I gather a heavy wool coat and put it on over my own. Find socks in my duffle bag and layer three pairs on my feet and one on my hands.

Shivering in bed under the covers, I write. It's awkward at first with socks on my hands, but then it's as if the memories have a mind of their own and take over.

I don't need to see what the words look like—I know they're right.

Funny—I'm not sure what day it is, but I can recall what happened between Pearl and me with absolute clarity. Like a movie I've watched too many times. I see the entire story on a loop, playing over and over, and I know every line of dialogue before it's spoken.

---

"Pearl White, will you marry me?" I walked into Tucker's man cave and got down on both knees. The ring cost eighty dollars at the thrift store. It was October 13. We'd been together three months, and we were celebrating since Tucker had business in Idaho.

"Will you?"

Pearl didn't answer, just started bawling. Snot ran from both nostrils over her lips and down her chin. I stood up and went to her.

"He's going to kill me and our son!" she screamed.

"Did he threaten you?" I held her hands.

She just laughed.

"Pearl, you told him you want a divorce, right?" I gently squeezed her hands.

"Oh yeah. Sure did." She nodded, and her eyes bugged like a maniac. "I surely did."

"What'd he say?"

"Nothin'."

"Nothing? Did you tell him you're pregnant . . . and in love with someone else?"

She stared across the room like she was far away.

"Pearl? Did you tell him about us?"

Finally, she nodded. Tears ran fast.

"Pearl?"

She looked at me and lifted her shirt.

"Motherfucker!" My jaw dropped, and my hand shot up to my mouth. Dark purple, fist-sized bruises accented by hues of blue and green covered her belly. "We're going to the police," I insisted. "Right damn now."

She dropped her shirt. "They can't stop him. Hell, half of 'em are in his pocket. I told you—if I file charges, I'm as good as dead." She buried her face in my chest.

I cradled her head in my hands and held her close. "Pack your things. We're getting out of here."

"He knows who you are and where you live. He said as soon as he gets back from Sandpoint, he's going to skin you alive, starting with your dick."

"What the fuck is wrong with him?" It sounded so ridiculous it was hard to believe, but something told me I shouldn't ignore his threat. "What the hell do we do?"

Pearl pulled away and faced me. "Kill him. I've considered every option I can think of, and it's the only way. Kill him before he kills us." She was serious.

"Pearl. We can't."

"If we don't, we'll wish we did. You don't understand how dangerous he is. We can make it look like a robbery gone wrong. Plus, he owes some very bad people a lot of money. I've thought about it for two days, and it's the only way out of this shit."

"No. It's not." I walked away and sat on the Cadillac couch.

"Listen, Tucker has a huge life insurance policy. If something were to happen to him, Bodie and I get everything. Do you know how perfect life could be for us? We could be a family. You, me, Bodie, and our baby."

A family. To me, the possibility of having a normal family with a mom and a dad was about as likely as flapping my arms and flying off to the moon. The idea of spending the rest of my life raising children with Pearl made me smile and nod.

She sat next to me, put her head on my shoulder, and held her stomach. "I know it sounds awful, but think about it. There's no other way."

"How in the heck are you gonna do it?"

She took my hand and moved to the edge of the couch. "You know I watch like every true crime show, right?"

"Yeah."

"I know how not to do it. I know how to not get caught. It's so simple it's ridiculous. Tucker gets back on the thirtieth, the day before Halloween. Halloween night, he's always shit-faced by ten. After midnight, a masked intruder breaks in. I wake Tucker and tell him I heard something downstairs. He goes down to investigate and . . . you shoot him."

"I shoot him?" I squealed. "I can't shoot someone. I don't even have a gun."

"I'll take care of that."

"I've never shot a gun."

"We can go shooting tomorrow—in the forest."

"I don't know. You're talking about killing someone. Murder."

She stood and pointed her finger at me. "It's him or us. You best decide if you're man enough to save your family or not. Before it's too late. Because if you choose wrong, you'll spend the rest of your life regretting it. Choose right—and we'll live happily ever after." She got up and walked out.

Shooting cans off a log was easy—agreeing to shoot Tucker wasn't.

That night, in his house, was a fucking nightmare. But I pulled the trigger. Saw the bullet nail him in the stomach. The violence was gut-wrenching, awful. I immediately regretted it.

But I don't regret not pulling the trigger when I had the gun pressed between his eyes. At least I don't have that vision haunting me.

Something runs across the porch. I don't move. Don't breathe.

The cabin's being surrounded, and I'm about to be arrested. At least it'll be warm in jail. I'll be where I was destined to be all along. With criminals and fellow murders who were set up by backstabbing bitches like Pearl and my mother. Yep, my mother. Mom. She let me take it in the ass for her.

When you're nine and your mom's screaming, covered in blood, you retreat to the safety of your shell. Like a turtle. That was where I went when things got ugly. The good thing about the shell was you can't talk to anyone outside of it, the bad part was you can still hear what's going on outside.

"Kenny! Kenny! Fuck!" Mom screamed, looking at her hands, covered in red. Her eyes were bugged out, her face freckled with blood. She was high. Again. Bouncing off the walls. Pacing back and forth.

"What the actual fuck? He tried to kill me. Did you see that? He almost fucking killed me!" The man was face down, and she kicked him. "Fucking asshole!" she screamed like he could hear her. Then, she looked surprised to see me.

"Kenny. He tried to choke me. Did you see that? He tried to fucking strangle the life right out of me. Fucker!" Her accelerator was floored. She paced back and forth, then grabbed the gun off the kitchen counter with her bloody hands.

"I'm not like her. You just wait. It was him. I don't care what they say. I didn't do it. Right, Kenny?" She hurried to the sink and turned on the faucet. "I'm not going to go to jail because that yeast infection tried to kill me." She washed the gun and her hands at the same time. "Hell no. Uh-uh. Fuck that." She looked at me. Then grinned.

I stood in the door, scared stiff.

"Oh honey." Mom wiped her hands and the gun, then came to me. "It's okay. No, no. don't cry, okay?"

I wasn't crying. I wasn't moving, or blinking, or breathing. I was in my shell, where nothing could hurt me.

"Here. Take this." She handed me the gun. "You take this and hide it somewhere real good, okay?" The heavy gun felt icy and slippery in my grubby hands.

"No one can ever find it. I need you to be a good boy and not tell, no matter what they say. They're a bunch of lying dickheads, okay? We don't ever talk about this to no one. Got it?" She kissed my forehead and picked up the phone.

I ran to the bathroom and hid the gun in the toilet tank. I was hiding in my bedroom closet when I heard the sirens, because when you're nine, you do what your fucked-up mother tells you.

And when the cops arrest you for killing the guy your mother shot because he was supposedly strangling her, and she confessed that you were the shooter, told them you pulled the trigger while trying to save her, you keep your mouth shut and take it, or else. Because "or else" meant being beat and locked in your room for days with nothing to eat or drink.

"Or else" would have been far better than five brutal years in a Stockton juvenile detention center. It's easy to look back and wish I'd told. They might have locked her up, and I likely could have gone to live with Tutu. But that's not what I did. I kept my mouth shut and never revealed the truth to anyone, including Tutu. Even when she visited on holidays and Sundays.

Every single Sunday for five years, Tutu was there. Smiling. That's 260 visits. I know because I did the math. There's plenty of time for stuff like that when you're incarcerated. All those visits and phone calls made me feel loved. When you're locked up, not getting raped and being loved are the only things that matter. Especially when your mother never showed up to visit—not even once. I figured she was dead. It was easier than believing she couldn't stand me.

Tutu always asked, said she knew there was more to the story, and why won't I please tell her the truth?

I miss Tutu. For her to get me out of juvie and take responsibility of me is beyond my comprehension. Way more than I deserved. Tutu doesn't *know* I'm innocent. Or maybe she does. I don't know. Maybe on some level, she knows that what really happened wasn't my fault. Or she just chooses to believe what's best.

I want to go home, eat vegetable lasagna, and hear Tutu laugh. I'm so lonesome. Have been for as long as I can remember. Guess that's what made it so easy for Pearl to work me like a puppet. Especially after I shared my criminal record—a murder conviction. She knew she had the perfect idiot. My mom did drugs, a lot, and I'm sure she did them while she was pregnant with me. Maybe it's why I do such dumb shit. My heart crawls into my throat and forms a sickening lump, which I try to swallow down.

"Kenny." It's Pearl. Footfalls race across the porch for the second time tonight. What's she doing here? How'd she find me?

"Fuck." I rush to the window, pull the curtain back with my socked hand, and look out. It's snowing, and the water trickling in the sink tickles my inner ear. I shake my head.

There's nothing out there. "No one." And as if on cue, my shoulder starts up, reminding me what an idiot I was for loving Pearl. Now my stomach hurts too.

I find my pills, pull the socks off my hands, fill a cup with whiskey, and gulp down four. That leaves two. Soon, I'm going to be in a lot of pain—and I'll freeze to death if I don't get some firewood.

"Shit."

I want to go home. As soon as it gets light out.

# THIRTEEN

A newborn baby cries. I'm trying to find him. To pick him up and soothe him. But it's dark and snowing and I'm lost. If I don't find him soon, he'll freeze to death. He wails.

I wake up weeping. I couldn't save him. My cheeks are wet, and an overwhelming sadness forces my head back under the covers. I'm so tired and severely confused, I can't sleep.

I've completely lost track of the days, but figure I've been here about a week, since my antibiotic pills are gone. Yes, a week sounds reasonably right. Should have written the dates down in the journal.

I can't get that crying baby out of my head, and I wonder if the dream had something to do with Pearl. With my son. Is he okay? Maybe there's something wrong.

I get out of bed, flip on my headlamp, grab my jeans off the floor. The sonogram is tucked inside my wallet in my back pocket. I've kept it with me since taking it from Pearl. The headlamp lights my foggy breath and the black-and-white photo of my son. He's probably a lot bigger now. Because that was taken weeks ago.

The sonogram is framed in white. Digital blue numbers line the bottom. I bring my headlamp down and the sonogram to eye level. I can't make out the dates. The numbers are worn except for the year. 2018.

"What?" I look closer, and there's no doubt the sonogram is dated 2018. "What the fuck?" I count backward. Four years ago.

I don't get it. Why would the sonogram be this old? How? I struggle to make it make sense, squinting at the numbers as if I'm staring at the TV when the antenna is jacked and the picture is fuzzy. You know it's there, right in front of you, yet you just can't see it.

Then, I catch a glimpse. The shadow of possibility. Bodie is four. Maybe she got them mixed up? Maybe my son's sonogram is somewhere else.

Or maybe Pearl lied. Maybe she's not pregnant. And she used me to kill her husband.

"No." My head is shaking.

"She wouldn't." I know it.

"She couldn't." I sound defensive.

"She'd have to have had the entire thing planned from the beginning." The thought makes my skin crawl. My bones ache. I'm coming undone.

We were never together in public. But only because she was worried someone might see us and tell her husband. It made sense. It was the smart thing to do.

What about my birthday? Sweat trickles down my temples. My armpits. She wore a wig and glasses, for God's sake. She was fucking in disguise so no one would recognize her. My stomach twists. It's all starting to make sickening sense. The burner phone for my birthday. The guy that caught us having sex in the cave was definitely not Pearl's husband Tucker, but he played the part well. So whoever he is—he had to be in on it with her. My heart is hammering.

"They set me up." She had a partner. Tears burn my eyes.

And dear God. "There is no baby." I grip the sonogram. I'm not going to be a father. No one will ever call me Daddy.

I run to the door and rip it open. Cold wind slaps my face as I puke, coughing up unidentifiable bits and spit. "Ohhh God!" The ache in my chest is worse than my shoulder.

Shivering, I go back inside. My face tightens, and tears pour out of me faster than the trickling faucet. I don't hold back. I let it all out, sobbing and moaning like a dying man. Like Tucker after I shot him.

I'm hollow inside, and I want to die. "Stupid fucking idiot!" I crawl into bed, curl into the fetal position, and beg for mercy.

I must have cried myself to sleep, because when I wake, the sun's coming up. The sonogram is on the pillow. I take it and eturn it to my wallet, which I shove deep into my back pocket.

I find my pen. Find where I'd left off in my journal.

In big ugly letters, I scribble;

Why did you do it, Pearl?

Why?

I loved you so much and you tried to kill me.

I turn the page.

Mom, you let your own child spend five years in detention and get jumped fourteen times for a murder you committed. Why?

Did either of you ever love me?

Even just a little?

I slap the journal shut and set it aside on the bed. The back of my neck itches.

I need my pills. I need a shower.

And I've got to go home. The last two pills go down like candy with a Jim Beam chaser.

"Trick-or-treat." I have no idea where that came from, or why I said it. I've never been trick-or-treating. So many random thoughts constantly popping into my head and preventing me from thinking straight. I'm fully aware I'm losing my shit, and I couldn't care less.

The Jim Beam doesn't burn my throat anymore, and I guzzle until the bottle is empty.

Eventually, I feel better. Almost good. Maybe God, or the universe, heard me. "Thank you," I say, because I'm grateful to whoever or whatever lifted some of the weight off me.

I still miss Tutu, but now it doesn't hurt so bad. She said she'd come check on me as soon as she could. It must not be safe. Which means the police probably know I killed Tucker.

As soon as I return, they'll arrest me. I'll try to explain. Tell them my side of the story and how Pearl set me up. But I can't prove any of it. According to my record, I'm a cold-blooded killer. I don't feel like a killer in the least. But I won't stand a chance with a jury or in the eyes of the law.

I'm not ready to go down. If that bitch Pearl wants to play games with my life, we'll play. "Vengeance is mine, saith Kenneth Tait."

First thing I need to do is get firewood, build a big fire, eat, and prepare for a life without pills.

----

I can't remember the last time I ate. I'm not hungry, but I feel like I should eat something before gathering wood. The split pea and lentil soup are on the counter. I go for the split pea and pop the lid. The smell makes me nauseous. I can't do it—I have to push the can away.

On the counter, the empty and torn baggie where my pills were taunts me, along with the empty Jim Beam bottle. I try not to worry. I have a high pain threshold. My shoulder is healing. I don't need meds. I can use snow as ice if it gets too uncomfortable.

Preparing to venture out, I remove my sling. Moving my arm isn't as painful as I thought it'd be. The meds are probably masking most of it. I pile on layer after layer of clothing to stay warm. My thermals. Two pairs of jeans. A wool sweater, puffy, and a wool jacket I raided from the closet. My beanie. Two pairs of socks on my feet and two on my hands.

Bending over to pull my boots on is a fucking effort.

Walking to the door reminds me of that kid from *A Christmas Story*, when his mom bundles him with too many layers. At least she cared.

Wind slashes at my cheeks the minute I step onto the porch and grab the ax. The air is so cold, it hurts my chest and makes me cough. There's nearly a foot of new snow, and it's still coming down. Just not as heavy as before.

But the sunrise is glorious. Otherworldly. Like nothing I've ever seen before, and it holds my focus a while. Purples and pinks explode through the clouds, glowing bright as embers on the horizon, casting colorful movement across the frozen lake. It fills me with hope as I set off in search of dead timber.

A brutal wind kicks up, bringing with it a wrinkled curtain of snow that blocks the brilliant sunrise. I pull my beanie farther down over my ears and trudge forward. Along the lake, snow drifts like sand. My boots crunch through tiny shards of polished ice as my lungs burn with the cold.

I stop and search in every direction for wood. Nothing. I put my head down and move forward. The forest is thicker and darker under the canopy of trees as I climb upward. The slope is thick and heavy, like walking through mashed potatoes. My quads spark to life.

Halfway uphill, light on the horizon reveals a dead tree leaning and stuck between two others. "Perfect." I suspect I could push it and drag it downhill and back to the cabin. At the very least, I'll bust some of the branches off with the ax.

The light under the canopy of trees is dim at best. By the time I reach the dead tree on top of the ridge, I'm sweating and out of breath. I look up, through the snow. Slivers of dark sky shadow it. The mountains have faded.

I struggle to wrap my head around what I'm seeing. Is it me, or is it getting dark?

# FOURTEEN

A twinge of panic fires inside my chest. I take a shot of oxygen to clear the fog in my head and watch darkness fall, along with more snow. How on earth did I confuse sunset for sunrise?

The pills. They've mangled my limited intelligence and warped my simple reasoning. Tutu warned me to only take three per day at most. And only if the pain was unbearable. The pain *was* unbearable—just not my shoulder.

Night and the temperature have dropped. I'm wasting too much time worrying about how confused I am. What matters now is that I need wood. And I need to get back to the cabin fast. Before it's pitch dark and I lose my way. I don't have my headlamp.

The dead tree is pinned sideways, branches covered in snow. I lift the ax with my good arm as my right assists with the aim. I hack a limb the circumference of a baseball bat and three times as long, but snow is the only thing that breaks free.

I repeat the process. Over and over. The limb finally gives and falls. I do it again, same thing, until I've busted off four good chunks.

My sweaty hair itches, and I pull off my beanie, shoving it in my coat pocket. My sock hands are soaked as I gather up the wood. It's impossible to carry the wood and the ax back to the cabin. I consider leaving the ax and returning for it tomorrow, but I'll need it to chop the limbs.

I pull the wet socks off my hands and bundle the wood along with the ax, using the wet socks to tie the ends together. It's awkward, but I get it balanced and cradled between both arms. My shoulder doesn't seem to hurt, or I just don't notice because of how my entire body aches with numbness. Deep down, my bones feel like they're warping

from the wet. I try not to think about the pain or the beautiful relief
the pills would give if only I had them.

My boots and an inch of fresh snow fill my previous tracks as I trudge
downhill. As the descent steepens, I stumble over a log under the snow.
"Fuck," I growl through a face full of powdered ice.

Just getting to my feet is an effort. Gasping, I stand and brush myself
off. I find the beanie in my coat pocket and pull it on over my frozen
and matted hair. My hands burn with frost. I press my fingers over my
mouth and blow heated breath to warm the feeling back in. It doesn't
help, so I shove my fingers in my mouth and suck. I can't feel warmth.

A fierce and fiery pain in my legs sends shivers that nauseate me. I'd
feel better if I could just throw up and move on. The bundled wood and
ax are above me—I think. I backtrack a few steps, find it, and decide
to drag it the rest of the way. Snow sticks to my face and eyelashes
with each step. I'm sweating my ass off while my teeth chatter so hard,
I think they might break.

After about twenty minutes, I should be near the bottom of this hill
or mountain or whatever this steep son-of-bitch is, but then I realize
I'm no longer following my tracks. I stop. I can almost feel insanity
stalking me, it's so dark. I can barely make out the snow, and there's
no sign of my tracks. Not one. I'm surrounded by trees. Swirling snow.
Imprisoned in a violently shaken snow globe. The sky offers no light,
no help.

"What doesn't kill us. Tutu said so."

A pathetic whimper escapes after the words, and all I want to do is
sit down and cry.

Going back up and trying to find my tracks seems pointless, since I
can't see and there's a good chance they're filled with snow anyhow.
The best option is to descend. It shouldn't be far, and once the snow
levels out, I might be able to see the lake and locate the direction of
the cabin.

"You can do this," I tell myself because I have to. Tutu isn't here to
save me this time. "Be a man." I'm so sick of myself. "Man up, bitch!"

After a while, the ground isn't as steep. Boulders pile up like blocks
and form a granite structure ahead. I try to go around but am walled
in and get nowhere fast. Right now, I have to get warm. Have to get
back to the cabin as quickly as possible. I look for a way down as wind
whips up a thick cloud of snow.

It's slow going, but I push on, picking my way through a never-ending maze of snow-covered cracks and crevices. Then the snow suddenly stops as if the supply in the sky just ran dry.

I slip and land on my knees. My hands are on fire. I can't take it another second, and I scream as long and loud as I can. "Help! Help me! Someone!" The cruel wilderness swallows my pleas.

Then, I cry. On my knees, it occurs to me that I might die out here. Alone. I bow my head, shaking with cold. I fucked up. Finding the will to keep going is impossible. I don't even know if I'm going the right direction. "God, help me."

Then, as if God took pity on me, I look up—the sky is clouded, but the moon is there. Like a beacon offering its light. I wipe my eyes and face with my wet sleeve and look around. straining to see something familiar. Something that could offer a glimmer of hope.

There's a wide, flat meadow of white. The lake. It has to be the lake. My chest heaves as sobs turn to intermittent laughter. I can do this. I will make it around the lake. The cabin isn't that far, because the lake isn't that big. The cabin sits on the north end, where the water runs in. I just don't know for certain which direction that is. If this is the lake in front of me, my instinct tells me to go right.

I do. Moving as fast as I can through a foot of snow with numb feet, frozen legs, and bundled wood sucks, but at least I'm moving in the right direction, my breath smoking up the vicious night.

The moon glows through rolling clouds. I can see the forest. The mountains. The frozen lake covered in thick white frosting. The triangle chunk of granite the cabin lives on comes into view and confirms I'm headed home. "Oh God. Thank you." I'm so far beyond happy to see that miserable, lonely little cabin about the length of a football field away. "Thank you." My pace quickens as I appreciate how precious life is.

The moon is full and magnificent, illuminating the landscape. I feel small but oddly significant. On top of the world. Grateful for a second chance to fix my life. To right my wrongs, as much as I can.

I swear to myself and whomever is listening, "I'll do better." As soon as get myself warmed and well or Tutu shows up, I'm going straight to the police. I'm going to tell the truth about everything, including the murder. Whether anyone believes it or not isn't the point. Being honest and doing the right thing is what matters.

I follow the lakeshore, dragging my wet firewood behind me.

# FIFTEEN

The cabin is like a mirage under a painted moon. I can't believe my eyes when it comes clearly into view.

As soon as I get inside, I'll get these wet clothes off. Put something dry on. Get a fire going. My fingers are an interesting bluish purple, shiny and hard. They look like ugly candlesticks. I've lost feeling in both hands, and I'm pretty sure the sock attached to the bundled firewood is frozen around my fingers. I'm not sure what frostbite feels like, but if I have to go around with a few less digits, I'm okay with that.

I hope I don't lose my hands—that would suck. But at least I'd be alive. I'm glad I wrote down everything that happened with Pearl in the journal, since I may not be able to write again. I don't think I'll burn it, but I'm definitely keeping it hidden from Tutu. I could learn to type with a pencil in my mouth or something.

Before I know it, I'm at the ten-yard line to the goal—the triangle granite where the little cabin waits. Nearing the far end of the lake, where the creek runs in, I cut across the inlet. A low knocking sound stops me. I wait and listen, and there it is again.

Fear spikes. A bang, bang, bang, like someone knocking hard on a window. It echoes across the lake, and I feel it. Then the eeriest moans I've ever heard.

It's Pearl playing with my mind—or maybe it's the pills. Long, guttural groans fill the night like a woman. Run, my mind says, but my legs aren't working right. They won't do what they're told.

Sound vibrates through me like electricity, then backwashes. A pressure squeezes in all around me like a loud time warp. A snap. Pop. Then a crack like a tree just before it falls.

The cabin flies upward. Wrong. It's me. Dropping.

Down through the ice. The water shocks. A thousand needles stab. Holy shit. I've fallen through the ice. I might drown.

This can't be happening. I'm so close to the cabin, so close to surviving the cold. I can easily reach the shore. Don't panic. Not yet. Think.

Holding my breath, I kick my way up and out of the darkness. I slap my arms out of the water and reach out over the ice, but there's nothing. Nothing to hold on to. Nothing to save me. With a full shot of adrenaline, the pain is muted, but not the fear. My bad arm escapes the sling and joins the fight.

I claw and claw at the ice with frozen fingers, butI can't pull my torso out of the water.

More ice breaks, and the cold intensifies, sucking me down. My heavy clothes and what feels like a current drag me farther away from the cabin. Back under.

Kicking, kicking, kicking, I break the surface again. Gulp in precious air. My arms flounder desperately while the waterlogged boots, heavy as bricks, try to sink me.

"Help!" Clawing violently at the snow and jagged chunks of ice, I reach for the bundled wood with the ax. If I can just get the ax, I could bury it in the ice and use it to pull myself out.

I swim hard. Use every last bit of strength I have to reach the sock attached to the wood with the ax. I'm not even close—it's too far away.

"Help!" I scream at the cabin. But it doesn't care. The mountains, and trees, and mothers don't care either. Moans frozen in time, while the rest of the world marches on. I try to swim, try to live, but I can't.

The worse thing about dying is having too much time to think about all the things I've done wrong. I think of Pearl, but only the good parts of being with her.

I can't feel my arms or my legs when Mom comes to mind. The Christmas morning when she convinced me it was Santa who left the new bike. Just us, on the floor, eating warm cinnamon rolls, next to the Christmas tree, where she loved me. There is no cold here. Only perfection.

Tutu smiling that huge, dimpled smile. Cooking. Loving me, always.

Eventually, exhaustion and water become lethal. I stop fighting. There's a weightlessness in the silence. The lonesome dark wants me, but it can't have me, because true love never dies. There is no end.

# THE CLEANING LADY

# ONE

Nine days ago, I left my only grandson, Pu, alone at Mosquito Lake. He's not had much experience in the wild. Add an early-season snow storm that likely pounded his little cabin with no electricity, and a bad shoulder, and I can't help but worry sick.

For years I worried, wondering where Pu was after my son, his father, died and his mother disappeared with him. Not knowing where he was, if he was safe, took its toll, turned my black hair gray in less than a month. When I heard that Pu had been arrested and sent to juvenile hall, I left the job I loved teaching preschool at the Aloha Academy in Oahu and went to California. He was only ten, and did his best to act tough, but when I was finally allowed to hug him, he cried like a baby in my arms. In that moment, I knew he was innocent—I'd have staked my life on it. Walking out of that jail and leaving him behind was like leaving my heart. The pain in my chest was physical.

That was when I nicknamed him Pu. My heart.

We were alone in the world, and he needed me as much as I needed him. I found a cheap place to live in Murphys, where I could visit him every Sunday and on holidays.

At the Murphys Market, I load six bags of groceries, a portable heater, and four propane bottles into the van and head uphill to Bear Valley. The excitement I used to get while driving to visit Pu is back now, and I can't wait to see his sweet face and kiss his chubby cheeks. It's only thirty-odd miles, but the road is icy, and I have to take it easy. Last thing I need is to get into a wreck or slide off the road.

The glare from sun and snow stings my eyes and warms my face. For a moment, it feels good, and I escape the fact that my sweet boy killed someone. I crave the bliss, but the memory of Teresa pulling bits of bone from Pu's shoulder crushes my chance. I made him a CBD salve for his injury. Poor kid. I can't believe the mess he's gotten into. Choking the steering wheel, I notice that the worry wart on my wrist is bigger.

After an hour of trucking up the mountain, I turn into the Bear Valley Outdoor Adventure parking. A huge banner is strung over the entrance: "WE RENT SNOWMOBILES." The yellow pipe gate across the highway will be closed, making it impossible to drive the nine miles to Mosquito Lake. Eighteen miles round-trip. In the snow. Walking, even with snowshoes, or cross-country skiing with supplies, might seem doable for some mountain man. Not me. I'm renting a snowmobile.

The icy lot is mostly empty as I impersonate a tightrope walker from the van to the shop. "CLOSED"—the sign in the window sucker punches me.

"No." I jerk on the door, but it doesn't budge. These guys on Hawaiian time or what? This is going to ruin everything. They're supposed to be open. I saw their ad in the paper—that's how I got the idea. Now what? I press my face against the glass, shading the sides of my eyes with my hands. Inside, a man is carrying a box. I knock on the glass door with my knuckle.

He sees me, and I wave. "Hi there." Please be a kind human. I offer my best smile, and he sets the box on the counter. Comes to the door and unlocks it. When he pokes his head outside, I hold my hand out. "Hi, I'm Talula."

"Anthony." Salt-and-pepper hair pulled back into a shoulder-length ponytail under a greasy red 49ers ball cap. Too old to be an employee. Probably the owner. He extends a lanky arm, and we shake. His hands are inked like a mechanic's, with black grime under the nails.

"Hi, Anthony. I'd like to rent a snowmobile." I clasp my hands together and stand on my toes.

"Oh, sorry. We don't open for the season until next week." He stays put in the doorway.

"Ah, nuts." I weigh my words carefully. "Anthony, listen. I was supposed to clean and prep a cabin at Mosquito Lake. Snow came early, and with the road closed . . ." I point to my beat-up Astro van. "I got a ton of stuff to take up and no way to get it there. Owners are coming up this weekend, and if I don't have that cabin stocked, I'm screwed."

He has kind eyes. Big and brown, they narrow in on me and my outdated thrift store snow clothes. I wait. Smiling. Unsure if I evoke compassion, pity, or disgust. I certainly reek of abject poverty. "How they getting there? The owners."

I hesitate. Think fast. "Skis."

"Oh."

"Any ideas? I'm desperate."

He looks at the sky as if searching for patience, rather than a solution. "No. Not really. Sorry."

"Dang." I press my palm on my forehead. "They're going to fire me for sure, then all their friends will fire me too."

He fiddles with the diamond stud in his earlobe. "Wish I could help."

"You can. Just rent me a snowmobile. I'll be in and out. Lickety-split."

"Wish I could. I really do." But Anthony shakes his head. Tapping into his compassion didn't work. He doesn't care about my troubles. Why should he? Probably has plenty of his own—most people do.

I cross my arms. "I'll give you five hundred bucks. Cash."

"It's not that I don't want to—it's not my call. The owners could lose their lease with the Forest Service. We're not allowed out there until next week."

"Come on—when's the last time you saw a forest ranger?" I interrupt.

"Heh," he titters, "like never, but I could lose my job, and I need—"

"Six hundred. Final offer."

He scratches at the silver stubble on his jaw, considering it, because he's not the owner, he's a rickety employee making minimum wage. I have eight hundred, in the van, in case of emergency.

"Come in." He opens the door. He has the permanent scowl of someone who's experienced his fair share of trauma. Kind of like my resting bitch face. It's why I smile more than I probably should.

---

Anthony hitches up a child carrier to the back of the snowmobile—"on the house," he says, because after I put six hundred bucks in his hand, he's happy to help. The kid carrier looks like a plastic spaceship with flip-up doors balanced on top of two big skis. He even helps me load the supplies, shows me how to work the machine, then gives me a thumbs-up once I'm on my way.

The trail is actually closed Highway 4 and is as easy to navigate as the machine. For a gal from a tropical island who's never ridden a snowmobile, it's surprisingly simple, and I wish Pu was riding with me. He'd love it.

The high noon sun warms the snow, and it falls in chunks from trees bordering the roadside. In less than ten minutes, I'm at Lake Alpine. Snow glints and sparkles like diamonds across the ice. Natural beauty always takes my breath away and makes me cry, but not today. Today, it's impossible to appreciate.

Two cross-country skiers move aside and wave as I slow and go around them. An older couple enjoying life with a black and white border collie. Imagine that. Someone to share life's burdens with. Someone to trust, to laugh with, and to love. Pu filled that space for me these last few years. I can't wait to cook him a good meal.

After a while, my rear is numb, so I ride standing up. A big group of cross-country skiers are heading back toward Lake Alpine. I worry if anyone would venture all the way to Mosquito Lake. No. They couldn't make it out and back before dark. The icy air burns my cheeks and I sit, taking cover behind the windshield.

My heart flutters, and I can't help but smile when the cabin comes into view. I don't trust the ice enough to ride across the lake. The snow is about eight inches of wet mush as I navigate the back way to the cabin. The canoe sits frozen in time, right where I left it. I keep my speed, so I don't get stuck like Anthony warned. About a quarter mile from the cabin, I bog down, and the next thing I know, I can't go—I'm stuck.

There's a shovel at the cabin. Pu can help me dig the machine out.

After half an hour of post-holing through the exposed sections of forest, I'm sweating and out of breath. The cabin is a bit farther than I thought. I'm in pretty good shape, but I'm feeling the altitude and huffing like a freight train. Less oxygen equals more effort.

As I near the cabin, I call to him. "Pu!"

Nothing. When I'm closer, I call again. Louder, with my hands cupped around my mouth. "Pu! It's Tutu!" He's going to be so surprised.

But there's no response. I watch the door, waiting, expecting it to open any second. It doesn't. I step up onto the porch and notice that all the firewood is gone as I open the door.

"Surprise!" I look around. "Pu?"

He's not here.

It's colder inside than it is out, and a familiar worry comes over me. I shake it off.

Water trickles from the kitchen faucet like it's desperately trying to tell me something.

# TWO

It doesn't take long to realize the one-room cabin is empty. I rush out and check the outhouse, but he's not there either. The fireplace is empty except for ashes.

Pu's probably out gathering wood. I hope he returns soon—that snow machine has to be back by four, and we still haven't unstuck or unloaded it.

I pull off my glove and hold my palm over the ashes in the fireplace, hoping for warmth. There isn't any. I grab the poker and stir the ash, looking for the glow of an ember, but I can't see a single one. Finally, I touch the ash with my bare hand. Stone cold. I'm not one to let negative thoughts infect me, but the feeling that something is very wrong can't be denied.

All his things are here, so he didn't leave for a better option. Unless, maybe, he had to leave in a hurry. The police haven't arrested him, because they're still looking for someone who, according to Pearl White, looks nothing like Pu. KCRA News reported Pearl's description of the murderer as a tall, heavyset, man wearing what looked like a brunette wig and a leather mask. She's definitely covering up, and not for Pu's sake.

Could Pearl have found him or hired someone and . . . no. I throw the ridiculous notion away. She doesn't know about this place. By now, someone would have come to me about him, and they haven't. Not even the police.

I've considered going to the police myself, telling them what I know, but that's like putting a gun to my grandson's head and pulling the trigger. I just can't do it. Maybe after I ask Pu and he agrees. It's his life. His decision. If he turns himself in, it will look better for sure.

Rather than sit around waiting, I busy myself. As I'm cleaning the place up, I notice the damn pain pills are gone. My thoughts ignite a sick feeling. The baggie is empty and torn. There were enough to last him a couple weeks. I told him to only take them when absolutely necessary.

An empty bottle of Jim Beam rests sideways on the counter. "Aw, not good." I throw it in the trash bag. Pu's not a drinker. Guess I should have taken it away, but the thought he'd mix pills and alcohol never crossed my mind. Maybe he's in a lot of pain. Maybe the wound got infected or wasn't healing properly. A bone fragment could cause him trouble.

I gather the empty cans and garbage off the counter, then push it down into the trash can and tie up the bag. Set it near the door.

The bed's a mess. I pull back the blankets, and the leather journal falls. I pick it up, open it, and see that he's been writing. A grin lightens my worry. I won't read it, but flipping through the pages, I see he's been hard at work. I hope it's helped him deal with what he's done and why. I really want to read it, but it's not right. Not without permission.

I set the journal on the table and make the bed. Fluff the pillows. Tonight, he'll sleep in a comfy bed after a good meal.

Behind the cabin, I find the shovel and trek back to the snow machine.

Digging occupies my mind and helps me set worry aside. After a while, I've dug a nice track to pull it forward along and hope for the best. The machine revs as I press the throttle and move forward. Slow at first, then I gun the engine while the front end lifts a little. I stand, lean my weight forward, and progress through the mush. Then, suddenly, the machine finds footing and jumps ahead. Speeding for a tree.

I turn fast. Too fast, and the trailer comes up onto one side, the contents crashing around inside like dumping a sack of aluminum cans. I jerk the handle bars the opposite way and keep going with nothing more than beginner's luck as the trailer rights itself.

With plenty of momentum, I turn around behind the cabin. Now that I have a track, this part of leaving Pu should be easy. I hope.

By three o'clock, I have the supplies unloaded inside the cabin, but I can't stop worrying that Pu's gotten himself lost. A bad vibe takes hold of me when I realize that if I'm going to make it back by four, like I promised Anthony, I have to leave now. The guy trusted me. And my six hundred dollars. I'm usually a woman of my word, but I can't leave until I know Pu's okay.

I bundle up, take the headlamp from the table, and put it around my neck. With the binoculars from the shelf, I start walking. Taking the snow machine would be nice, but it would never work. I'd get stuck in a minute.

I circle the cabin, looking for tracks. A sign. Anything.

"Puuuuu!" I scream as loud as I can. Then I listen for a long, long while to nothing but the guttural sigh of wind whipping the treetops.

After a lap around the house, I'm more than a little concerned. There should be tracks. Where are his tracks? It hasn't snowed in a few days. No tracks means he hasn't been near the cabin in a while. If he left the cabin in the last few days, there'd be tracks. What's going on? Dread has its way with me.

Maybe there were tracks, and the sun melted them, I reason, but the urge to cry is overwhelming. I fight back tears and scream for him. "Puuu!" I can't breathe, and my legs go soggy.

"Pu!" The setting sun eats me alive. I haven't felt fear like this since the night they called to tell me my son rolled his pickup down the canyon. I knew he was dead long before they said it.

My hands shake as I hold the binoculars and scope the sea of trees. Back and forth and up and down and side to side. In segments, starting behind the cabin. I take ten steps to the north and repeat the process, over and over again, until I've worked my way to the frozen lake.

Through the binoculars, something catches my eye. Something odd, out of place on the ice, just past the mouth of Mosquito Lake where the water feeds in. I pull off my glove and adjust the focus.

There it is. Perfectly clear. A stack of tree limbs, with something white around one end.

I run as best I can through the pasty snow, following the lake shore around the long way as not to cross the ice.

As I near the object, chills stop me cold. Some sort of tracks. I get closer and pull the binoculars up. Focusing on the tracks, I still can't make them out. They're big—maybe a bear. Then I remember . . . when sun hits tracks, it melts the surrounding snow, making them appear larger after a day or two. Whatever it is, they lead from the shore to the wood stacked out on the ice. It makes no sense.

Chaotic thoughts swirl around in my skull. I step forward and catch something in my sights. Another step forward. Then I see it, and a force stomps my chest, makes it hard to breathe. Clarity comes crashing down—painful as Satan's fist.

Wood and the ax bundled on the ice. Hacking into me. Gutting me. Leaving me hollow and weak. Pu was out on the unstable ice. The world falls silent except for the sound of my own breath billowing in short bursts. My mouth waters as nausea swells. "No!"

My head falls back, trees mutilating what was just a blue sky. I rush out onto the ice.

# THREE

My pitiful sobs soak into the white wilderness. I can't live without him. I won't. I'd rather die. But what if he's not there? What if he got out and somehow survived? I have to know—I keep sliding my feet across the frozen lake.

Tears blur my vision, but I notice the ice has turned the softest hue of pink I've ever seen. I stop and turn around. The sun dropping between granite peaks lights frosted pines in neon pink and tangerine. Natural beauty, so real it hurts.

I scream and shake my fists at the sun, then turn my back and don't stop until I reach the spot where limbs and ax are bundled with what appears to be socks. I look around for a hole, but there isn't one. I scan the area for what I don't know, something to confirm what happened to Pu. I shake my head and call his name again.

Maybe he didn't fall through the ice. Or maybe he did, but he got out and now he's lost out here. I can't come up with a logical theory, other than that he fell through the ice and the hole refroze.

If he's in the lake, there's nothing I can do but join him. My future is laid out before me. Alone. Never-ending days and longer nights filled with resentment and blame. Trying in vain to understand why, while bitterness festers until all the good in me has rotted away. I'd rather not.

In the momentary silence, the subtle sound of a baby crying stops my world from spinning. Listening carefully, I wait for the silence to strangle me. When it doesn't, I turn and trudge toward shore with ice and snow crunching beneath me. Cries echo all around me. There's a baby out here. I spin. Listening. Looking.

With the binoculars, I search amid the gritty light and trees. How can there be a baby? My mind churns, struggling to make sense of it. Then a blast like gunfire engulfs me. I drop. The icy water shocks like a thousand electric needles, jolting me to life. Instantly, I want nothing more than to get out of the freezing cold lake. My arms flail as I gasp for breath.

"Ugh, ugh, ugh!" I spit and blink back water so cold it burns. My feet hit bottom. I can stand, my shoulders just above floating shards. My fists hammer the ice and bust it to bits, but not enough to make it to shore. My breath runs faster than my thoughts.

Two seconds ago, I wanted this. Wanted to die. Now all I can think of, as my body numbs, is how to survive. I can't will myself to stop fighting and let the water have me. The will to live is involuntary, and I don't try to understand. There's a reason. There's always a reason.

I use the jagged ice like the side of a pool. Pressing my palms down and leaning forward, I gather my strength and kick my feet. In one swift motion, my torso flops onto the ice like a seal, while the rest of me dangles in the water. Teetering on the precipice, I squirm myself forward. More of me is on the ice than in the water.

Gasping, I army crawl toward shore. It isn't far, but by the time I reach it, I'm exhausted, shivering, and I can't feel my arms or legs.

Pu's not down there. Wouldn't I have seen him if he was? Or would the current have carried him to deeper water? My mind is agonizingly numb as I struggle to my feet and zombie-walk back toward the cabin. Each agonizing step feels like it'll be my last.

I refuse to let bitter cold destroy me, refuse to consider not making it back to the cabin. I'll be there soon. I'll get these wet clothes off, start the little heater, and crawl into bed. That's what I tell myself—I'll be there soon. Have something hot to eat. Split pea soup in bed under the blankets. I'll be warm.

The baby cries again, wailing now. So close, then so far away. My body stiffens as if rigor mortis is setting in. I don't think I'm dead, but who knows?

Maybe I'm still under the ice, looking for Pu. Thoughts tangle as I pull the gloves off my stiff and shaky hands. Removing my clothes is impossible. My fingers won't work.

I can't pull the coat zipper down, though I keep trying. Finally, I work the thing halfway down. "Hallelujah!" I wrestle the coat to my waist. From there, I wiggle and work to shed the coat like a heavy cocoon.

A weight has been lifted as I leave the sopping mess behind. The cabin isn't far—only a few hundred feet. I'm going to make it. Tonight, my hot flashes will be a welcome nuisance.

The baby screams. This time, it's clear and close. In the rocks to my right. I look, but I keep moving. There's no baby out here, I tell myself. "No. Sorry. No." I'm pretty sure hallucinations are part of hypothermia—auditory hallucinations, I decide, because I really don't know.

"Whaa—whaaa—whaaaa." The poor thing needs help. Then it's silent again. A branch snaps. I turn, catch movement in the growing dark, but keep going. If I stop, I'll die.

When I reach the porch, I use my hands to lift my legs up the steps. It takes both obstinate hands to twist the knob. The door cracks open, and I can't help but let out a sorrowful victory squeal.

It's dark inside, and I pull the headlamp from around my neck. I doubt it will work, but I give it a go and switch it on. Light slices the dark, and I hurry to the propane heater. Violently shaking, I set it on the table, press down on the ignition, and twist as best I can. To spite my efforts, I can't get the darn thing going. "Damn it!"

*Okay. Fine. Get your clothes off and find dry ones,* I tell myself. "Come on. Get moving, Tutu."

In Pu's duffle bag, I dig out a sweatshirt and pants two sizes too big. The plastic bag of cash peeks out from the bottom. I'd put it there in case he needed it. If he had to run. Now what? What next? Get warm. *Dry clothes,* I think.

Getting undressed takes a ridiculous amount of effort and time, but I manage. Like dressing an uncooperative mannequin when it's a matter of life or death and the clock's ticking. There are a half dozen sweaters and a fleece jacket in the closet, and I layer on one after another.

I can't find socks or slippers for my frozen feet, so I take bath towels and wrap them up as best I can, then shuffle back to the table and give the heater another go. The rotten-egg smell of spent propane fills the cabin. How ironic it would be to die in an explosion after nearly freezing to death. I laugh when suddenly, the heater whoomps to life, and a beautiful orange glow lights up my life. "Ha! It's the little things. Always the little things."

I swing the knob to high. The heater hisses as I hold my hands to the glowing wire mesh, certain they're thawing though I can't feel a thing. I wonder if the guy, Anthony, thinks I stole the snowmobile. Maybe he'll come after me—or send someone.

After what feels like an eternity, the cabin isn't freezing. Constantly moving my fingers and toes has brought some life back into them.

What I wouldn't give for a cup of hot tea, but there's no wood for the stove. Instead, I roast marshmallows on a fork next to the heater, gooey sweetness sticking to my throat and forming a knot in the pit of my stomach. I hope the calories and warmth help me recover.

With the headlamp off and hanging from the bedpost, I crawl under the covers. Every once in a while, I shake, but it doesn't last long. My hands and feet feel like they're filled with broken glass, stabbing from the inside out as they warm. It's excruciating, but I know it will pass. Unlike thoughts of Pu.

What are the odds he's still alive? Instantly, I'm wracked with guilt for even thinking such a terrible thought. Where is he? Sorrow claws at my heart. Crying doesn't ease one ounce of pain, but I can't stop. It's as mandatory as breathing.

The crying baby joins me. Still out there, haunting my sanity all night long.

# FOUR

Somewhere in the middle of the night, the heater coughs and quits. My shivering has finally quieted, but I'm still exhausted and too tired to get up and replace the propane bottle. "Good night, Pu." I fall back to sleep.

Later, I wake again—cold. Finding the headlamp, I light up the emptiness. My shadow looms large as I replace the propane bottle. The heater lights on the first attempt this time.

Back in bed, I try to ignore the cold, but it's impossible. "How did you do it, Pu? You must have been miserable. I'm so sorry."

The bedframe creaks and moans as I switch the headlamp off and hang it back on the bedpost. Pedaling my obstinate legs and squeezing my hands open and shut to increase circulation is a chore. I lack the strength, and quit after a minute. "I hope you're not cold anymore. I hope you're someplace wonderful and warm."

Numb and weak, I stare up at the shadows of branches creeping across the ceiling. At least the howling baby has finally quieted. That, or my deep sleep prevented me from noticing.

Images of Pu under the ice intrude, causing my lower lip to tremble and my chest to tighten. I rub my hand over my heart in a circular motion while willing the awful visions to stop. It's like the universe is telling me where he is—that he's gone—but I don't want to hear it because it's too much.

"I'm sorry, Pu," I whisper. I never should have brought him here. Should have gone straight to the police. Jail is better than this. Growling, I snatch fistfuls of hair and pull until it hurts. Pain is a decent distraction—until the baby bawls again, sounding like it's coming from the back of the cabin.

I'm not getting up to investigate. The screams are not real. I'm distraught. Sleep will make them go away. I stare at the dark for what seems like hours, waiting for daylight that never comes.

Then I consider the journal. Wondering what's inside gets the better of me.

I sit up, pull the headlamp down, and switch it on.

With the journal against my chest, I reconsider a moment, then begin.

---

The cabin is dead silent when the morning sun finally crawls across the floor. I read the last few lines Pu wrote.

*Mom, you let your only son spend five years in detention and get jumped fourteen times for a murder you committed. Why?*

*Did you ever love me? Even just a little?*

The fact he was innocent and took the blame for two sorry women who damaged him beyond repair stirs something primal inside of me. My pulse quickens and bangs in my ears.

"I knew it." Five years in juvenile hall for a crime he didn't commit. No wonder he fell for that Pearl the instant she showed him a little attention. She set out from the very beginning to use him. He was the perfect pawn. Previously convicted of murder, gullible, and desperate to be loved.

I love him. But a grandmother's love is to be expected—and is never enough.

Once he got her pregnant, she could manipulate him in any way she wanted. Pu only shot her husband to protect his unborn child and the woman he loved. The police wouldn't be able to keep her safe. It suddenly all makes sense.

That baby inside Pearl *is* the reason I'm still here. The reason I fought my way out of the water. The reason cries came through the wilderness to find me. The reason I didn't freeze to death. The reason to live.

My great-grandchild cried out to me for help. So Pu can go on, so I can go on. My mind spins faster and faster. My first instinct is to go to the police, tell them what I know, show them the journal and get them to drag the lake.

At Na Pali, when a person drowns, it is customary for us to let them be. It is said that their soul becomes part of the water and part of forever. After reading Pu's journal, I'm almost certain it's best to keep Pearl White in the dark. Let her worry and wonder if he's coming for her.

According to the journal, Pu never told her about me. The less she knows, the better. I must be mindful of each and every decision. Think things through carefully. All I know for sure is I want custody of my great-grandchild. No way Pearl White is going to ruin another human. Not while I'm around.

My stomach growls as I crawl out of bed, but the thought of food makes me nauseous. I decide to leave everything as is, including the faucet trickling, if by some miracle Pu returns. I don't know whether to leave the money or take it. Both options feel wrong.

My boots are stiff with frost. I find two plastic grocery bags under the kitchen sink and unwrap the towels from around my feet. With a foot inside each bag, I work the boots on. It's not at all comfortable, but it'll work, and I'm out of ideas.

Outside, the air is crisp. The snow froze solid overnight. I notice animal tracks around the snow machine. The prints are not deer, that I do know. They're not bear either. Bears are busy hibernating right now. Too big for coyote, and there aren't wolves in these mountains.

By process of elimination, I suspect a mountain lion—maybe two, because there are lots of tracks. They circled the machine more than once. Three, maybe four times. I investigate and follow. The animal or animals circled the cabin as well, and even came onto the porch.

Something cracks and snaps. My heart lurches, and my head whips around. I'm expecting to be attacked. A clump of snow falls from the top of a cedar.

"Oh . . . kay." I slap my hand over my heart and take deep breaths until I calm down.

The sun is hard at work, thawing the day as I scan the surrounding forest for predators. It dawns on me that the cries and screams I heard last night were more than likely a lion. As if I couldn't be any sadder, the thought that the child wasn't reaching out to me from beyond stirs more sorrow. I look up, stare at the deep blue sky that comes with cold sunshine. Miles away, clouds decapitate mountaintops.

Waiting. Watching. Feeling for the answer. I place a hand over my heart and close my eyes, but roll them toward my forehead. Breathe deeply. Focus energy from my heart to open my third eye, to show me the way. There in the snow, the universe of color energizes my third eye. I feel it vibrate and activate my pineal gland. The powerful light from my heart, breath, and soul transcends the physical. Allows clear intention. Awareness.

It doesn't matter if it was a mountain lion crying or an auditory hallucination. Either way, it *was* a greater force pulling me back. Bringing me to life for the child-to-be. A child that is real needs me.

A distant purr interrupts my epiphany. My eyes open, searching, expecting trouble. Eventually, I glimpse movement between the tree trunks.

The constant purr gets too loud. An engine revs and releases. Revs and releases. A snow machine, coming in hot.

Anthony looks mad. I wave. He doesn't wave back, just jumps off the machine, yelling as he stomps my way. "What the fuck lady?" He throws his arms up for dramatic effect. "You trying to get me fired?"

When he's close enough and quiet, I respond. "No."

"Well, shit. I thought maybe you broke down. Got stranded out here. If my boss finds out, I'm history. Tried to do you a favor, and this is the thanks I get. No good deed, right?"

"I fell through the ice and almost froze to death last night. Sorry."

"You what?" He looks me up and down as if my appearance will confirm deceit.

"Wasn't trying to take advantage. Just trying to survive. Can we go now?" The sight of me must convince him, because his face morphs from anger to what looks like concern.

"Holy shit. You went into the lake? Are you okay?"

"No." I don't tell him I'll never be okay again, as a lump forms like a rock in my throat. I swallow hard and blink back tears as I climb onto the snow machine. Why bother explaining what may or may not have happened here? It's too complicated for me to understand.

"Whoa!" He's looking down and pointing at the snow. Stepping back. "You see these?"

I don't answer, and he looks up at me. His eyes widen.

"These are lion tracks." he says.

"Thought so," I say.

"See how wide and round the toes are? No nails. Claws only come out when needed."

"More than one?" I ask.

He kneels, studying them closer. "Adult lions seldom travel in pairs. This looks like one hungry loner. Long stride. Probably an old female. They get brazen the older they get."

I nod, understanding perfectly. "Nothing left to lose."

# FIVE

I'm not a violent person. I've never hit or hurt anyone. I never even spanked my son. Never. But the pain of missing Pu and what Pearl White did taunts me. Stirs a fire in me I never knew I had, and turns grief to fury. I often catch myself thinking about killing that woman.

I called the Sheriff's Department to ask if I had to wait forty-eight hours to report someone missing. They said no, especially since Pu is a minor, so I drove to San Andreas and filed a report. I gave them Pu's photo and explained—no, lied about—why he was staying at the cabin. I explained that Murphys Diggins was a retirement village and no one under the age of fifty-five was allowed to stay more than two days. Pu had nowhere else to go—the cabin was only temporary. It seemed reasonable, and I almost believed it myself.

Deputy Hannah Baxter promised sympathetically that she would forward the report to the national database after seventy-two hours and include search-and-rescue in implementing a sweep of the cabin and surrounding areas. "Unfortunately, due to the impending inclement weather and the location's inaccessibility, our search will likely be limited." She spoke so fast I caught myself squinting for no reason other than a feeble attempt to keep up.

"What does that mean?" I asked as her phone rang, signaling that my time was up.

"We cannot put staff at risk unless the circumstances of the missing person appear dire or concerning. But there's a volunteer group, El Dorado Backcountry Ski Patrol. They might be available." She reaches for the phone. "I'll contact them and let you know."

"Thank you." I smile and go, glad I did something right by taking the journal and cash from the cabin. That would have been a huge red flag.

For the next few nights, I lie face down on Pu's bed and take in the sweaty hair smell that lingers on his pillow. I roll over, stare up at the discolored popcorn ceiling, which looks like old snow.

"Where are you?" I wait and wait for the answer I believe will come. "Please, please, please come back, okay? We'll go away. Someplace warm." Then it dawns on me like a sensational sunrise. "Kauai." I sit up and clap my hands. "Yes. Na Pali. Yes, yes. Back to the good life. Back to ke ola nani. It's where we should have gone in the first place." I lie back down, plotting it out to the best of my ability. "No one will ever find us deep inside Na Pali. We can do it, Pu. I know we can." My hands are clasped over my heart, and I catch myself smiling for the first time in days. I take a deep breath and close my eyes. "You'll love it there. I promise. Then when the baby comes . . ." I'm clueless how to go about getting Pu's child away from Pearl and to the island.

It's impossible to function. To sleep. To shower. To clean houses, including my own.

Figuring out the right steps to a favored outcome is convoluted at best. While meditating the next morning, visions of beating Pearl to death with the journal make me laugh. I can't stop—I double over hysterically until I cry.

Drumming my fingers on the kitchen table, I realize I'm losing my marbles. How does one know for sure? Without a doubt, my marbles are scattered. Some have even rolled under the sofa to play with the dust bunnies.

The kettle on the stove screams. I jump. I don't recall turning on the stove, but I must have, so I brew some chai tea. Cradling the cup in my hands, I inhale, and think of the baby Pu left behind. I imagine holding him or her in a few months. Boy. Girl. Doesn't matter. I catch myself smiling.

I've reread the journal and prayed for the right answer so many times, I've lost track. If I go to the police and show them the journal, will it be enough to convict Pearl? Especially since the words were written by a convicted murderer? Do I want her arrested while she's carrying my great-grandchild? No. Definitely not. Not yet. Prison isn't the place for a pregnant woman. She could be beaten and lose the baby.

Maybe the county would protect a pregnant woman, place her in a safe section of the prison. Is there a safe place in prison? I'm more and more confused with each passing day. If only I could ask someone in law enforcement. Someone who could best advise me.

"A lawyer!"

Why hadn't I thought of it before now? I could consult a lawyer without repercussions. Right? I jump from the kitchen table, knock the chair over, and rip the junk drawer open. Finding the phone book, I search the Yellow Pages for attorneys.

"Family law, family law, divorce, personal injury, injury, injury. Crud. Does anyone practice criminal law?" My index finger scratches down the opposite page.

I call the first attorney listed under criminal defense. Thomas Owens. He's unavailable. When I explain it's an emergency, the woman on the phone promises he'll get back to me as soon as possible if I'd like to leave my name and number. I don't.

"I'll try back later. Thanks." I hang up. Leaving my name and number feels wrong. If I'm mistaken about speaking to an attorney, I could easily dig myself in deeper. I don't want what I say to come back and bite me later.

Next, I try Susan B. Torres. An answering machine, so I hang up. After four more calls, I've gotten nowhere. I flip the yellow page and find an ad in big, bold letters: *CRIMINAL DEFENSE ATTORNEY.*

I dial the number. It rings twice before a woman greets me with, "Law office of Edward Manetti."

———

The next afternoon, I meet Edward Manetti at his office in Angels Camp. A consultation he calls it, and only charges a minimal fee for the brief session. Mr. Manetti shakes my hand. His hands are soft, much softer than mine, and with nicer nails. Must be nice to sit at a desk all day, but then, as he pulls his chair in behind his desk, I notice his aura. It's weak. Not only can I feel it, I can see it on his face. The drab skin, the tired and faded brown eyes, but worst, he has no spark. A desk job probably isn't all it's cracked up to be. Cleaning houses isn't that bad.

I hand over copies of Pu's journal pages and begin summarizing what's there. The second I utter the name Pearl White and her involvement in her husband's murder, Mr. Manetti throws his hand up and stops me. "Wait. Whoa. Stop, please. I'm sorry."

I wait for an explanation as he hands back the journal copies.

"Since you refused to explain your case over the phone, I didn't know we would be discussing the Tucker White murder. I must recuse myself immediately and insist we stop here."

"Why?"

"Ms. White contacted me this morning, requesting I represent her. Which I agreed to, so this—"

"Represent her? She needs a lawyer?"

"I cannot discuss her situation with you." He stands.

"She's been *arrested*?"

"Please, Miss Jones, I really am sorry, but I can't help you." He can't get to the door fast enough. "Don't worry about the fee." He opens it.

I stand. "She's a murderer, you know." I head for the door. "Shame on you for defending trash like that." I hurry out and focus my breath on the sky. It's all about the money. People will sell their soul for the right price, which reminds me I have houses to clean today and I'm very late.

---

Cleaning houses has always been a way to clean the cobwebs out of my head. That, and meditation. I listen to an iPod with headphones that Pu gave me two or three Christmases ago. It's a modern miracle how something so small carries so much music and Solfeggio frequencies. Guns and Roses' greatest hits occupy the space in my head while I scrub iron stains from a toilet in a vacation cabin.

"Sweet Child of Mine" triggers tears and makes it hard to keep cleaning. Anger rears, and retribution creeps in. I hurl the scrub brush against the mirror, then slap the toilet lid down, hard enough to hear it through my headphones.

I flush the toilet and switch from music to the Solfeggio frequencies. I choose 417 Hz—the healing frequency to calm and balance my mind. The set of nine electromagnetic tones were used in the Gregorian chants hundreds of years ago to heal and raise consciousness.

I pull a crystal from opposing pants pockets. In one hand, I hold obsidian, which will help me process my emotions and aid in letting Pu go. The gem is black, smooth, and cold as ice. In the other hand, amethyst to heal and purify me. Mostly, the purple crystal will enhance my willpower, allow an opening for spiritual wisdom to show me the way.

Sitting on the toilet lid, I take deep breaths and close my eyes, gently squeezing a crystal in each hand, cleansing my mind of intrusive thoughts. Allowing the power of the stones to work through my palms, up my arms, all the way to my heart.

My right hand warms, the amethyst causing a slight tingle. Then, an undeniable vibration shakes loose the ultimate truth. I see it, clear as light in the dark. The only thing that matters is not only in the here and now, but from now on.

With eyes wide open, I accept the knowing. I'll die before I'll allow Pearl White to infect and destroy another one of my grandchildren.

# SIX

Keep your friends close and your enemies closer. In all my life, I've never hated or disliked anyone so much as to consider them an enemy. Not even my ex-husband. But Pearl White is an animal. A predator—biting, gnawing, and consuming me, stalking my every thought. Evil as she is, she's carrying my great-grandchild, so from now on, every move will be with resolute purpose.

Deputy Baxter called to inform me that volunteers from the El Dorado Backcountry Ski Patrol skied into Mosquito Lake yesterday. She said they searched the area for six hours, including the cabin, and found no sign of Pu. No news isn't good news. I guess I should be happy, but I'm not. With Pu gone, it's like I'm missing a limb.

When I get too down, I think of Pearl. Having a purpose is the only thing that gets me out of bed in the morning.

Exhausted and starving, I drag myself to dinner.

Margo, the server at Murphys Irish Pub, brings a tray with a frothy Guinness and vegetable soup to my table as she sings with Linda Ronstadt. "You're no good, you're no good, you're no good, baby you're no gooood." She's good and adds a basket of warm sourdough to the table. The earthy smell of bread and beer nurtures my well-being.

"Thanks, Margo."

"Of course. Let me know if you need anything."

I dig in, and in no time, I'm halfway through dinner. Then I hear, "Talula, right?"

A man approaches with a black apron around his waist.

"Yeah," I say around a mouthful, wiping my lips and looking up at him. He's middle-aged, clean-shaven, with close-cropped gray hair. I don't know him, but he stands there with his hands on his hips, like

I should. He's not smiling, but I am, because it's what I do when I'm nervous or confused.

"How's it going?" I can't think of anything else to say.

"Not that great." He crosses his arms. "Lost my job thanks to you." His expression doesn't shift as his dark eyes rake over me. It takes me a second, but then I see his name badge. Anthony. The snow machine guy. Cleaned up, he borders on handsome.

I place my hands in my lap. "You got fired?"

"Yes, ma'am. Sure did." He unties his apron.

"Really? I'm sorry." I swallow. "But, um—so, you work here now?" I try to sound encouraging. Like, how great is that?

"It's only part-time." He folds, then rolls his apron.

"Can I buy you beer?" I can't help but feel like a jerk.

"Yeah. It's dead, so I got the rest of the night off. Be right back." He turns and walks behind the bar, stashes his apron and name badge somewhere under the register, then fills two glasses with Guinness and returns. He sets the beers on the table and takes a seat across from me.

"I'm really, *really*, sorry you lost your job. You work there a long time?"

"A few winters. Springtime, I hunt mushrooms in the Pacific Northwest. Summers, I'm in Alaska. Cheers." He offers his glass, and we toast.

"Cheers."

Anthony does most of the talking, telling me how tending bar is like being a therapist. How everyone has a story and assumes the bartender has nothing better to do than listen. Eventually, he gets around to asking me about the kid that went missing from the cabin at Mosquito Lake.

"Kenny Tait's been the topic of conversation lately, and since you were up there . . ." He waits.

"He's my grandson. He stays at the cabin. I lied to you. I wanted take him supplies.  Owners don't know about it."

"Did you lie about falling in the lake?"

"No." I shake my head. "I was out looking for him, and went down through the ice."

"Shit. I'm sorry. Shit." Anthony reaches across the table and squeezes my hand. "I'm sorry you have to go through this."

"And I'm sorry I lied to you. Really sorry you got fired because of me."

"Don't be. I actually like this job. The owner gave me a room upstairs, and with what I was paying for rent, it comes out pretty close to the same as running snowmobiles. And food's included here, so I'm not complaining." He swigs his beer and licks the froth off his upper lip. "If we're being honest, it's my own fault I got fired. I didn't have to take your money or give you the sled. I could have said no. I knew the owner was just looking for an excuse to fire me—other than the *real* reason."

"Why?" I sip.

"The owner's wife, Laura, has had it out for me since I caught her screwing around. And not with her husband."

"Oh, no." I lean in, the beer heating my cheeks along with my spirits.

"Yeah. You heard about that dude that got shot on Halloween? Tucker White?"

My heart sputters, then speeds up. I nod, gulping my third Guinness and practicing patience.

"He bought a snowmobile from Laura last winter. She took him out more than a few times for what she called"—Anthony's finger shoot into air quotes—"a guided tour." Only thing she was guiding was his dick into her mouth. Shit. I'm sorry. That was inappropriate."

"No. It's okay, really. So, you saw them?"

"Yeah, one night in the shop. I'd forgot my damn phone in the office and went back. She knew I saw her sucking—I mean, giving him oral sex. I even *excused* myself for crap's sake, but she never said a word about it."

"You think she's involved with Tucker's murder? Or her husband maybe found out and shot him?"

"Hell if I know." He shakes his head. "Neither seem the type. But . . . you never know, right?"

"You tell the police about Tucker and Laura messing around?"

"Yup. Called the Sheriff's Department soon as I heard what happened—which was like three days after the fact, but still. I don't know if they even questioned them."

"What? They had to."

"Yeah, no kidding. I read somewhere the average murder investigation takes two and a half years from start to finish, so who the hell knows. Not my monkeys, not my circus, but I know the clowns." He throws up his hands.

"Tucker's wife got attorney," I say. I can't stop myself. "I think she's involved." Alcohol has never improved my judgement, and it's so nice having a conversation with someone other than myself. "That's what I heard, anyway." I shrug, as if it's just gossip and I don't know it's true.

"Pearl White? No way." Anthony shakes his head, then swigs his beer. "She goes to my church and was absolutely heartbroken after the murder. No way you could fake that. Her and her little boy—we all pray for their healing every Sunday. No way Pearl's involved—she doesn't have it in her."

"What church do you go to?"

"First Congregational." Anthony grins. "You should join us Sunday."

"For sure. I'd love to."

# SEVEN

Church bells sound strikingly similar to temple bells. A murky sky bears down on the white steeple of the First Congressional Church. Guilt and vengeance battle for position as I smile and nod to fellow struggling worshipers. *WE ARE ONE*, the banner above the entrance reads.

Inside, a dozen stained-glass windows brighten the small chapel despite the darkness outside. Cheerful faces, organ music, and candle smoke fill me with temporary good will. The oak pews are mostly empty, but I'm early, so I take a seat in the back, searching for Pearl White while integrating with a devout smile. Directly in front of me, someone has planted a row of red pleather Bibles one foot apart, like seeds waiting to sprout and offer nourishment. I pluck one and flip through the pages. I've read it all before, hoping for enlightenment that never came.

I thumb through it until I find Exodus and read. An eye for an eye, a tooth for a tooth, a hand for a hand, a foot for a foot, a burn for a burn, a wound for a wound, a bruise for a bruise. I look up and around to be sure no one is watching while I slowly rip the page from the bible. Then I fold it in half and slide it into my coat pocket. Last, I replant the Bible.

Worshipers fill pews, but I don't see Pearl. Maybe she's not attending today. Folks pass with a "hello" or a welcoming nod, and I reciprocate. Anthony slides in beside me. "Nice skirt," he says.

"Thanks." He smells good, like my favorite lemongrass soap.

"Glad you could make it." He hands me a trifold pamphlet.

"Wouldn't miss it." I skim the bulletin.

A white woman with short white hair and a long matching robe steps behind the pulpit, smiling like the rest as she watches us. Her hands hold the bulletin below a large, gold crucifix hanging near her navel. Her head bobs while she waits for the organ to conclude.

"That's Pastor Connie. She's awesome. Very open-minded."

I nod, then straighten my crinkled cotton skirt. Wearing a red skirt with gold sequins was a mistake. I stand out like a bloody zit between the Virgin Mary's eyes.

A feeble, bent man gets up from his seat in the corner and hobbles to the door. He fights to kick the doorstop up and eventually wins. Just as the door falls shut, it suddenly opens again.

The old man holds the door and greets a captivating redhead that can only be Pearl White. She's bewitching. Fear washes over me. Why am I afraid? She's the one who should be scared. I take a deep breath.

Pearl loosens her long fur coat and scurries to the pew in front of me like a rat. A skinny rat, shedding her fur. By my calculations, she should be somewhere between two to three months along, but I guess she isn't showing yet. It dawns on me that she might have gotten rid of it. Had an abortion. My stomach does a triple-gainer, ending in a tragic belly flop. I feel sick. She's already killed two people. Why not a third?

Pastor Connie nods and waves at Pearl. The door closes, and Pastor Connie slips on a pair of red cat eyeglasses rimmed in diamonds. The organ quiets.

Someone coughs, and Evil takes a seat right in front of me, her long red hair pulled into a high ponytail. I can see the little red hairs at the nape of her narrow neck. My heart races, and I'm sweating like crazy. I crack my knuckles as quietly as I can.

"Welcome, everyone. Whoever you are and wherever you are on life's journey, you are welcome here." Pastor Connie lifts her bulletin and glances around the room, smiling. "Did everyone get today's bulletin?"

A few random "yeses," and Pastor Connie gets right to business. "Stapled inside"—she opens the bulletin—"you'll find your pledge envelope." She fingers the envelope. "On the front, you'll find a prayer request." The pastor folds it over. "On the back is a neat little guide to giving based on your level of income." She says it like she's preaching the gospel, and I wonder if God answers prayers based on your donation amount. It reminds me of what I dislike about religion.

"Breathe in God's spirit, and help us keep the lights on."

The organ begins, and plays for way too long. Candles are lit, and the service finally starts as I stare at the back of Pearl White's head.

We stand and sit and sing and read from the bulletin.

"Praise God. Let us pray in silence." Pastor Connie closes her eyes. I bow my head, lace my fingers, close my eyes, and attempt to welcome the light. Let it warm my soul. But Pearl is sitting right there in front of me like an eclipse darkening everything.

Silence allows Pu's sweet smile to blossom then rot into visions of him frozen under the ice. Something presses down on me. I can't breathe. I'll never see my Pu again. Hear his laughter. Loving him is killing me.

Everything is as it should be, I tell myself. But the pain in my heart is so bad, I wonder if I'm having a heart attack. I squeeze my eyes shut and my hands together. Tears escape as Pearl's sacrilegious being taunts, then disgusts me. Pain turns to vengeance, and I like it. For the first time in my life, I truly want to hurt someone. Pearl White. I don't want her behind bars. I want her dead.

I imagine my hands reaching forward, grabbing fistfuls of her flaming hair and bashing her skull against the back of the pew until every ounce of blood empties from her wicked soul.

I catch myself smiling. Laughing. I open my eyes, giggling aloud. Anthony is looking at me suspiciously.

"Amen." I smile sincerely, grateful for the epiphany. I'm done fighting back the urge.

---

After the service, Anthony and I walk outside. Groups gather along the sidewalk in the cold.

"Wanna grab a bite later? I have to work at noon, but I'm off at five."

"Okay." I'm pleasantly surprised at the thought of Anthony being interested in me in any way, shape, or form, but I don't let on. Instead, I tighten the belt on my wool coat and look away.

"Come to the pub anytime after five."

"Okay." I play it cool.

Pearl White exits the church behind us.

"Can you do me favor?" I ask Anthony.

"Will it get me fired again?"

"No. Just . . . if you can introduce me to her?" I point to the vixen as she soaks up Pastor Connie's sympathies.

Anthony tucks his chin. "Why?"

"So I can be of service to the congregation and I think she could probably use some help around the house."

"Oh." He nods approvingly. "Yeah, sure. That's a great idea." He seems impressed with my offering, and tells me how lucky he is to have a small studio above the bar that seldom needs cleaning.

As Pearl nears, Anthony greets her. "Hi, Pearl. Good to see you."

"Good to see you, too." She squeezes both of his hands.

"Where's Bodie today?" Anthony asks.

"He has a cold," Pearl says.

"Bummer." Anthony turns his palm upward, presenting me to Pearl like a prize. I smile like I don't know what she's capable of.

"Hi," I say.

"This is my friend, Talula."

"Hello." She has one of those big, impressive Colgate smiles.

"Nice to meet you," I lie.

"Nice meeting you." She draws it out like a slow song. Like she means it.

"She has a housecleaning service, best in the county, if you're ever in need," Anthony says.

"Oh, really? That's great. I'll keep it in mind." Pearl nods.

"Here." I dig out my business card, for "The Cleaning Lady," and hand it to her. "Just give me ring if you need anything." Then I sweeten the deal. "First cleaning's on the house."

"Wow!" Anthony chimes. "That's a smokin' good deal—even I can afford that."

"That's very kind," says Pearl. "Thank you." She tucks the card along with her hands inside her coat pockets.

"Pearl, dear—how are you doing?" a tall man interrupts, cradling a gallon-sized Ziplock like a baby. "Jim and I baked you and Bodie brownies." He hands Pearl the bag.

"Thank you." Pearl hugs him. "Bodie will love them."

"We want you to know we're praying for your healing." He tears up. "Hang in there, honey."

"Thank you. Really. I appreciate it." Pearl's face twists as she pretends to cry without tears. She's good. "I'll see you next week. Tell Jim thank you." She walks away as everyone tries to act like they're not watching.

"That poor darling dear," murmurs the brownie man.

I fight the urge to punch some sense into his sympathetic face. What's happening to me?

# EIGHT

I meet Anthony at the Pub a little after five. I tried to wait until closer to six, so I didn't appear too anxious, but who am I kidding? I hadn't been on a date since 1985, and nine months later it ended in the birth of my son.

Is this really a date? Maybe Anthony just feels sorry for me. I shouldn't read too much into it or try to analyze, just enjoy positive energy and time spent not suffering alone in the dark.

Anthony lights up as I approach the bar, then escorts me to a corner table set where flowers and a bottle of Jameson Irish Whiskey wait.

He pulls out my chair. Yep. This is definitely a date. I take my seat as Anthony fills two shot glasses. After passing one to me, he holds his up.

"Here's to a sweetheart, a bottle, and a friend. The first beautiful, the second full, the last ever faithful." We clink glasses and take our shots.

Whiskey burns down to my core, and I blow out a fiery breath. "I don't drink much," I confess.

"Would you like a coffee or a Coke, or . . . how about water?"

"I'm fine, thanks." But I'm not fine. I feel guilty for even being here. The urge to rush home and mourn Pu tugs at me, even though that's exactly what I did right after church. After balancing my chakras. The release was intense, and I cried for two solid hours. "I'm starving."

"I made us meatless shepherd's pie. That cool?"

"How'd you know I'm vegan?"

"I could tell just by looking at you. Long, lavender hair. Silky-smooth olive complexion. Mostly it was your sparkling brown eyes. You reek of health." He tilts his head and grins. "And Margo told me."

"Oh," I laugh. "You don't have to abide by my choices. Really."

"No. I don't mind. I think it's great. Wish I had that sort of discipline."

After dinner, drinks, and effortless conversation, I can't stop grinning and giggling like a girl.

The jukebox grabs my attention with a sweet symphony of violins. "This my jam!" Whiskey has fine-tuned my performance. "At . . . last," Etta James and I sing, "my love has come along."

"My lonely days are over," Anthony sings as he stands and offers his hand.

I give him my hand. "And life is like a song." We sing like two drunks.

"Hey Anthony," Margo yells from behind the bar.

"Yeah?" he answers.

"Who sings this song?" Margo asks.

"Etta! Etta James, man!" Anthony replies.

"You should let her sing it." Margo laughs and goes back to hanging copper mugs behind the bar.

"Oh . . . ya, ya . . . at last! The stars above are blue." Anthony sings louder and pushes aside two tables, making room for us.

He brings me to him. My arms wrap around his neck. Our hips sway. I like how simply snug we fit together. Like Birkenstocks on a summer morning.

Floating somewhere between the whiskey and Etta, I look up at Anthony. His strong, stubbled chin and kind smile. His lips meet me halfway. I'm not sure if he's kissing me or I'm kissing him. But, sweet spirit in the sky, we're kissing, and it's not just any old kiss. It is *the* kiss. Tongue and all. The kind that first melts then stirs a fire I thought had gone out long ago.

I'd all but given up on relationships. The two men I'd been with soured me. Since then, risk outweighed reward. Most men my age want young, gullible, and hot. I'm a lavender-haired grandmother. I don't put up with narcissistic bullshit, and the only time I'm hot is in the middle of the night when I'd much rather be sleeping.

The song ends, but he doesn't let go. Neither do I. Until this moment, I hadn't realized how badly I missed being touched. Being affectionate. Being of interest. This is the most alive I've felt in years, maybe decades.

Anthony steps back and takes my hands in his. "Not to be dramatic," he says, "but I think you're the answer to my prayers."

"You hear that from a drunk at the bar?"

"No. And not ashamed to admit I've prayed on it more nights than I care to count."

His honesty hits home. It makes me wonder if like me, he's spent nights so long and lonely you'd almost rather die than spend another minute feeling so unbelievably abandoned.

We return to our corner table, and he pours us both a drink. Hands me mine. I hold my glass out to him. "Here's to not being alone tonight." I say.

A crooked grin grows as his eyes narrow in on me. "You mean . . . you want to spend the night?" He holds his glass out. "With me?"

I clink my glass against his, too insecure to admit I'd love to sleep with him. We shoot whiskey, then slam our glasses on the table. I let the fire burn.

Anthony runs his hand down his mouth and chin, obviously troubled. He takes a seat and clasps his hands on the table, as if ready to pray. His eyes cast down. "There's something you should know."

# NINE

Sex isn't everything. It turns out Anthony had prostate cancer in his early fifties, and had his prostate removed, which resulted in him jokingly referring to himself as a "limp lover."

It was the best sex I never had. Anthony went deeper into me than any man. The knowledge and energy he brought to pleasuring erogenous zones with kisses, touch, and tongue left me breathless. He saw me. All of me, because he cared enough to look.

We shared every bit of ourselves intimately, then both cried after he gifted me with not one, but two transcendent orgasms. We held tight to each other until morning.

Orgasms, it seems, may be the cure for negativity. Better than any healing crystals, drumming, or yoga poses. It was all I needed to find a hint of joy in living again.

Before leaving Anthony's apartment, I made it perfectly clear that he shouldn't feel obligated to call or ever see me again. I assured him he did not owe me a commitment of any sort.

He called the next day to ask if I'd be in church Sunday and if he could sit next to me again.

After nearly a week of waiting and hoping Pearl would contact me to clean her house, I start second-guessing my decision not to go to the police. My inability to concoct a flawless plan caused me to gather Pu's journal and my nerve and drive to San Andreas. I'm going to hand over all I have and let law enforcement figure it out.

I sit in the van parked outside the Calaveras County Sheriff's Department. After a minute, I tuck Pu's journal into my sling bag and get out. Walking to the entrance, I wonder where and how to start.

Inside the generic waiting area, a young man sits behind plexiglass with a speaker in the center. He leans in to the microphone and looks at me. "How can I help you?"

"I have some information about a case, and I'd like to talk to someone."

"Okay. Have a seat, please. Someone will be with you shortly."

I sit one chair away from the only other person waiting, a woman in a baby-blue skirt suit. She's digging through a briefcase and looks up.

"Hi." I smile and nod.

She returns my smile but grunts more than greets me. She looks concerned about whatever she's digging for. Wrapping her hair behind her ears, she grunts again.

My palms are sweating, nerves firing—most of me wants to leave.

The woman gets up and knocks on the plexiglass with a single knuckle. The young man returns to his seat, chewing and wiping his mouth with a napkin.

"Jake, can you make me a copy of the charges? Please." She sounds desperate. "I asked Amanda to put them in my case, but it didn't happen. Again."

"Surprise, surprise. Yeah, I gotcha." He types on a keyboard.

"I owe you. Thanks."

"Just pay it forward," he says, and shoots her with a finger gun.

I really want to leave. It's clammy in here—or maybe it's just me. The kid behind the plexiglass shoves a paper into the tray and pushes it through to the other side. The woman grabs the page and bows to the boy. "Thank you." She studies the paper as she walks back to her seat.

"You're a lawyer?" I ask softly.

She glances up at me and looks back at her page. "Uh, yes."

"Can I ask you a quick question?"

She shoots me a you-can't-be-serious look, with her perfectly plucked eyebrow raised. "Thought you might want to pay it forward. Sorry. Never mind." She wouldn't dare not respond in kind now. "What's your question?" She doesn't bother faking nice, which is cool with me.

"Just hypothetical."

"Okay." She doesn't look up from her page.

"For a book I'm writing."

Now she looks up. "Don't quote me."

"No, I won't. It's fiction anyhow. See, the main character leaves behind a journal about a murder he committed. He tells all about the woman he loves, but ends up that she set him up. Would that be enough to convict her?"

She shakes her head and rolls her eyes. "Not even close. That's nothing more than he said, she said. It's a lead, so investigators might take a closer look at the implicated person based on the accusations in the journal, but it can also work against the investigation." She leans in and lifts her index finger. "The minute a suspect realizes they're a suspect, evidence disappears. Criminals prioritize their innocence, lawyer up, and cover their tracks. The best suspects are the ones who think they've gotten away with it. Who don't have a clue they're being investigated."

I nod, attempting to contain my disappointment and chew my bottom lip "Even if a killer's confessing to the crime?"

"A killer is considered an unreliable source. A decent defense attorney would have it thrown out. Nowadays, prosecutors have to produce reliable witnesses, scientific evidence, DNA. Jurors expect it and typically won't convict without it. Too much *Forensic Files* and true crime podcasts."

"Thank you very much."

I walk out not knowing the answer, but knowing this isn't it. If Pearl knows there's new evidence against her, she may get nervous and run. Seems all I'm doing is chasing my tail.

---

By Sunday, I'm a wreck. I haven't slept a wink since attempting to hand over Pu's journal. I want to do the right thing, but I don't know what that looks like. I've never had this much trouble discerning right from wrong. The layers of injustice form a sticky cloak around me, making movement impossible. I decide to believe the answer will come when it comes. I have to be patient. Good things come to those who wait.

After Pastor Connie explains the importance of tithing, we sing. She shares the message of Thanksgiving, of being thankful for all we have. All I can think about is what would have happened if the natives had let the pilgrims starve. What would America look like today?

I see Pearl make her way to the restroom. I excuse myself from Anthony and join her. In the compact ladies' room, I pretend to wash my hands until Pearl exits the stall. "Hello." I smile and move aside so she can use the sink.

"Hi."

"I'm Talula, we met last week." I ratchet down a length of paper towels.

"Oh, yeah. The cleaning lady."

"Right." I hold out the paper towel and offer it to Pearl.

"Thank you." She dries her hands.

"Ready for Thanksgiving?" I ask.

She shrugs and makes a face. "No. Don't feel much like celebrating."

"Oh. Yeah. I'm sorry. That was insensitive. I didn't mean . . . I try to make you feel better, and just make you feel worse."

"I couldn't feel much worse. Please, don't worry about it." She walks out, and for a split second, I actually feel sorry for her. She got what she wanted, and she's still not happy. I can see it in her eyes, her sagging shoulders. I look at myself in the mirror and feel better believing she's miserable. Because miserable people want more than anything to be happy. I would know.

That night, Anthony comes to my house for dinner and brings a gift bag. "What's this for?" I ask.

"You seem to be in crisis. Am I right?"

I stop untying the bow and look at him, but I don't answer.

"Inside might be the answers you seek."

"What the— Why do you think I need answers?" An unreasonable defensiveness takes over.

"You talk in your sleep. It's obvious something's troubling you, and I'd like to help if I can. This"—he nods at the gift bag—"is how I quit fearing death when I had cancer."

I dig through the pink tissue paper without a word and bring out a black eye mask. If I find fuzzy handcuffs, I'm out. No handcuffs, just four lemons, a stainless-steel grinder of some sort, and a plastic baggie of dried mushrooms.

"Do you trust me?" Anthony takes my hands and brings them to his chest.

I think about it for a second, then nod. "I guess so."

"Lemon Tek is the best way to ingest Azzies." He opens the baggie and palms a perfectly preserved mushroom, stem and all. "Psilocybe azurescenes. Among the most powerful little mushroom in the world. Picked them at the Oregon coast last year. Fort Stevens."

"I don't know about this." Apprehension scratches at my spine as Anthony slices, then squeezes lemon juice into a glass. He adds the dried mushrooms to the grinder and pulverizes them into a fine powder. Then he shakes it into the lemon juice and stirs the concoction.

"The acid in the lemons brings out the good stuff—speeds up the digestion process and alleviates nausea." He hands me a glass. It looks as innocent as lemonade.

"I've never taken hallucinogens before," I confess.

"Okay, look, I'm here to take good care of you. I promise. But it's totally up to you. If you're not ready, that's perfectly fine."

I think, staring at the glass. Do I hold the answers in my hand? Curiosity soon gets the better of me, and I down the mix in one big, sour gulp.

Anthony leads me from the kitchen to the couch. There's not much ground to cover, and I lie back. He adds pillows behind my head.

"Close your eyes." Gently, he places the silk mask around my head. "And try to relax. Let the world come to you." He slides the mask down over my eyes and kisses me.

I try to relax, to clear my mind, but thoughts of Pu, Pearl, and the baby sneak in. Smiling. Laughing at me as I reach for them.

Visions of trees come first. Greener than they've ever been. Like they're lit from the inside with an energy. Then wind, a force of nature, causes the sturdy pines to double over in laughter. It's so funny. Hilarious, and I can't stop laughing because I'm a tree. Stuck right where I want to be in the new world.

A vibrant, breathing, Technicolor world where it's perfectly clear everything is connected. A system of plugged-in, pulsing roots, entangled in the atmosphere like an enormous ball of twine. This is Earth. This is us. We are one or none, and the epiphany is so beautiful it makes me cry.

I look up, allowed to stare at the sun without pain or words. There are no words to communicate the complex bliss lifting my soul, the rapture while inhaling the meaning of life without remorse.

Walking on the beach has never felt like such a privilege. With open arms, my mother emerges from the florescent sea. I run to her. Hug her. Love her.

"Come home, Lula" she says. "Come home." She cries, and her tears fill my lungs.

We float in the waves. Purging our past. Holding hands. Alive. Until she dissipates like octopus ink in glowing water.

A shadow cascades. The sky provides demons that turn the world upside down. I look up and fall. Death is certain but not frightening.

Then, I'm rising. Flying. Riding a featherless, headless turkey. I ride it all the way to hell, where the demon opens the door to Pearl's house. She smiles with blood on her hands and gives me the baby. A girl wrapped in gold foil, like a gift from God.

Then everything becomes fuzzy. Out of focus. The world fades, dulls, and disappears. There is no concept of time. It could have been days, hours, or only minutes.

I pull off my mask. Anthony is there. Smiling. "Hello."

"Hi." The air feels clean.

I'm light. Like a helium balloon. A thousand years of therapy in a few hours. I felt the suffering of the entire planet, but somehow understand that everything is exactly as it should be.

"I've created my own suffering." I swallow. "I did nothing to fix it." I'm half floating, half climbing a mountain. I kiss Anthony's hand. "I got it."

"Got what?"

"A solution. But I need a turkey."

"You're still high."

# TEN

Anthony attends to me all night and in the morning brings me tea. No one has ever brought me tea. He is either the most caring man I've ever met or he's after something I don't have.

The next day, I don't think twice about going to the market and using Pearl's money to buy the necessities for a Thanksgiving feast.

Early Thursday morning, I start cooking. The dead turkey gets me. His or her wings that once flapped and maybe flew. The neck missing its head. I push through, pull out the insides, stuff the big bird, and get the creature in the cooking bag. Once it's in the oven, I prepare the pumpkin pie from scratch.

By noon, I'm tired, but vengeance gives me stamina. I box up the entire dinner, load it into the van, and head to the Whites' residence. Finding the old winery is easy. Faded signs still point the way.

Her gate is shut when I pull up. I roll down the window and press a speaker button. I wait and wait. Maybe the thing's broken, but I press it twice more. And wait. Maybe she's not home. All this work for nothing.

"Yes." A woman's voice cracks through from a speaker.

"Hi, Pearl?"

"Yes."

"It's Talula, from church. I have something for you."

"Who?" There's a long pause.

"The cleaning lady." I lean hard on the words through a clenched jaw.

"Um, oh yeah, okay."

"I brought Thanksgiving over."

"What?" She sounds groggy.

"I made you turkey and all the fixings. I wanted to drop it off for you and your son."

"Oh, okay. I, uhhh—hang on."

The wrought iron gate slowly swings open.

"Just follow the driveway up hill."

"Okay. Thanks! See ya in a sec." My sugary-sweet tone is too much. I'd better not overdo it. Pearl White is not a dumb bimbo.

The wet asphalt snakes its way up to the horror show house on the hill. It cast an eerie shadow as I approach. Ivy creeps up weathered sides. I slow the van to a crawl, looking up through the windshield, taking in the crusty windows framed with decaying shutters that loom down at me like knowing eyes. Gripping the steering wheel, I shiver and take a breath. "Perfectly macabre." I shake my head, wondering if Pugsley or Wednesday will come running out any minute. "So cliché."

I park, get out, then grab the aluminum roasting pan as the wind kicks up. In the front yard, a dying pine tree shoots dead needles my way. Pearl probably never bothered to water the poor thing. The smell of cooked turkey flips my stomach upside down. I shut the door with my foot, turn, and see her. Pearl White in the flesh, standing on the porch in her robe and slippers. Her hair is twisted into a messy bun. Only she could look this good without trying. Maybe she's ill. Maybe morning sickness, I hope, and smile.

"Hi! Happy Thanksgiving." Turkey in hand, I follow the stepping stones across the lawn as cats run for cover under dead rose bushes.

"I can't believe you brought an entire meal," Pearl says.

"I hope you didn't cook?" I make it a question.

"No. Actually didn't even realize it was Thanksgiving."

"Are you not feeling good?" I hand her the turkey pan.

"I'm fine."

"Your place is incredible," I say admiringly. A little boy wanders out. He hides behind Pearl and peeks at me. "Hello there." I kneel and smile. "What's your name?"

"Bodie," he says with a finger in his mouth.

"Nice to meet you, Bodie. I'm Talula. You can call me Tutu if you want."

He laughs. "That's funny."

"What's so funny?" I ask.

"Tutu!" He steps toward me, laughing.

"You think my name is funny?" I tickle his belly. Most people care enough to ask about the unusual name or meaning of Tutu, but not Pearl. She doesn't ask because she couldn't care less. "Tutu means grandmother where I come from."

"Gram-moter?" He bends forward, accentuating his confusion.

"Yep. You have a grandmother?" I only ask because I need to know who else might fight for custody of Pu's baby.

Pearl shakes her head and crosses her arms. "He's got a kooky old great-grandma in Louisiana, but that's it. Not much family left." A creepy grin cracks her porcelain facade. "You don't look old enough to be a grandmother."

"Oh, thanks. I started young." I reach out and tickle him again. He squeals and hides behind his mom. "You like turkey?"

He shrugs, fingers back in his mouth.

"Maybe you can come help unload the dinner?"

"Yeah!"

The three of us unload the van and bring the feast inside. The old house is missing a few walls, exposed ceiling beams like bones.

"Please excuse the mess. I'm remodeling."

The kitchen looks like someone forgot to clean up after a party. Dirty dishes are piled everywhere, and the trash can is overflowing. The wood flooring is filthy, and the stove looks like a grease fire waiting to happen. Pearl pushes aside pill bottles, wine bottles, and a variety of crap to make room on the counter for the food.

"I'm sorry, the kitchen is such a disaster, I meant to . . ." She trails off.

"No worries. I'm no one to judge. You hungry?" I ask Bodie.

He nods vigorously.

"All righty, let's get big bird in the oven and warm him up."

"Yeah." Bodie opens the oven door.

"Umm . . ." Pearl reaches into the oven and snags a stack of dirty pots and pans. "Sorry."

"No. Don't be." I set the roasting pan in the oven and turn to Pearl. "Look, I don't want to make you uncomfortable. It's just, I don't have anyone to spend Thanksgiving with and want to do something nice. Makes me feel better. Sort of penance, you know. I'll leave you in peace and you can enjoy your day. Everything's cooked. Just needs heating. Except for the pie. Oh, shoot, the pie. It's in the van. Let me grab it."

"Can I come?" Bodie asks.

"If it's okay with your mom? She's the boss."

"Of course." Pearl smiles and sets the temperature on the oven to 450 degrees. She's Cajun—maybe she prefers blackened turkey. What do I care? Then she looks at me and asks, "Is that the right temperature?"

"Maybe down a little. I'd go 300—325 at most." I'm such a pushover. "Oh, and the whipping cream. You know how whip cream?" I ask as Bodie follows me outside. I hear Pearl laugh.

"No," Bodie says.

"You beat the heck out of it. "

"Whaaat?" The boy doesn't get it.

"I'll show you." I open the passenger door.

"Can I see inside your car?" Bodie asks.

"Sure." I grab the cardboard box with the pie, sugar, and carton of cream and set it on the ground. Bodie climbs in, and I help him.

"Wow." He rolls off the seat and into the back of the van. "It's like a army fort. Umm . . . a tank."

"Yeah. A tank with rubber wheels."

He nods. "Can we go for a ride?"

"Maybe another time. Let's go beat up the cream."

"Kay." He reaches for me, and I lift him out. He's a beautiful boy, and I want to hug him, but I set him down instead. He sees the pie under the plastic wrap.

"You like pumpkin pie?" I ask.

"Me have it now?"

I laugh. "You're silly."

Bodie laughs like that's just fine with him as I hand him the bag of sugar.

"We have to get supplies in the fridge, fast! Now march, soldier!"

Bodie marches inside, carrying the sugar above his head. I march behind with the rest.

The smell of coffee brewing hits me as we stomp into the kitchen. Pearl opens the cupboard above the counter. "Would you like coffee?" she asks.

"I'd love some. Thank you," I lie. I don't drink coffee, but I will today.

Bodie opens the refrigerator. The stench of something rotten wallops me. I set the pie inside, noticing the shelves are mostly empty other than a few bottles of beer, milk, and family-sized condiments.

"Can we kill the cream now?" Bodie asks.

"What?" Pearl pulls mugs from the cupboard.

"I think he means whip the cream. You have mixer?"

She sets the mugs down. "I don't know. Maybe." She opens three drawers and searches, finding the mixer but only one beater.

"That'll work," I say, and we go to work whipping the cream and adding the sugar until the sweetness is just right.

"Can he have this?" I ask Pearl, ejecting the beater from the mixer while Bodie reaches for it.

"Oh sure," she says, and I hand Bodie the cream-covered beater.

"Good stuff?" I ask as Pearl pours coffee.

"Mmm-hmmm." He nods and licks, his tongue and nose covered in white.

She hands me a cup of coffee. "Thank you," I say.

"No, thank you. You didn't have to go to all this trouble. It's so . . . much."

"Enjoy it. I know things are rough. If I can add a little happiness, it's worth it," I say, knowing full well I'm going straight to Hell.

Pearl looks at me, grins, then looks down. Tears fill her eyes.

"Can you do me a favor?" I ask.

"Of course." She wipes her cheeks.

"You go take a shower, get dressed, and let me get dinner ready."

"You've done so much already. I just—"

"Please."

"Really?"

"Yes."

Pearl looks at Bodie licking the beater. "Okay." She grins. "Thank you."

As soon as she leaves, I go to work.

# ELEVEN

While Pearl's upstairs, I poke around the kitchen for some sort of clue confirming or destroying a pregnancy. Bodie is busy chasing a cat he wants to show me while I search drawers and cupboards. No iron pills or vitamins, but she could keep them in her bathroom. A pill bottle prescribed for Bodie catches my eye. Zithromax, an antibiotic, three times daily until gone. The label is dated September 29, and the bottle is still half full. She obviously didn't follow doctor's orders. My great-grandchild will not suffer at the hands of a negligent mother.

In the filthy downstairs bathroom, I lock the door, sidestep a heap of dirty towels, and look through the medicine cabinet. Just the basics, as far as I can see. Razors, toothpaste, hair gel, men's deodorant, and shaving cream—must have all belonged to Tucker. Under the sink, baby shampoo, toilet paper, tampons, and two boxes of unopened black hair dye. Interesting, but not the answer I'm looking for.

Behind the small trash bin next to the toilet is a bottle of drain opener. Aren't these things supposed to be kept out of reach of children? I pour the entire bottle into the toilet, flush, then replace the empty container. The chemical smell burns, and I pull my sweater up over my nose, breathing as little as possible.

In the tub, I dump the contents of the trash and replace each item back in the can as I go. Disgusting, yes, but if there's proof of feminine products, then I'll have my answer. Not the one I want, but an answer just the same. I find nothing but empty toilet paper rolls, spent razors, mystery tissues, an empty bubble bath bottle, and a half-eaten lollipop. I put the trashcan back and wash my hands twice.

In the hallway, a calendar hangs next to the phone. I flip through the months—every square is empty. Not one word on one day. Not one stinking doctor's appointment. Most folks probably use their phone for that sort of thing, I guess.

"I gots her." Bodie struggles to bring me the captured feline, but she claws her way to freedom, and Bodie fights back tears.

"It's okay, sweetie." I hug him, and he cries on my shoulder. "Let's get things ready for Mom, okay?"

He nods and follows me to the kitchen.

By the time Pearl returns, showered and dressed, the kitchen is clean. Dishes washed, floor swept, trash taken out, and dinner table set. Mashed potatoes and gravy, stuffing, green beans, Jello salad, and yams.

"Wow!" Pearl's eyes light up. She's in skinny jeans and a long, cream-colored sweater, no makeup and still undeniably stunning, but it's like trying to see the beauty in a poisonous snake when they make your skin crawl. As the venomous bitch slithers closer, I'm torn between wanting to run or stay and chop her head off. Fully aware that I'm descending toward a darkness I never knew existed, I ponder forgiveness. Then I think of Pu. My disgust and utter hatred for this woman is undeniable.

"This is incredible." She clasps her hands under her chin.

"It's no big deal. I cooked everything at home, so it was super easy."

Bodie sets the cranberries on the table. "Did you help Miss Talula do all this?" Pearl strokes his silky hair.

"No, Tutu."

My heart fills a little. "He's a good helper."

"I smashed the potatoes!" Bodie exclaims.

"Good job, Bode." Pearl helps him into a chair as I set the golden-brown turkey on the table. "Well, that's everything."

"This is amazing. I don't know what to say."

"Don't say anything. Just eat and enjoy. Please." I grab my coat off the bar stool. "Happy Thanksgiving. See you at church."

"Oh, no, you can't go," Pearl grabs a plate and silverware from where they're drying in the rack and sets a place at the table. "Please stay. Sit."

"Yeah. Eat by me," Bodie says with a mouthful of potatoes.

"I'd love to, but I can't."

"Really?" Pearl takes her seat at the head of the table.

"No. Thank you, I have a date."

"Ooo-hhh." She says it like a friend in high school might, insinuating that she's surprised and sort of impressed.

"What's a *date*?" Bodie asks, attempting to scoop cranberries onto his plate but spilling most of it on the floor.

"It's when two people have fun together." Pearl pours a full glass of chardonnay. She shouldn't be drinking, but maybe it's okay to have one glass. Research seems to change every few years. Do this, don't do that—I'm not up to date. I notice she won't help Bodie, who's still struggling to serve himself cranberries.

"Tutu and me have a date," Bodie chirps.

Pearl and I laugh as I dish the cranberries onto Bodie's plate. Part of me wants to stay. Not for Pearl, for the boy. But I've been as deceitful as I can for one day. It's exhausting. All I wanted to do was get my foot in the door, see what I could learn about Pearl's pregnancy.

Bodie mixes his mashed potatoes and cranberries.

"Bode, that's disgusting," Pearl snaps.

"I used to do that when I was pregnant. I loved mashed potatoes and cranberries," I lie.

"Maybe you're pregnant, Bode."

"What's that?" His face twists.

"When a baby is growing inside a mommy's tummy," Pearl explains.

Come on, Bodie. Ask. Please, please for the love of God—ask if Mommy has a baby growing in her tummy. Come on.

"That's dumb." Bodie tears into his turkey leg.

"You have kids?" Pearl asks.

"I did. A son. He passed a few years ago."

"Oh my God, I'm so sorry." She slams her hand over her heart to seem sincere, but I know better.

"Hey, speaking of pregnancy, any chance you know a good OBGYN? A gal I clean house for just found out she's expecting and can't find a doctor nearby."

"I don't—sorry."

Damn, damn, damn. "See ya, Bodie," I say, slipping my coat on.

"Can you come back tomorrow?" he whines.

"Yeah." Pearl puts her fork down and stands. "I hate to admit it, but I could really use some help around here. Obviously."

"I'd love to." I'm practically salivating, "I can start tomorrow."

"Actually, we're heading to Cabo tomorrow."

"Cabo?"

"Cabo San Lucas, Mexico."

"Oh. Wow. Mexico?"

"Yeah. They're going to start construction, replace the heating, flooring, a bunch of stuff, so I thought I'd get out of the house. Take a little vacation. Teach Bodie to swim."

I nod. Son of a bitch. "Great. Is Mexico safe? I read somewhere that kidnappings in tourist destinations are on the rise. And Americans shouldn't risk going—"

She cuts me off. "It's fine. I stay at a resort. There's security. I don't exactly feel safe here right now."

"Oh. Yeah. That's understandable." I can't think straight. Thoughts careen, bang off bone and leave behind nothing but twisted muddle. I'm no good at scheming. Pearl is world class. "How long will you be gone?"

"Two, maybe three weeks. I rented a time-share for a month because the rates were better, so who knows. I'm hoping the house will be done by the time I get back."

I nod because there's nothing else to do.

"Can you start when I get back? Say around the first of the year."

Wait until January 1? Are you freaking kidding me, you rotten, no-good, phony bitch? "Sure." I smile.

Night comes early this time of year. I drive around until dark with no final destination in mind. Somewhere near Dorrington, I pull over and park alongside the wooded two-lane.

A burst of absolute desperation sends me from the van to wandering the forest in a foot of hard-packed, dirty snow.

Last Thanksgiving, Pu and I went for Thai, came home, ate pumpkin pie, and played Monopoly. The next day, he hugged and thanked me, said it was fun hanging out together. When he said he didn't just love me, but that he actually liked me, I was so overwhelmed I cried.

Now my Pu is gone, and Pearl's going to the beach. Nothing in this world is right. I want to punch, kick, and demolish something. More than anything, the urge to scream shoves me into a full run. I have no idea where I'm going. What I'm doing. I have to move fast to keep from coming apart.

Soon, I'm out of breath and stop, throwing my head back. The frigid night stings as I fill my lungs. My exhale rises—and I purge a scream so long and loud it shakes the tree tops.

I grab my head, my hands trying hard to crush my skull. "Pu." I clench my teeth and swallow down the explosion of useless grief until I'm seething.

The taste of hate holds tight all the way home. When the time comes, the hatred I have stored for Pearl White will send her straight to Hell.

# TWELVE

On the living room floor, I end morning meditation with some dragon breathing exercises. Hands on my belly, I inhale through my nose, relax my jaw, and release through my mouth with a soft roar. I consider the Pearl situation and fill my lungs again, open my mouth, let my tongue touch my chin. Then I exhale, with a much louder roar this time.

"All I need to do is confirm Pearl's pregnant. That's all." It sounds simple when I say it out loud.

I have a gun. The one Pu left in the van, under the driver's seat. "I could put a gun to her head. Make her pee on one of those pregnancy sticks." Sounds like a Quentin Tarantino script. Besides, she's gotta be on a plane flying south, or at least at the airport.

"Follow her to Mexico. Hire someone to kidnap her and make her pee on a stick. If she's pregnant, keep her locked up until she's gives birth. Then take the baby to—" I cover my mouth with both hands. Scary how quickly I fell from grace and swiftly descended into Hell.

I can't go to Mexico. I don't even have a passport, and getting one will take way too long. Even rush jobs take weeks.

Walking across the Southern California border isn't realistic. I wouldn't even know where to start, let alone how to survive the journey. Seems I recall someone saying crossing into Mexico from Tijuana is a breeze. It's getting back into the States that's difficult if not impossible without a passport.

Maybe I can wait her out. It's only a few weeks, a month at most. Who am I kidding, though? That sounds like a lifetime. But patience is a virtue, and if, God forbid, Pearl's already gotten rid of her child, there isn't a darn thing I can do about it.

I'll sit tight until she returns. Keep busy somehow. But what if she doesn't return? She knows she's a suspect—she may just disappear somewhere in Mexico. She has the money to make it happen. Then, like a beautiful sunrise, I realize I don't think murder suspects are allowed to leave the state, let alone the country.

Life always comes down to choices, and right now, I have two. I can let Pearl leave, wait around and hope she comes back. Hope she still has my grandchild inside of her. Or, I can tell investigators what I know and risk Pearl getting arrested, risk her giving birth in prison.

The phonebook is in the kitchen drawer. I tear through the pages until I locate the Calaveras County Sheriff's Department and dial.

"I need to speak to someone regarding the Tucker White murder investigation," I say as calmly as I can.

The woman on the other end asks me to hold, but it's not a question, because she doesn't wait for an answer, just puts me on hold. I'm pacing, my hand on my hip. I'm tethered to the wall by a long, curly yellow phone cord. After what seems like forever, the same woman says that Detective Rocha is unavailable and asks if she can take a message.

"No. This is an emergency. I need to speak to him immediately. A murder suspect is about to get away—she's on her way to Mexico if someone doesn't stop her.

"If you'd like to leave me your name and number, I will relay the information to the detective."

"Now? You'll get the message to him this instant?"

"Ma'am, I'll try. I can't guarantee he's in a service area. He could be in the middle of something. I don't know. I *will* call him."

"Okay. Thank you. Thank you so much. It's just, this is really important."

"Name?"

"Talula Jones."

"Phone number."

I give her my number and hang up, wondering if he'll call back. And if I've done the right thing.

Waiting is worse than disappointment. Even if the outcome isn't what you had hoped for, you can move forward. Take the next step. I drink a glass of lemon water, then stretch my hands over my head, bend at the waist, and touch the floor. In a downward dog position, more deep dragon breaths. Roll forward, lower my hips, on my stomach. Chest up, head back, arms push into cobra pose—breathe in. Child's pose to corpse pose. Nothing's working. Yoga usually helps settle me, but not this time.

I look at my watch. It's been fifteen minutes, and he hasn't called back. Pearl could be walking through airport security right now, and all it would take is a phone call to stop her. I consider calling back. Instead, I open the cupboard above the washing machine and find my sage bag. Pulling out two sticks, I state my intention.

"Let me live in harmony with the child." I focus my thoughts only on him or her.

I light the sage on the stove. Sitting cross-legged, I rest the backs of my hands on my knees. With both bundles smoking in one hand, I chant, "Let me live in harmony with the child. Let me live in harmony with the child." I continue the mantra throughout the cleansing process.

Starting at my heart, I fan smoke inward, where dense negative energies accumulate and tend to hide. Slowly, I proceed toward my crown chakra, then move downward to my root chakra until I am fully purified and protected and the sage is nearly spent.

After thirty minutes, I have to pee. While I'm on the toilet, the phone rings. "Of course." Stopping the flow midstream is impossible. Pu was right—I should have a cell phone.

I run to the kitchen with my pants half down and grab the phone. "Hello?" There's a pause, and my heart skips a beat when I think he's hung up.

"Talula Jones? This is Detective Edward Rocha."

"Yes, thanks for calling back."

"I understand you may have some information about the Tucker White investigation."

"Yes. I do. About his wife, Pearl White. I know she hired an attorney and assume she's a suspect?" I say, hoping he'll confirm.

"I'm not at liberty to discuss the investigation."

"Well, I know she hired an attorney because I tried to hire him too. Ed Manetti. He said she hired him, that's why he couldn't help me. And I thought you'd want to know she's on her way to Mexico. And I know for a fact she had her husband murdered. My grandson—"

"Ma'am, ma'am, please slow down." The detective interrupts my babble.

"Sorry, I just thought you'd want to stop her before she gets on a plane and disappears."

"Mrs. Jones, Pearl White hasn't been charged and is free to travel where she likes."

"Oh." I deflate.

Lightheaded, I grab a chair from the table, slide it over, and sit. "What if she never comes back? She's getting away with murder. You're letting a murderer walk away."

"Do you have evidence to back up those accusations?"

"Sort of."

"Could you be more specific?"

I suck in a deep breath and begin. "My grandson left a journal. He's the one who shot Tucker White, because Pearl White convinced him to do it. Said she was pregnant and her husband was beating her."

"What is your grandson's name?"

I pause and pull my hair back off my forehead. "Kenny Tait."

"Where can I find him?"

# THIRTEEN

It takes Detective Rocha less time to knock on my door than it took for him to call me back.

He's the spitting image of Homer Simpson. We sit on the couch, and I start from the beginning.

From Halloween night, when I found Pu shot in the shoulder, but I don't throw Teresa under the bus. She went out of her way to help me and even stopped by to check on him. I convinced her that Pu was sleeping, that there was no sign of infection and the wound was healing well.

I implicate myself when I tell Rocha how I took Pu to the cabin, but the detective doesn't react. He waits, letting me tell the story my way.

"When I saw the ax and the bundled wood, I thought he'd fallen through the ice. I never should have left him alone up there. It's all my fault." I can't help but cry. "I should have forced him to confess." Tears soak my cheeks.

Rocha pulls a folded white handkerchief from inside his blazer and offers it. I take it and sop my face while he gives me time to purge my guilt.

"I appreciate your honesty, and since you came forward and turned over potential evidence, the DA will likely forgo aiding and abetting charges. I know it's hard, but rest assured, we'll locate him."

The thought of pulling Pu out of the water, dripping with bloated death, is like a knife plunged into my heart. Telling Detective Rocha that Pu shot Tucker White made it all too real, brought the entire shit show to a head, and I'm about to burst. "Excuse me." I rush to the restroom, hope the man in my living room can't hear me throwing up and crying, but I'm sure he can. I rinse my mouth and splash my eyes with cold water, then look at the mess I've made of myself in the mirror. I bury my face in the bath towel hanging behind the door. Eventually, I return, somewhat improved, and take my seat on the couch.

"I promise you, my Kenny's a good boy. When you research his record, you'll find out he was arrested and sent to juvenile hall for murder. I know you can't take my word for it, but he didn't do it. It was his mother. She shot that man, then convinced a little nine-year-old boy to take the fall. Same as Pearl."

Rocha writes something on a yellow legal pad. He's filled several pages already.

"She's pregnant—with Kenny's child, my great-grandchild, and said her husband found out about the affair. She told Kenny he beat her up. Punched and kicked her in the belly. When she showed Kenny the bruises, he wanted to go to the police, but she convinced him Tucker would kill them both. Said he had friends in the sheriff's department." I stand, make the short walk to the kitchen. "Can you make her take a pregnancy test?"

"We can't force her—it's like a polygraph test, though. It looks better for her if she agrees voluntarily. I'll contact her attorney and request one."

I scoop the journal off the kitchen table. "With all that DNA stuff, you can prove the baby's Kenny's, right? That she was sleeping with him."

"Possibly. It's complicated, to say the least."

"Yeah, tell me about it." I hand him the journal, like a child handing over a bad report card. "The truth about what happened to Tucker White is all in here. While he was at the cabin, Kenny wrote down everything that happened."

Detective Rocha takes it as if it's the gift he's been waiting for. "Thank you."

"I'd like it back when you're done."

"I'll try. Let me sift through it carefully, and I'll let you know where we're at."

I look him in the eye. "Is she gonna get away with it?" I ask.

He stands. "If she did it, we'll get her. Sooner or later, she'll slip, and I'll be there with the cuffs. But understand, homicide investigations can take a while. It's not like on TV where crimes get solved in a few days. Sometimes it takes years."

"Years?"

"Yes. There's a big difference between knowing someone's guilty and being able to prove it in a court of law. The district attorney won't prosecute unless she's confident she'll win."

I walk him to the door and open it.

"I'll be in touch." He offers his hand, and I shake it.

When he leaves, I try not to slam the door, but it's the only way it shuts. So, I wait. Watch him walk to his black Ford Explorer. The neighbors are surely peeking out their windows by now. I shove my shoulder into the door until I hear it latch. Something shifts. I'm not sure if it was me or my aura. Likely both. Breathing is easier. I'm lighter. The weight of the world hasn't been completely lifted, but now Rocha is carrying a fair amount.

---

The following week, I busy myself cleaning houses and hanging out with Anthony. We cook eggplant parmesan. And for dessert, he massages my feet with a healthy dose of lavender oil. He's working his way up my calves when the need to share the ugly truth kicks my conscience. For some odd reason, the burden of keeping secrets weighs heavily tonight. I haven't told a soul other than Detective Rocha. I need to trust someone, and Anthony's it. The one I want on my side, as if it will somehow improve the odds of bringing Pearl White down.

Once I conquer my apprehension, and Anthony crosses his heart and hopes to die if he doesn't keep my secret, I spew like Kilauea. The truth flows faster than red hot lava that will not be stopped, burning up everything in its path.

Anthony's jaw drops and stays that way throughout the second half of my confession. Sharing what I know about Tucker's murder isn't nearly as difficult as I thought it'd be. Deep down, I'm relieved when Anthony laughs. "That's the craziest shit I've ever heard," is the last thing he says before we fall asleep.

November turns to December, and I haven't heard from Detective Rocha about the investigation or finding Pu. Our local newspaper, the *Calaveras Enterprise*, lists him as a missing person. Technically, he's only missing, not yet suspected of murder. The paper doesn't mention the Tucker White case.

Another week passes, and I buy a cellular telephone. My very first call is to Detective Rocha. He doesn't answer, and I leave a message.

"Hi, it's Talula Jones. Sorry to bother you, I'm just checking in. Wanted to see if you've found my grandson yet. And how things are going with the investigation. I'm not trying to be nosy—I'd just like to know about the pregnancy. Pearl White's. The child is my grandchild. Great-grandchild, and you were going to put in a request, remember? Okay, thanks. Bye."

I know he's busy. I understand, but my patience has worn thin. And when I don't hear from him two days later, I call again. And again.

When he does call back, somehow my ringer is off and I miss his call while in the shower. He leaves a message:

"Mrs. Jones, this is Detective Rocha. I'm sorry it's been difficult to connect. Rest assured, Search and Rescue has been working diligently. Conditions have hampered locating your grandson. I'm very sorry. But with the current weather forecast, I'm afraid the search will have to be postponed until conditions improve. The ice is unstable, and we can't risk the lives of rescuers. As for Pearl White, I'm unable to discuss the situation at this point. Feel free to give me a call anytime."

"Give you a call anytime? You never answer your phone, you dick!" What does he mean he can't discuss the situation? I have a right to know if that bitch is carrying my great-grandchild. It's after five, and he's likely gone home for the day, but I drive a half hour to the sheriff's department anyway.

It's raining, and though we need the water, I could use some sunshine. I think of Pearl White in her bikini on the beach in Mexico. Hope her white skin is fried to a crisp. She's consuming me—I'm well aware of my bitter obsession.

"Bitch!" I strangle the steering wheel and drive way too fast around wet curves on Highway 4. When cell service improves outside of

Angels Camp, I dial Rocha. It rings and rings, and I fully expect his voice mail when he answers.

"Detective Rocha."

"Hi. Hello. This is Talula Jones. You're a hard guy to get a hold of."

"Hello, Mrs. Jones. What can I do for you?"

"For one, it's Ms. Jones, not Missus. Second, don't I have the right to know if Pearl White is carrying my grandchild? Why won't you tell me what's going on?" I press my fingers into my brow and squeeze.

"I understand your frustration. I do. At the moment, there's not much to tell, but to be perfectly clear, I don't and won't share details of a homicide investigation with anyone outside of my team."

"Did she take a pregnancy test?"

"Look, I can't—"

"Please!"

"Yes. She did. She's back in the county and volunteered. They did a blood test yesterday."

"And?"

He's silent.

"Hello?" I say. "hello?"

"I'm sorry," he says.

"You're sorry? Sorry about what?" My heart is punching at my breasts from the inside out. I pull off the road and skid to a stop. "Sorry about the test results? Or sorry you can't tell me?"

"Miss Jones, try to understand—my hands are tied. Health records are confidential. I'd be violating California HIPAA laws if I disclosed her test result to you. I could lose my job. I know this is hard on you, and I'm sorry."

"Sorry. Everyone's sorry. Sorry is just a useless word spewed to replace a lack of inspiration." I hang up.

My windshield wipers are hypnotic. I should have gone to Mexico when I had the chance. Should have kidnapped Pearl, pushed the gun to her temple while she peed on a pregnancy stick.

Too late now. She's back home.

But I have a gun. Pu's gun. And I have a mask. A Pleatherface mask.

# FOURTEEN

Yesterday, I bought a Christmas tree, a Santa suit complete with a wig and white beard, and two pregnancy tests in case one gets messed up. In a situation like this, you want to make double-damn sure the results are correct. A second positive will alleviate any doubt.

As I'd been doing all week, I replayed the sequence of events, visualizing down to the very last detail, over and over to manifest the desired outcome.

I'll do just like Pu did and park the van behind the huge stack of logs. In the back of the van, I'll pull on my rubber gloves. The Santa suit will go on over my clothes in the van. I'll wear two puffy coats under the suit to add weight to my appearance.

Next, I'll situate the wig and strap on the beard. I'll have stuffed the toes of the extra-large rubber boots with rolled socks, so the tracks left by the intruder look larger than mine.

I've written the note directing Pearl to take the test. Used my left hand so the handwriting in no way, shape or form resembles mine. It could have been written by a child.

My long hippie hair will be in a short ponytail. I've already chopped it off and bleached the lavender out. I now resemble a grandfatherly Jackie Chan.

The note, along with the tests and gun, are inside a blue velvet bag I bought at the second-hand store.

"Shoot." I realize I've forgotten the Duct tape for her mouth. Surely the first thing she'll do is scream. The last thing I want is to scare Bodie.

There's tape under the kitchen sink. Waterproof Gorilla tape. Extra heavy-duty adhesive—that sow might not talk for a long time. I add it to my velvet Santa sack.

It's easy to convince myself I can do this, but I wonder if I'll have the nerve to go through with it when the time comes. How did Pu convince himself to go through with it? The same motive that's convincing me. Pearl White's pregnancy.

After reading the Clearblue pregnancy test directions, I learn that the most accurate results are obtained with the first urine of the day. I'll have to go extra early in the morning. Before Bodie wakes up—3 a.m. should work. I don't think about what I'll do if the tests are negative because I don't want to. I'll know soon enough.

I hide the Santa disguise and the velvet sack in a trash bag and put it inside the van. In twelve hours, I'll be in Pearl's bathroom holding a gun to her ugly forehead while she cries and pisses on a plastic stick.

In the recliner, I leave Anthony *another* voice message. "Hey, there. It's me. Just haven't heard from you in a while, hope everything's okay. Call me when you get a chance." I haven't heard from him since the day after I told him about Pu and Pearl. I must have scared him off, and I wish I'd kept my big mouth shut. It was nice having him around. He's interesting and intelligent and I loved not having sex with him.

By eight, I'm beyond restless, so I drive to the pub where Anthony tends bar. The rain is relentless and makes for another dreary evening. Main Street is mostly empty. I pull up in front of the pub and park.

Inside, Margo's behind the bar and offers a wave as I push my dripping hood off. Her white T-shirt exposes arms sleeved with a tangle of rose and bird tattoos.

"Hi." I nod back and wonder if Anthony is upstairs. I could just go knock, but I don't want him to know I care that much. It will certainly scare him off.

I hang my wet raincoat on the rack and take a seat at the bar. Two grizzled old men, retired locals named Jim and Jake, sit at the far end, each with a pint. They offer a polite nod. A man in a sloppy suit sits a few stools over, and there's a mix of patrons at bordering tables.

Everyone's attention is on the stout blonde at the mic singing "Danny Boy" a cappella. She's good. Really good.

"Hey, love the new do," Margo says.

"Thanks."

"Drink?"

"*Yes*. Something warm, please."

"How about a naughty toddy?"

"Sure." I lean on the bar. "Is Anthony here?"

"No. No one's seen him all week."

The singing stops, and everyone cheers, including me. I brush my bushy wet bangs off my forehead as the singer hands the mic off to a man in a cowboy hat and boots.

"I'm gonna bless y'all with a bit of cowboy poetry," he begins with an exaggerated and likely unearned Texas drawl. Oh God, it's Wednesday—Open Mic night.

Margo sets a glass mug on a napkin in front of me, steaming with a cinnamon stick. "Hot cider with a little sumpin'." She smiles and waits for my approval.

I sip. The sweet apple and whiskey fill my nostrils and open my lungs before the tang hits the back of my tongue. "Oh, that's perfect. Thank you."

"Of course." She rubs at the back of her neck. "Hey, I know you and Anthony were . . . friends. That's kinda shitty he didn't say bye."

"I just hope he's all right."

"Look Lula, I'm gonna give it to you straight. His shit's gone—he cleared out his apartment."

"Oh." I pull out a twenty to pay for my drink and set it on the bar.

"It's on me, girlfriend." Margo pushes the twenty back at me.

"Thanks, hon. Cheers." I take a swallow as the cowboy poet rides off the little stage. I straighten on my stool and watch Margo refill sloppy-suit-guy's beer. He loosens his tie.

"Merry Christmas, everybody." A sugary voice comes through the speakers. "I'd like to share a . . . a—um, my favorite Christmas song." She's slurring her words a little, and the voice is familiar. I turn and see Pearl White at the mic, a Santa hat cocked on her red head.

"Any Elvis fans in here?" A few claps and one "yeah." "Okay. This is . . . for you . . . and Tuck."

The place goes silent. Margo rolls her eyes and shakes her head. Has she been drinking? Is she drunk?

"I don't need a lot of presents to make my Christmas bright. I just need my baby's arms wrapped around me tight. Oh Santa, hear my plea. Santa bring my baby back to me." She stops. Laughs for a split second, then closes her eyes, pulls off the Santa hat, drops her head and the hat. It's like watching evolution in reverse.

When she drops the mic, I jump off my stool and start toward her, but she hustles from the stage. I halt and watch her throw herself through the ladies' room door.

Margo picks up the hat and the mic. "Anyone else?" She looks around the bar. Drunken laughter comes from parts unknown. "No?" No one responds to anything other than their drinks.

As she wiggles the mic back into the stand, I rush after Pearl.

# FIFTEEN

I find her in the first of two stalls. The door's open, and she's sitting on the toilet, unwinding toilet paper from the roll. Jeans at her knees.

"You all right?" I ask.

She doesn't look up, just sniffs back tears. "No." She covers her eyes with a handful of toilet paper. "Everything's fucked," she whines, and her face morphs as if someone else is speaking. "You can't be with him. You can't love him. No, no, no, bad girl." She looks at me. "It's fucking *unbearable*. I can't take it no more!"

"Have you been drinking?" I try not to sound accusatory, but I'm certain she has. I know what alcohol does to a fetus.

"Have you been drinking?" She mocks me in a sarcastic tone typically reserved for hormonal teenagers. "Who are you, my husband?" She laughs and looks at me. "No, he's dead. You're that cleaning lady."

My face is on fire as my blood boils. "That's right. I clean houses. And I'm not drunk, so why don't you let me drive you home? I bet Bodie misses you."

"Yeah, my Bode. He's fine. He's sleeping. I have to piss." She tries to stand. Stumbles forward, and I grab her. Noticing her stringy undies are down, help her back onto the pot. "I really have to pee."

"Go ahead," I say, holding her shoulders as she sways and rocks like a leaf in a storm. "I got you."

I hear the release of urine. "You know, you shouldn't drink—" I hesitate, then think, *fuck it.* "When you're pregnant."

She takes a moment to open her eyes and respond. "Pregnant!" She laughs. "You're too old to be preggers."

"Not me—you!" I push her back against the toilet tank. "You're pregnant and drinking."

She shakes her head. Faster and faster, like it's fun. Then she halts, reaches a hand down between her legs. Looks up at me grinning from ear to ear.

I step back as she proudly dangles a bloody tampon. "Merry Christmas. Hang this on your tree." She flings it at me. It hits my leg and lands at my feet. "Clean that, cleaning lady."

Pearl stands, pulling up her pants. Her mouth is moving, but I can't hear anything other than my blood rushing in my ears. For a moment, I think I'm having a heart attack. The pain in my chest is acute, and my arms tingle. I don't think I'm breathing.

The world stops as I realize I have absolutely *nothing* left to lose, and I shove her backward. Hard.

She falls into the narrow space between the wall and toilet. Like a spider on her back, I watch her struggle, and I snatch her by her long red hair.

"What the fuck?" She yells.

I pound her head against the wall as she screams at the top of her lungs.

"Shut up!" I smash her again.

"You guys okay in here?" I didn't hear Margo come in. She's looking right at me.

"She's stuck!" I pull and come up with two fistfuls of red hair, but Pearl stays wedged. "I can't get her out."

"She's trying to kill me!"

I shake my head at Margo. "She's wasted."

"Not the first time." Margo crosses her arms.

"I offered to give her a ride home and"—I tap the floor near the bloody tampon with my toe—"she threw that me."

"Oh, my *gawd*!" Margo covers her mouth. "That's disgusting!"

"She's all yours," I say.

"I'm *so* sorry."

"Not your fault. She needs help."

"I'll see if I can get her a ride home." Margo says.

I rush out of the bathroom. My hot toddy is now cold on the bar. I gulp it down, pull the twenty from my pocket and set it under the empty mug, then grab my raincoat.

Outside, rain cools my face. Cold air soothes my fire as I pull my coat on and cry. There's no baby. Was there ever a baby? Either way, there's nothing now, and I'm as empty as Pearl White's uterus.

Raindrops mix with tears as I head for the van and notice Pearl's Subaru parked across the street. Without a second thought, I locate the tire iron in the back of the van and run across Main Street.

"Fuck you, Pearl White!" The taillight bursts on impact. Next, I bat the fogged back window, and it shatters.

Between blows, a scream comes from inside the car, and I freeze midswing.

# SIXTEEN

I step back on the wet pavement. A shadow crawls across the foggy windows and cries. I drop the iron and press my face to the passenger window.

"Bodie!"

"Mommy."

"Bodie! Open the door! It's me, Tutu. Please, honey. Unlock the door." I point to the lock while digging my cell phone from my raincoat. Bodie doesn't move. He's crying so hard, there are long moments of silence while he holds his breath.

I dial 911.

"Open the door, honey, come on. It's okay."

As the dispatcher assures me help is on the way, I toss the tire iron into the bed of a truck parked in front of Pearl's Subaru.

Before help arrives, the car beeps and unlocks. Pearl stumbles across the street with the cowboy poet and two others playing catch-up. Sirens in the distance.

I open the back door and grab Bodie. His little arms wind around my neck. He's shaking. "It's okay, sweetheart. I've got you. You're okay, now." He buries his head in the crook of my neck.

"What the fuck are you doing?" Pearl screams. "Don't you touch my son, you fucking cunt!"

She comes at me, and I step back. She halts when she sees the damage to her car. "What—the—fuck!" Her arms flail, stretching her long neck like an ostrich. "Look at my car!"

I walk away, but she catches up, pulling me back by my coat. I stop and turn toward her.

"Give me my son, you psycho bitch." She grabs Bodie. "Come to Mommy, Bode."

I don't fight her for him. I hand him over and he clings to her. It's all he knows. A deputy arrives, stops in the road, and parks. He turns off his siren but leaves the lights flashing.

I rush toward him as he steps out. "She left her son locked in the car while she got wasted in the bar!"

An ambulance arrives.

As soon as I get home, I gather up every last crystal, all my sage, and toss them into the trash. I will never waste another minute meditating or cleansing my chakras. It doesn't work. Looking back, it never has. I only convinced myself of the healing power of crystals and all the rest because I wanted it to be true. Just like I want Pu to be alive and Pearl in prison.

A few days later, Margo tells me Pearl was arrested the night she left Bodie alone in the car, but not charged. She's still getting away with murder. Still has her son, and what do I have? This woman has taken everything from me.

They've put off searching for Pu until the lake ice melts and it's safe. Probably May. Could be June, depending on the weather.

On Pu's bed, I stare at the cobwebs on the ceiling. A long, miserable life stretches out before me. I don't know how I'll cope.

Days come and go unnoticed. Christmas arrives, and I celebrate with a baggie of ten-year-old weed. Some days, I don't even get out of bed. Sleep is the only time I'm not miserable.

Most nights, I'm at the pub. "Misery loves company" is a cliché, but it's also very true. I pay my tab with Pearl's murder money. I tried church, even donated five hundred dollars, but it didn't take. It reminds me of how much I miss Anthony. I guess I was wrong to trust him. Wrong to tell him my secrets. Wrong to ever expect to love and grow old with someone.

After my last Sunday at church, I got wasted and ate a cheeseburger for the first time in thirty years. I thought it'd make me sick, but it didn't. Oddly, I felt strong and full of energy. Probably the iron.

New Year's Eve, I'm home, opening a box of rosé, when there's a knock on the door. I peek out the hole, see the back of what looks like a guy in a pink beanie. "Who is it?" He turns. "Anthony." I open the door. "Hi." He doesn't look like himself, but it's him.

"Hey, girl." We friend hug—brief and a little awkward. He steps back and smiles. Pale. Dark circles under his eyes.

"Happy New Year," he says.

"Happy New Year. Come in." He steps inside, and I slam the door so it closes. "You don't look so hot," I say. "Sit down." It looks like he's back on the shit. Been there, done that—tried to get my ex clean for six years. Never again.

He sits on the edge of the couch.

"Can we talk?" he asks.

"Sure." I cross my arms and wait.

"I want to apologize for leaving without saying goodbye."

"No need." My jaw tightens, and I suck a breath.

"You know how when people say it's not you, it's me, they're usually lying?"

I nod. "Yep."

"My leaving had nothing to do with you. Every time something interesting happens, first thing I want to do is call and tell you about it. I fall asleep thinking about you, and it's kinda creepin' me out." He pulls off his beanie and rubs his bald scalp. "What do you think?"

"The pony tail's better." I smirk.

He tears up as he shakes his head.

"It'll grow back. No big deal." I smile.

"God damn it, I swore I wasn't gonna get fucking emotional." He tosses the beanie on the coffee table. "I have a proposition, but before you answer, I want you to know—" He looks up at me. "I don't love you." Tears run down his cheeks.

"I don't love you either." I shrug. "What's the deal, Anthony?"

"I bought a camper van. One of those ridiculously overpriced yuppie-mobiles. Figure I can make the payments for a few months, while I take a good look around. See the sights. And, well, I was wondering if maybe you'd come with me?"

My eyes narrow in on him, and I cross my arms. I did not see that coming.

"Before you answer, you should know it's not permanent. Just a few months." He takes a big breath and sighs. "Cancer's back. It's in my pancreas and I left 'cause I didn't want to put you through that. I'm not asking you to take care of me, that's the last thing I want. Just, you know, want to enjoy my time. And I'd love to enjoy it with you. I really want you to come. You wanna come?"

"When do we leave?" I hug him like I love him, and he holds me like his life depends on it.

"Really?" he asks, because he doesn't know he just saved me from a fate far worse than death.

We laugh and cry.

When he pulls away, he cradles my face in his hands and looks me in the eye. "I don't love you."

I grin. "I don't love you either."

# SEVENTEEN

We make years of memories in a matter of months. Like an old married couple, Anthony and I come to know and rely on each other. As he drives, I navigate our way deep into the Canadian Rockies. It's negative six outside, but we couldn't care less. The mountains layered in limestone and shale bring a perfect palate of color along with the white snowy tips, and we have them all to ourselves. I finally comprehend the meaning of breathtaking as we hike to the Athabasca Glacier.

A dog sled tours us deep into the Yukon territory of Whitehorse, where we spend the night in a vast arctic land. Cuddled up next to a campfire, in quiet darkness, we gaze at the sky, waiting and watching for the first sign of Northern Lights to appear.

It starts with a splash of florescent green, then comes alive. Violet, shifting sand swirls in outer space and dances as if perfectly orchestrated yet somehow unpredictable. Performing just for us.

"It's like the universe is on magic mushrooms," Anthony squeezes me tight, kisses my neck just below my ear, and whispers, "I don't love you."

"I don't love you too," I lie, and squeeze him back. Massive beauty in the smallest of moments. I never thought I'd experience bliss again. I'm glad I was wrong.

By the end of February, we've experienced the magic of winter in Glacier National Park, Yellowstone, and now Yosemite thanks to La Niña and snowplows. Neither of us has seen the Firefall. It only happens from mid to late February, and the stars must align. Enough snow must have accumulated on top of the glaciers. The weather must be warm enough to melt the snow, creating a waterfall. The sky must be cloudless. You have to be lucky enough to find a place to park, since the lots are filled with thousands of sightseers. Then you have to be able to hike two miles one way to Horsetail Fall and wait for the setting sun to hit the fall at just the right angle, creating the illusion that it's on fire.

We got lucky. The sun sets the fall on fire, and we share a universal awe. Anthony and I, along with the masses, applaud Mother Nature's finale.

Anthony swears he's feeling fine every time I ask. Describes his condition as wonderful, fantastic, even magnificent. He blames it on me and a miracle March. But deep down, we both wonder how it's possible he's feeling so good. Neither of us is used to this much happiness, and it's unnerving.

We drive south out of Yosemite and make our way to Mammoth Lakes, where Anthony teaches me to fly-fish. We catch our limit in trout but keep only two for dinner.

Three days of snowmobiling to a dozen natural hot springs that scatter the snow-covered valley floor is like floating through a dreamscape. The hot mineral water, jagged granite peaks, and red wine are curative. We sleep like the dead.

By April, Anthony has maxed out his credit cards, and I have $2,300 left in the money bag. I decide to list my mobile home. It's not worth much, but I don't plan on going back. When our vacation is over, I'm going home. Back to Na Pali where I belong.

The sun sets the desert aglow. It's mid-May, and we're only a few miles outside of Joshua Tree National Park when I get a voice message from Detective Rocha. It seems Mosquito Lake has thawed enough to allow Adventures with Purpose to search. They're a group of scuba divers who use sonar to locate missing persons in bodies of water. They arrived from Bend, Oregon today and were planning on searching tomorrow, but since the lake is so small, they just went in today. They scanned the entire lake in under two hours and didn't find Pu. Rocha says he's sorry.

My mind races. How can he not be in the lake? Where the heck is he? I roll my window down and let the desert air refresh me. Hope trickles in. Could he be alive? I slap my hand over my mouth. Just the possibility brings tears to my eyes and a smile to my face.

"What is it?" Anthony asks.

"Rocha called. The lake thawed enough, and a group of divers went in with sonar today. They scanned the entire lake, and Pu's not there."

"What?" Anthony pulls the van over to the side of the road and looks at me. "Could they have missed him?"

I shrug. "Maybe, but I watched these guys on the news. They're very successful. The sonar doesn't lie."

"Holy shit." Anthony leans on the steering wheel, and we stare out at the setting sun, considering the possibilities.

"I know it's crazy and highly unlikely," I admit, "but stranger things have happened. I mean, what if . . ."

"I agree," says Anthony. "But how? Like, where would he have gone? He couldn't survive the exposure. Could he? I mean, anything's possible. There are plenty of crazy survival stories."

"Exactly and I really like the thought he's not dead." My lower lip quivers, and I cry happy tears as Anthony holds me.

"Wanna go back?" he asks. "It's okay if you do. Really."

I consider it a while. "No." If they can't find him, how could I? Besides, I'm having the time of my life. Pu would want that.

———

At Joshua Tree, we camp at Jumbo Rocks campground and read in opposing eye sockets of Skull Rock. Anthony's into *A New Earth* by Eckhart Tolle, and I'm starting *A Walk in the Woods*. A hot air balloon ride has us marveling at 1,235 square miles of canyons, oasis, red rock formations, and oceans of wildflowers. I had no idea how alive the desert is or how cold it gets after sunset.

No matter how many amazing sights we see, I feel guilty, especially if I catch myself having fun. It's silly, but I can't stop believing that Pu is still somehow alive. Then I wonder if I'm just convincing myself because that's what I want to be true. I *want* him to be alive. Just like I wanted the crystals to work.

I call Rocha every few days and learn that the volunteers who searched for Pu last winter will be back as the snow melts. He promises to keep me informed. Not a day goes by I don't feel guilty about not being there, but Rocha says there is absolutely nothing I can do. I've quit asking about convicting Pearl White.

The mystery of the moving rocks in Death Valley reminds me that some things can't be explained. I don't have to know how or why. It keeps Anthony and me spitballing possibilities all the way to San Diego, where we board a fishing boat and fish for a week along the Baja peninsula. I eat my body weight in fresh tuna, mahi-mahi, and wahoo. Days of diving and snorkeling the warm turquoise waters have us agreeing that coming here was the right thing to do.

Although they've searched a radius of one mile from the Mosquito Lake cabin, there's still no sign of Pu. Tourists, fishermen, hikers, and campers are flocking to the lake and would have stumbled onto something. Even Rocha admits it's odd. I'm starting to believe he escaped. Maybe caught a ride with someone. But I can't see him leaving all the money behind. He would have had to eat.

When summer heat threatens our southern paradise, we work our way north. Into Southern Utah. Canyonlands, Zion, and Bryce Canyon consume the better part of June, and as July approaches, I notice Anthony struggling to keep up. His eyes and skin have jaundiced rapidly, and he's constantly scratching due to the bilirubin buildup. His clothes hang off him now, and he seldom feels like eating. Our walks are brief; mostly we sit around camp, reading and lounging in the hammock.

In Colorado, we spend eight days and seven nights in Rocky Mountain National Park, where we watch elk watch us, spot an elusive black bear, and happen upon a moose on the way to dump our trash. Outside of the park is the Stanley Hotel, a colonial revival said to be haunted and the inspiration for Stephen King's *The Shining*. We agree to splurge on a room, share a bubble bath, and watch a spectacular display of fireworks. Anthony puts his arm around me and says, "I don't love you." Then he kisses me.

His pain's getting worse. I rub CBD cream on his lower back, but it doesn't offer the relief it did a week ago. Neither of us wants to think or talk about tomorrow, but I feel it creeping up, lurking just ahead like a malevolent shadow.

We're heading for the Grand Tetons, camped outside of Jackson Hole, Wyoming, when I wake to sunshine. The grandeur of the Tetons outside the van window is like a painting come to life. I stretch stiff morning muscles and roll over to kiss Anthony, but he isn't there. I sit up, look around.

"Anthony?"

I pull a hoodie on and step outside, searching our little camp next to an unnamed creek. "Anthony!"

I go back inside to make coffee and dress for our day kayaking Jenny Lake. On the counter, I find a paper plate with my name written across it. Fear shoots through me as I flip it over and read.

*The last time I left without saying goodbye. So goodbye. Don't you dare be sad I'm gone. We had a lifetime of fun these last few months. Remember how much I don't love you.*

*—Anthony*

Tears blur my eyes as I pull away a folded paper taped to the plate and unfold it.

Handwritten, it reads:

*I didn't write this. I'm not that poetic. I just thought if you miss me sometime you should remember these words.*

**Do not stand by my grave, and weep**
**I am not there, I do not sleep—**
**I am a thousand winds that blow**
**I am the diamond glints in snow**
**I am the sunlight on ripened grain,**
**I am the gentle, autumn rain.**
**As you awake with morning's hush,**
**I am the swift, up-flinging rush**
**Of quiet birds in circling flight,**
**I am the day transcending night.**
**Do not stand by my grave, and cry—**
**I am not there,**
**I did not die.**

I sob. How many times can a heart break before it quits working?

# EIGHTEEN

After waiting and wondering why searchers haven't located Pu, I occupy August and half of September alone on the road. There's a big difference between being alone and being lonely. Some people are okay being alone. They don't want to die when that lonesome pain gnaws on them in the night. Good for them. Since Anthony left, I've read three books by psychologists trying to convince me otherwise, but it didn't take.

I've decided to go back to Murphys. There's a cash offer on my home, I've accepted it, and need to sign the paperwork.

Fall is unusually warm, which is nice since I have forty-five days to clean and be out of the house. After two yard sales and three trips to the dump, the place looks decent. The recliner, TV, and my bed are all that's left.

In the recliner, I'm flipping channels when a knock sounds on the door. Detective Rocha stands on my porch under a fading sun. I open it.

"Hi."

"Hello," he says.

"What's going on?" I ask.

"May I come in?"

"Sure." I step back and allow him in. That familiar twinge of worry sets off an explosion of panic, and I know. "You found him, didn't you?"

"Maybe." He digs out a plastic bag from inside his blazer and hands it to me. "Can you identify this?"

Inside is the obsidian-and-quartz necklace. "I gave it to him the last time I saw him at the cabin. For protection." My head and hand and heart are shaking as I give it back. "Obviously doesn't work." I sit on the couch.

"Two hunters found remains that fit the profile."

"Where?" My voice cracks.

"Under the root ball of a downed tree about a quarter mile northeast of the cabin. Looks like a lion cache. He could have drowned in the lake, then gas formed, and when he surfaced, the lion likely dragged him." He pauses. "Explains why we couldn't locate him."

My mind rushes to the old mountain lion that cried all night at Mosquito Lake. It was her. She did it. Was she trying to tell me? Was she sorry? Doesn't matter. The back of my nose tingles, my eyes swell, and tears wash away all hope of ever seeing Pu again.

"It's Alpine County, so they're handling the forensics." He fills the silence. "Probably take a few weeks, if we're lucky."

"It's weird."

"What is?"

"The awful relief—like the most sorrowful joy . . ." I can't finish.

"That feeling that's swirling around inside you—that's every day for me," he says. "This is the case I go to sleep thinking about, and it's the first thing on my mind when I wake up."

"I'm sorry." I stand, take his hand, and offer a soft, sympathetic squeeze.

Before I can stop myself, I'm hugging him around the waist. He takes a while, but then hugs me back. "I hope this gives you some closure."

"I'd rather you find a way to prove Pearl White is a murderer."

"Me too. It torments me. I can promise you—we're working on it. Thing is, after twelve months, a case becomes classified as cold. We're past the twelve months, and the clock's ticking down."

"What's that mean? You're gonna stop investigating?"

"It will no longer be a priority. It'll get moved to the back."

"That's about right."

Detective Rocha starts toward the door. "You moving?" he asks.

"Yup. This beauty is someone else's problem now."

"Where are you going?"

I shrug. "Do some traveling. See the world."

"Good. Good for you. Enjoy yourself. I'll call you the minute there's a positive identification."

Selling the Astro van was a piece of cake. Teresa stopped by, saw me taping a For Sale sign to the windshield, and said she'd love to have it. She'd been looking for a van to convert to a camper. When she returned the next day with the cash, I asked for one last favor.

I explained that I hadn't learned to navigate the internet on my phone yet and asked if she'd help me search for an old friend. Sheila Kamaka once owned a livestock transport business that shipped horses and cattle from the states to the Hawaiian Islands and back. I wasn't even sure she was still in business. Teresa pecked on her phone—there were only a handful of companies that shipped livestock from the US. In less than five minutes, Teresa located Kamaka Livestock Transport.

"That's it!"

I dialed the number, left a message, and later that day, she called.

Hearing Sheila's voice again after something like twenty-years was like going home. Like we'd never been apart. Growing up on Na Pali, we were inseparable until we left and for no good reason drifted apart.

When I told her I was coming back, she immediately offered me a job attending horses being shipped from the port in Oakland to Honolulu and then on to Kauai. On November 1, Pu and I will be sailing South for Na Pali. Soon, we will be where we should have been all along.

The bank hasn't repossessed the camper van yet, probably because they can't find it. I'll leave it parked in Oakland and get on the boat.

The sun works hard to burn away most of the clouds, and by noon, the sky is a brilliant blue. The fall foliage is wet from a morning shower, and it smells like sweet, fermenting earth. I'm busy sweeping the front porch when Rocha pulls up.

This is it. The end—I think. He has confirmation that the remains discovered at Mosquito Lake are those of Kenneth James Tait. My Pu is officially dead. All that is left is to confirm the cremation, pay $895, and I can have him back next week.

When Rocha leaves, I drink too much boxed wine and hate on Pearl White, until I blow and beat the crap out of an innocent vacuum cleaner. Bits of plastic and debris explode as I slam it against the floor, then hurl it as far as I can.

The next day, I meet with Brie, my enthusiastic real estate agent, at the pub. She wants to celebrate her first sale, her first divorce, and pay me the cash minus the commission, with dinner and a drink. I regret it the second I walk in the door. The place is packed. It's the Saturday before Halloween. Brie waves from a corner table, and I push through the crowd.

"Hey. Hi," Brie says as I sit.

"Hi."

"I ordered us some nachos." Brie seems overjoyed. Everything she says and does is with extreme enthusiasm. She smiles and digs into the purse hanging off her chair, then hands me an envelope with my name written across it, along with a smiley face.

"Thank you," I say.

"No. Thank *you*." Her grin stretches out across her face. I'm not sure if counting it in front of her is rude, so I don't, just slip it into my sling.

"Aren't you gonna count it?'

"No. I trust you. And I don't want to flash all this cash around a bunch of drunks."

"Oh yeah, guess you're right."

Margo brings nachos and a martini. "Hey, Lula. Long time no see. How are you?" She carefully places a martini in front of Brie.

"I'm okay."

Margo cradles my shoulder. "Thanks for the postcard. Sorry about Anthony. Sounds like you two had one hell of a good time."

"That we did." I nod and swallow the lump in my throat.

Brie feels the need to fill the silence. "I hear the Sheebie Jeebies are playing Pearl's Halloween party." She waits for Margo to respond.

"Yep." Margo keeps her eyes down on her notepad. "Something to drink, Lula?"

"You're kidding me, right? You're playing for Pearl White?"

"Yeah. I'm kind of obligated. Jess sold Pearl half interest in this place. So, technically she's an owner—and my boss. Which means instead of leaving her kid locked out in the car while she gets ripped, she brings him in here and locks him in the office."

"Margo! Come on!" someone shouts from across the room. She raises her middle finger high in the air.

Heat builds in my chest. I picture Bodie that night in the car—terrified and alone, shaking like a lamb as he clung to me. It's hard to breathe. I can feel my pulse. Something shifts.

Margo lowers her voice. "I wish Child Services would fucking do something. Jess said she saw Pearl pouring sloe gin in his juice cup the other night."

"What? Why doesn't someone report her?" Brie asks.

"She's *been* reported, but she hired some clever attorney, and now the county is scared shitless. She could get away with murder 'cause everyone's scared of her. I think she gets off on it, actually."

"Well, most everyone I know is going to the white trash bash at her vineyard. They must not be too scared of her." Brie shoves a cheesy tortilla chip into her mouth.

I snap and slam my hands on the table. stand. "People suck!" Everyone's eyes are on me as I get up and stomp out. I'm too old and too fed-up to wait for someone else to do something about Pearl White. She's going to turn Bodie into a miserable deviant. He deserves better, and I can give him that.

# NINETEEN

Pearl and Dracula are going at it hard and fast in a freaking coffin, of all things. That's when I make my move from the party cave to the house. To be safe and unseen, I stay in the trees above the dirt road.

With Pu's Pleatherface mask pulled down, I slip my hands into blue latex gloves and test the back door. It's unlocked, and I walk right in. Quietly, I shut the door behind me and look around. New stainless-steel appliances. New rustic chic kitchen table and chairs. Stone flooring that must have cost more than my entire wobbly box, covered in dirt and food remnants. Trash can overflowing, just like before the remodel. New countertops covered in dirty dishes, bags, and random groceries that belong on a shelf. Money can't buy class.

For a moment, I reconsider. If I leave now, the only crime I've committed is breaking and entering. My hand is on the doorknob. All I have to do is turn around and walk out. But what if she kills again? I can't look back a year from now and wish I'd had the guts to do something when I had the chance. I can't live in a world where Pearl White gets away with murder and no one can do a damn thing about it.

Halfway up the stairs, I lift Pu's mask up to catch my breath. Bodie's room is on my left. A flatscreen lights his room as a cartoon plays. Cheaper than a babysitter, I guess.

On my hands and knees, I crawl into Bodie's room. Next to his bed, I pause. He's snoring, uncovered and sprawled sideways across the bed. I reach up and pull the blanket over him. He stirs. I drop to the floor in child's pose and notice a wine bottle between his bed and nightstand. I roll it toward me and lift it.

It's not wine. The label reads Mystic Sloe Gin, and it's empty. Was she giving Bodie gin?

I put it back. Looking around, I find a sippy cup on the windowsill. There's still some red juice inside. I pull the lid off and sniff. Still not sure, I sip. The tang of alcohol warms my chest. Bitch. I can't wait to get my hands on her. I jerk the television cord from the outlet. The room goes silent and dark.

As soon as I'm comfortably cross-legged in Bodie's closet, I realize I have to pee. Of course. My need to urinate could ruin everything. What if Pearl walks in while I'm using the bathroom? I'll hear her coming and hide in the shower, I guess. I can't do this with a full bladder.

At first, I stay low, crawling out of Bodie's room. Look both ways and listen. Nothing—all clear, I think. I stand and run to the bathroom. Close the door without latching it. My heart hammers as I feel my way to the toilet in the dark.

I sit but can't go. For a moment, I'm in urination limbo. What the hell is going on? I strain to relieve myself. On to the next dilemma. To flush or not to flush. Holy shit—I'm losing it. Don't flush. Too risky. Get back to the closet or you're going to blow this, I tell myself.

Slowly, I crack the door and listen, but all I can hear is wind and my heart drumming in my ears. I peek out. The coast appears clear. Go. As I scurry to the closet, the familiar roar of a diesel engine and squeaky brakes grind to a halt somewhere outside.

Inside the closet, I hide and wait.

By the time I hear Pearl stumble up the stairs, my legs are asleep. There's a thud—maybe she's fallen and broken her neck, saving me the trouble. For a while, it's silent, and I wonder if she really did take a tumble. Then footsteps again, and a muffled "shit," and banging. Wood cracks. It's quiet. Quiet for a long while, but I wait, then wait even longer to be sure she's deep in drunken slumber before making my move.

When it's time to go, I pull Pu's mask over my face and emerge from the closet, too focused to be scared. Everything that was and all that will be comes down to these next few moments. I refuse to fuck it up. The stairs to the attic moan and creak with each step, no matter how soft and slow I take it. Please let Pearl be drunk enough to not notice.

Above the stairs, I drop. Like a mountain lion stalking my prey. Slinking on all fours, graceful and silent, deadly. Down the narrow hall to Pearl's room.

I make it to her door. Thank God it's not closed. With my gloved hand I slowly push the door open and step inside. Step by step, I creep toward the bed, my shadow emerging and spooky. I'm so close, within reach, watching her sleep. She looks dead with her skull makeup. Ironic.

I've dreamed about getting my hands around her neck for so long, it seems surreal. With fingers spread wide, I make my move. Her neck is narrow as I squeeze. She doesn't move, and it's easy to clamber up and straddle her waist, squeezing as hard as I can. It's feeling like her head's about to pop off when her eyes open.

Panic as she tries to scream, but can't. Our eyes bulge close to one another as she reaches for the nightstand. I squeeze with all my strength.

She tries to roll, and I scissor my legs—cutting her in two, I hope. The grip I have on her neck is working. She's fading. I hear a bone crack in her neck, and the next thing I know, her fists connect with my head. One nails me in the throat. I cough and gasp.

If I don't finish her now, she wins. The beast in me stirs. I growl, unrecognizable as I wring her neck with every fiber of my being.

She thrashes and kicks, and I know it's her final effort.

She looks into my eyes and then quits. It's almost over.

Until I hear—

"Mommy?"

# TWENTY

Bodie's standing at the door, holding his sock monkey and sucking his thumb.

"Mommy?"

I release my hold on Pearl's neck. Her head lolls to the side, eyes closed. She's dead. No—her chest rises—she's still breathing, still alive. I dismount, ripping off the mask, and rush to him. "Bodie, hi honey. It's just me. Tutu. Mommy wasn't feeling good. She ate too much candy at the Halloween party."

I pick him up, grab Pearl's cell phone off the nightstand, and shove it in my pocket. Then I close the door tight before hurrying downstairs to Bodie's room.

"I wanna trick-or-treat. Mommy didn't take me. She lied."

"Do you have a costume?" I ask.

He shakes his head.

"Okay. Here, you can wear my mask." I hand him the Pleatherface mask. "Where's your shoes?"

He rushes to his little cowboy boots and pulls them on.

"Okay. Good boy." I grab a hooded jacket from the closet. "We're gonna have so much fun."

"Yeah." Bodie puts his little hand in mine and keeps the mask in the other as I lead him down the next set of stairs.

"Are you ready for a big adventure?" I ask, and snag the cordless hand phone as we pass through the hallway on our way out the back-door.

"I ready." Bodie skips.

The boy is amazed at the inside of the camper van, and he doesn't fall asleep until I pull into the Oakland Airport. We sleep a few hours.

On the camper stove, I scramble him eggs for breakfast and tell him about my favorite breakfast—loco moco with extra gravy. I hadn't planned on taking him, but I had considered it. After all, how could I leave him to a foster family that may or may not abuse him? This way, I know he'll be looked after and loved. Where we're going, there's no doubt.

Last week, I picked up Pu's ashes. He's in a small plastic bag inside a small carboard box. I packed him in my backpack.

Bodie and I take a cab from the airport to the Port of Oakland, which drops us at berth twenty-one.

"Our lucky number," I say.

"Our wucky number," Bodie mimics.

The air is damp and briny as we board the ship. Captain Alex, Sheila's son, greets us.

I called Sheila early this morning from a payphone—I destroyed and dumped Pearls' phones, along with mine, somewhere along Highway 5. She seemed to believe me when I lied about Bodie being my grandson. After explaining that I had to take care of him due to his mother's incarceration, she agreed, because she's that kind of friend. Besides, she didn't have a last-minute replacement for me. The horses require an attendant or she'd have to cancel the trip. She'd lose more money than I make in a year.

We watch the beautiful horses as their owner's assistants lead them onto the ship. A red roan stud named Nibbles is our favorite. Bodie wants to be a cowboy now. I tell him about the island cowboys—the paniolos. He can't wait to ride, and I promise to take him. By 8 a.m., the ship's horn blows. Bodie and I wave goodbye to our old lives as the ship leaves the harbor.

———————————

Five days at sea, and Bodie knows each of the thirteen horses by name. He helps me feed, shovel manure, and check the automatic water system. We spend hours visiting each horse, and I note their overall health three times a day.

When we're within fifty miles of Honolulu, Captain Alex blows the horn three times, and the ship slows. Bodie and I rush to the upper deck just in time to witness a pod of migrating humpback whales, so close we can see their barnacles, feel the mist of the spray from a blowhole, whiff the sour smell—and witness the magic of humpbacks migrating for the winter.

"Whoa!" Bodie screams with excitement.

"Look!" I point behind the ship just as the massive mammal breaches, then slams down and sends a tsunami of water. Bodie squeals and covers his mouth with both hands, laughing. "Can you believe this?"

He wraps his hands around my neck, and I hug him. "You know how special whales are? We call them kohola."

"Kowla."

"Yes. And thousands of years ago, they helped show people the way to their new home in Hawaii. Do you think they're showing us the way?"

He nods. "Can we wide them?"

"Not now, but later, in our dreams. And when you get older, you can swim with them."

The koholas wave goodbye with their tails and fade into the sunset. A spectacular sight to behold.

It's dark when we dock in Honolulu. Bodie is asleep in our cabin, while I help unload nine horses. The remaining four nicker, letting me know they'd like off this ship too. "Not much farther." I offer hay cubes from my hand, then pat and rub each of them as we set sail for Kauai.

Two days later, we dock in Nawiliwili Harbor. Sheila greets us, and after the horses are delivered in Lihue, she pays me two thousand dollars in cash, lets me borrow a car, and offers her cottage on the beach for the night. After shopping for new clothes, food, leftover Halloween candy, and supplies, we stop on the side of the road and each get a blue and red shave ice.

At the cottage, we play in the tropical surf. I'm teaching Bodie to swim. He loves putting his face in the water and looking through his goggles. When he sees a turtle, he throws his arms in the air and yelps. He seems truly happy. Truth be told, I think he's having the time of his life. And so am I. We spend the night pretend camping on the lanai in our new sleeping bags because Bodie wants to practice camping for our next adventure.

Sheila picks us up early and drives us to the Kalalau trailhead. We get there early, before the crowds of tourists, so as not to be seen. I hug

Sheila and promise to meet her back here in one week. She'll pick me up and take me to her Lihue cottage. She'll pay me to clean, so I'll have a steady income for whatever it is we need. The woman understands island life.

As I turn to go, Sheila stops me. "I wanted it to be a surprise, but you know, I can't keep a secret. They're building you a new hale."

"You're kidding?" Tears fill my eyes. The thought of everyone working together to build us a bamboo-and-palm home fills me with so much gratitude and confidence that I'm doing the right thing. I hug Sheila tight.

"Everyone's happy you're back, including me." She squeezes, and I wish more than anything that Pu was standing here, feeling loved.

———————

Bodie's backpack fits him well. He's eager to get going and runs ahead of me. "Wait up." I cinch down the shoulder straps on my pack and catch up to him.

The hike along the Kalalau trail takes twice as long, because Bodie is amazed at everything. It's like he's never seen a flower, a bird, or a stream. Even rocks impress him.

At Hanakapiai Beach, we take a break, remove our shoes, and sit cross-legged on the white sand. We snack on granola bars and banana chips before heading east into the mountains.

"How much farther?" Bodie asks.

"About twice as far as we just came. We can take another break in the Bamboo Forest. Listen to the spirits singing through the bamboo. Then it won't be too far."

"And we can have a campfire? And swim in the waterfall?"

"Yep. That's right. But you have to learn to swim first."

"And fish too." He jumps up and down. "Let's go, Tutu. Come on."

# TWENTY ONE

It's been nearly a week. Bodie seems so happy here, but he finally asked where his mother was last night. I told him I wasn't sure, and that he could write her a letter and we could mail it to her. He said maybe later, then never mentioned it again, reassuring my conscience.

There are eleven other children here that range in age from two to thirteen, and they welcomed Bodie right in. He swims, fishes, and plays tag with them. Jojo, a ten-year-old girl, is his new best friend. She's teaching him to read.

Yesterday, he saved a baby sea turtle and watched a seal birth her pup. He's like a sponge, absorbing his beautiful new world. I've yet to regret the decision to give him a better home. A better life.

The morning breeze hints at high off-shore winds. "Today's the day," I tell Mai, one of the few old-timers who never left. "The ocean has sent the wind to take him home."

"Yes. The spirits are ecstatic. Let's go," she says.

We gather at the cove, all thirty-two of us scattered along the rocks as the wind carries our chants and drumming over a sparkling blue ocean. Awakening the spirits. I open the plastic bag containing Pu's ashes. The wind wants them now, and they swirl from the bag.

I climb out onto the lava bed, then into the waves, and hold the ashes high above my head.

"My Pu, my heart. I love you. Swim in peace with your people. You are forever free."

I shake Pu's spirit free. The wind catches him instantly and gently carries him into eternity.

I stare out into the never-ending blue, and there in the distance a whale breaches, giving me chills. I smile at the perfection as the chant and drums come to an abrupt end.

Our little hale is made of palm fronds, sea grass, and bamboo. At night, Bodie and I bring the solar lights inside and place them in all four corners. A warm breeze swings bamboo chimes that lull Bodie and me to call it a good day. We take turns listing what we're grateful for. When Bodie lists Tutu, I tear up and kiss his forehead.

I read him the story of Pele—the goddess of volcanos—and when I get to the part about her bad temper and how she can destroy things, he asks, "What destroy means?"

"Like wreck. She can turn things to ashes with her power."

"People too? Like today. Did Pele do that?"

"No." I will never tell him it was a combination of the women in his life, including me.

"Does Pele kill people?"

"Sometimes. But we're safe here. Pele doesn't come to this island. She's old now and stays home on the Big Island."

Bodie thinks for a moment, then nods his acceptance. "I wish Mommy stayed on the Big Island."

"Why, hon?"

"So she couldn't hurt Daddy."

I pause. "Mommy hurt your daddy?"

His lower lip quivers, and he nods, looking about as scared as a kid can look.

"How did Mommy hurt Daddy?"

"With a gun—on his head." He touches his forehead.

My heart skips a beat. "What do you mean, Bodie? Did you *see* your mommy hurt your daddy?"

He hangs his fingers from his missing teeth. "Mmm-hmm." He nods. "I saw his blood came out."

I cover my mouth, then take his hand and kiss it. "Bodie, honey, I don't want to upset you, but this is really, really important, okay?"

This is more than important—this is everything. This is Pu not being a murderer. "You have to tell Tutu the truth."

"Kay."

"Did you see Mommy use a gun to shoot Daddy in the head?" I know kids can lie for no reason. Maybe Bodie just imagined he saw something. Or maybe he overheard a conversation.

"I'm not supposed to say it. Mommy will get mad at me."

"Mommy's not here." I lie down in front of him. "I promise you, I won't tell her you told. I will always love and keep you safe."

"They were yelling. I went down the stairs, and Kenny ran away, and then I hid under the table and Mommy came down the stairs and she hurt Daddy—with a gun in his head."

"I'm so sorry you saw that." I grab and cradle him against my chest as the possibility that Pu didn't kill a man hits me. Satisfaction with a sweet and sour twist.

"Did you tell the police what you saw?"

"No."

I rock him and sing, "Twinkle, twinkle, little star, how I wonder what you are . . ." And I keep singing until he's asleep.

How on earth do I give Rocha this information without risking me and Bodie? He'll want to know how I know this. They'll want to talk to Bodie because, just like with Pu's journal, it's just he said, she said.

---

Sheila is waiting at the trailhead parking lot by the time I reach Ke'e Beach.

"Hey, Lula." We hug and kiss cheeks. She smells of citronella bug repellant just like always. She's allergic to mosquito bites.

"Aloha."

"You look great. How's the little keiki?"

"I'm so glad we came. He loves it and seems happy."

"I think about going back sometimes." She pulls onto the narrow road.

"You could do it. Leave the business to Alex. Come back. Please," I beg, and squeeze her forearm.

"I'm too spoiled. I like air-conditioning and my Serenity bed."

We laugh and reminisce all the way back to Lihue. I consider telling her everything, but not yet. Not until I have the inkling of a plan. I can't simply call Rocha—they'll track the call. I can't email. They can track that too. I can't mail a letter without a postmark.

The cottage is hardly dirty, yet Sheila insisted it needed a good scrubbing, so I oblige while she's at the harbor, shipping another load of horses back to the States.

Cleaning still clears my head and at the very least takes my mind off my worries. I wash windows, scrub both bathrooms, and mop floors. After I've cleaned the refrigerator and wiped down the outside of all the cupboards, I'm done. Completely spent, and I still don't have the slightest clue how to tell the police what Bodie saw.

Between the four-hour hike out of the mountains, the mental stress of knowing Bodie saw his mother kill his father, and cleaning, I put my feet up, right on the polished coffee table. Switching on the television, I open a cold bottle of beer.

Lester Holt is reporting the Nightly News. Russia is still launching attacks on Ukraine. Another school shooting. Children's hospitals overwhelmed by mystery virus.

Why would I ever want to expose Bodie to any of this crap? I take a big gulp of my beer. I'd turn the news off, but the remote is too far away, and I'm too lazy to reach for it. I let my head fall back on the couch and stare at the bamboo ceiling fan spinning overhead.

"And in a strange twist of events," Lester says, "Pearl White, the mother of missing child Bodie White, has confessed to plotting the murder of her husband, Tucker White, last year. Also involved in the diabolical scheme is fugitive Jackson Davis Lejeune." I jump off the couch, spilling my beer.

Standing directly in front of the TV, I watch as a photo of the happy couple, Tucker and Pearl White, fills the screen. Then it cuts to footage of Detective Rocha standing outside the Calaveras County Sheriff's Department. My heart somersaults and bangs against my chest.

"I'd just like to start by saying that the facts of this case are still unfolding." He clears his throat and looks up at the camera. "Things like this don't happen often in our little community. It was a difficult case to say the least, and thanks to the diligent good work of our detectives, we have Tucker White's murderers in custody. Ms. White and Mr. Lejeune have confessed to plotting the murder. It was Ms.

White who delivered the shot to her husband, after the intruder, Kenneth Tait fled, that ultimately led to his death."

I scream and jump up and down, "Holy fucking shit!" I cover my mouth with both hands.

"There is still a missing boy, Bodie White." Bodie's smile fills the screen. "If you've seen this child or have any information, please contact the nearest Federal Bureau of Investigations office."

My hands are on my head. I'm walking back and forth. Lester's yapping about something else, but I'm about to burst.

"She confessed. That bitch confessed! But why? What happened? Did she find Jesus? Who gives a shit!" I jump up and down. "She confessed! They know Pu didn't do it. He didn't do it." I say it so I can comprehend everything I just heard. "He's *not* a murderer. Not ever!" The satisfaction of believing all along—knowing in my heart that Pu was no killer is the best feeling in the world.

I fall to my knees, throw my fists up in triumph and my head back. Tears of pure joy wash away all pain and suffering from now on. "My sweet, sweet, good boy. I love you, Pu. I love you."

I stand. Dry my face with my T-shirt and take a breath. The world has been set right. All is as it should be.

"A child for a child."

# DEAR READERS

Thank you for giving *The Lonesome Dark* a chance. I hope you enjoyed reading it as much as I enjoyed writing it. Please let other thriller lovers know by leaving an Amazon and Goodreads review.

A huge thank you to my wonderful read team for their input on my first draft of *The Lonesome Dark*. Read team includes Frank Riley, Robert "Obie" Beukers, Dawn Crikman, Paula DiFalco, Lori Gallant, and my editor Dylan Garity.

If you'd like to become part of my read team be sure and sign up for my seldom sent newsletter at https://www.lisamichellestories.com

A special thanks to Calaveras County Deputy Alan Serpa for his brilliant insight and expertise with my endless procedural questions.

I'd love to keep in touch. You can contact me at https://www.lisam ichellestories.com/

Follow my Amazon author page for updates and discounts. https://www.amazon.com/stores/Lisa-Michelle/author/B0847SPYKD ?ref=ap_rdr&store_ref=ap_rdr&isDramIntegrated=true&shoppingPo rtalEnabled=true

I'm on Facebook @ https://www.facebook.com/lisamichellestorie s/and Instagram at https://www.instagram.com/lisamichellestories/? hl=en

Goodreads: https://www.goodreads.com/author/show/20063065. Lisa_Michelle

Thanks again!

Lisa Michelle

# EPILOGUE

To read Pearl White's *CONFESSION* go to https://www.lisamichelle
stories.com

Sign up and click on ***THE CONFESSION*** where the ugly truth will
be revealed. Once you're signed up you can also access a FREE copy of
*Mountain Misery* and take part in my awesome read team where you'll
have the opportunity to offer feedback on my early manuscripts.

# ALSO BY LISA MICHELLE

**IN READING ORDER:** Feel free to contact me for personalized signed copies.

LisaMichelleStories@gmail.com

*BLUE MOUNTAIN* available at Amazon: https://www.amazon.com/dp/B09GZK77ZF

Barnes and Noble: https://www.barnesandnoble.com/w/blue-mountain-lisa-michelle/1143740107?ean=9798484341535

*CALAVERAS* available at Amazon: https://www.amazon.com/CALAVERAS-THRILLING-SUSPENSE-Lisa-Michelle/dp/B08DBVZYFC/ref=sr_1_1?crid=12A33TJLFZNN2&keywords=Calaveras&qid=1693329876&s=books&sprefix=calaveras+%2Cstripbooks%2C179&sr=1-1

Barnes and Noble: https://www.barnesandnoble.com/w/calaveras-lisa-michelle/1143740123?ean=9798647815392

*FOREST CREEK* available at Amazon: https://www.amazon.com/gp/product/B0BGQJ6K1R?ref_=dbs_m_mng_rwt_calw_tkin_2&storeType=ebooks&qid=1693329876&sr=1-1

Barnes and Noble: https://www.barnesandnoble.com/w/forest-creek-lisa-michelle/1143740949?ean=9798355163617

Made in the USA
Monee, IL
23 October 2023

45050964R10163